Seoulmates

Seoulmates

SUSAN LEE

Recycling programs for this product may not exist in your area.

ISBN-13: 978-1-335-91578-8

Seoulmates

For questions and comments about the quality of this book, please contact us at CustomerService@Harlequin.com.

Inkyard Press
22 Adelaide St. West, 41st Floor
Toronto, Ontario M5H 4E3, Canada
www.InkyardPress.com

Printed in U.S.A.

To my dad...who always used to tell me I could be anything—
from Miss Korea to the president of the United States. :)
Well, I chose storyteller...and I hope this would have made you very proud.
I miss you.

CHAPTER 1: Hannah

Nothing says "I love you" more than patting your boyfriend's back as his head is in a toilet, barfing up warm Bud Light.

He groans miserably.

I switch to rubbing circles and throw in a "there, there."

It's not my dream date, but it's a good place to be, all things considered. I started high school with no close ties and now I'm going into the summer and my final year with a perfect boyfriend and a built-in friend group. It's funny how life can change so suddenly when you're least expecting it.

We've come a long way, Nate and me. We've known each other since he was a big, clumsy kindergartner and I was a small, mouthy one. We used to hate each other when we were kids. But fate has a way of showing up when we least expect it.

I ran into Nate at the beach last summer, the day after my sister moved to Boston. I was feeling particularly raw, and Nate was being surprisingly charming. "Why would anyone leave San Diego?" he asked me. "Worst decision ever. Best way to get back at someone who leaves is to take advantage of everything the city has to offer." And then we went to Carlsbad and walked through the flower fields, something I'd never done before. It wasn't cheesy like I thought it would be. It was nice.

And that's when I knew he was on my side. Because really, why *would* anyone want to leave San Diego? Nate gets it. He gets *me*.

The knock on the bathroom door elicits another groan from Nate, sending a whiff of something pungent my way. I swallow hard, pushing back the gag reflex to avoid my own fiasco.

"We're busy in here," I yell.

I hear the snorts and giggles from the other side of the door.

"Um, not that kind of busy," I rush to explain.

The last thing I need is for the rumor mill to make up some scandalous story about me and Nate in the bathroom at Jason Collins's end-of-year party. Trust me, the smell in the air does not make me want any nooky, that's for sure.

There's another knock at the door. What, is this the only freaking bathroom in this house or something?

"Hannah? Is everything okay in there?"

Oh, thank god, a familiar voice. Maybe Shelly can call us an Uber and help me get Nate outside. But then again, she's also kinda the biggest gossip in our friend group. I try not to tell her anything I wouldn't want the entire school to know the next day, and I'm sure Nate wouldn't want everyone talking about how he can't hold his liquor. I don't think he'd appreciate Shelly posting about it all over and seeing people write stuff like "Nate is a lightweight." People can be merciless in the comments.

It's fine. I can handle this. I can take care of Nate myself. Despite the current situation, I can't help but smile. I like being the reliable girlfriend. I like being needed.

"We're good, Shelly. Everything's fine. Nothing interesting is happening in here. Thanks," I call back. Hopefully she'll find some other drama to report elsewhere.

"Okey dokey! I'll be downstairs if you need me," she says.

A moan comes from inside the bowl. I look down at the back of Nate's head. "Oh, babe, are you gonna be okay? What can I get you?" I ask him.

"Hannah?" He turns his head slightly to put his cheek against the toilet seat. I try not to worry about all the germs now transferring to his beautiful face from the porcelain throne. Nate's voice is weak, and his breath is rank. I suck in a breath and avoid breathing through my nose. I take the wet washcloth on the counter and wipe his neck, fascinated at the little blond hairs there. Sweat has darkened the rest of his head to a sandy blond, but those tiny neck hairs are almost white.

My heart softens at the sight for some reason. Even though he's a big, strong guy, he's got these small baby hairs. Cute.

"Hannah," he calls to me again, drawing me back.

"Yes, Nate?" I reluctantly lean in closer over him.

"I..." He takes another breath, looking mildly unsure if he's going to hurl again.

"Shhh. It's okay, Nate. I know, babe, I know."

"Hannah, we..."

We. Awww. "Yup, it's you and me," I say.

"I... I think we should break up," he says, rolling his face back towards the inside of the toilet.

"No thank you," I say.

Time stops. My entire body numbs except for the sinking in my stomach. This shaggy bathroom rug suddenly feels scratchy and rough on my knees, and the room is entirely too small. It's a warm San Diego night, and a house full of mostly drunk kids isn't making for the best air circulation. Still, I don't think sweating this much is normal.

Don't panic, I tell myself, closing my eyes to center my suddenly spinning world.

I replay his words in my head. We haven't dated long enough for him to decide we need to break up. I heard it wrong.

We should wake up. Yes, time is ticking and we've gotta take life seriously.

We should prank up. Ha ha! Gotcha! Good one, Nate.

We should steak up? I mean, I love a good cut of beef. I'm down.

A large hand wraps around my wrist, drawing me out of my panic. But when I look into Nate's red-rimmed eyes, notice his runny nose, and try hard not to stare at the suspicious chunk of something stuck to his cheek, my throat tightens.

It's not love I see. It's not even anger. It's...pity.

"Nate, babe, you're not thinking straight. You're drunk and sick," I reason with him, voice shaking.

"I'm sorry, Hannah. I've been trying to tell you all night.

But I didn't want to hurt you," Nate says, punctuating his platitudes with another moan reverberating back into the bowl.

"But...but you're my person," I say, the last word almost a whisper. My voice sounds pathetic and small.

"We can still be friends. It's just not working between us," he says. He sounds miserable. I want it to be because he feels bad for breaking my heart and not because he currently has his head in the toilet.

"What's not working? I thought we were having fun. We're here, at this party, um, having fun, right?"

I look down at Nate, who definitely does not look like he's having fun.

"Hannah, we...we don't have anything in common," he says.

"What do you mean we have nothing in common? We have so much in common. We're basically the same person." I struggle to come up with the list, the list of all the things that we both enjoy. It's a black hole right now in my brain, but I don't work well under pressure.

"We really don't. You don't even like the things I'm..."

"We both like *Riverdale*," I cut him off, finally thinking of an answer. See? I knew there was something.

"You hate it. You make fun of Archie every episode."

I let my shoulders fall at his words. He's right. Busted.

"You hate tomatoes..."

That's a deal-breaker when it comes to love?

"...and cats..."

This is true. But can't we agree to disagree?

"...and you don't know anything about K-pop or Korean

dramas. I just can't talk to you about the things I'm passionate about."

K-pop? Korean dramas?

I let out my own groan. No, not Nate, too. Another person swept up into the sudden worldwide fascination with all things Korean. And of course, apparently, I'm the only person in the world that isn't, even though I am…Korean.

"Nate, we can fix whatever you think isn't working."

"Hannah?" He turns his head to look at me again.

Yes, good, he's regretting his words already. I nod to myself and smile. We'll be fine.

"Nate," I say back assuredly.

His eyes widen in panic as he opens his mouth and throws up all over my sandals.

I tuck the phone into my neck so I can suck the chocolate off my forefinger and thumb. I ate the entire Toblerone, starting from the top, biting off exactly at the crease of each piece, holding the same spot at the bottom so that just enough chocolate would melt onto my fingertips for me to suck off at the very end. Strategic consumption for healing a broken heart.

"I couldn't just get dumped in front of the lockers or in the parking lot of In-N-Out like everyone else. Nope, I have to have chunks of chicken nuggets swimming in sour beer vomited in between my toes. Great." Shelly is quiet on the other end of the line. She's probably gagging at the thought of it, too.

"Since when did not liking the same music become a reason to break up with someone?" I ask.

"Nate told Martin Shepherd who told Mandy Hawkins who told Jason Chen who told me that when he asked you who your bias was, you said you had a bias towards 'justice, equality, and Sasha over Malia Obama.'"

"I didn't realize Nate felt so strongly about Malia."

"It's a K-pop thing." I can hear her eye roll through the phone. "Your 'bias' is your favorite person in the group."

"Okay, but how does everyone know this but me?"

I reach for the bag of peanut M&M'S on my nightstand. I ate all the other colors, and now only the green ones remain. A feast of green M&M'S is my recipe for healing.

"Seriously, though," she goes on, ignoring my question, "I can't believe Nate dumped you right before summer. What are you gonna do now about all those plans you guys made? You can't do them alone."

Dumped.

Alone.

The words slap me in the face so hard I can still feel the sting. She's right. Other than my internship, I thought I'd be spending all other waking hours with him.

"Like lifeguard camp? It's nonrefundable, you know." Shelly's reminder breaks through the haze of my misery.

Ugh, lifeguard camp. I hate the smell of chlorine and the thought of all the damp places for germs and diseases to fester. But Nate had all these ideas and plans for us the "big summer before our senior year," our first summer as a couple. And he got me kind of excited about it all. Well, maybe I should just count my blessings that I don't have to go to the pool anymore. Now that I'm…

Dumped.

Alone.

No boyfriend. No summer plans. No life. A Times Square billboard reading "pathetic" in bright, blinking lights to the tune of Celine Dion's "All by Myself."

"Maybe I should talk to Nate..."

"Well, like, give it a day or two. Make him miss you. Plus, if you're gonna try and win him back, you'll want to be strategic," Shelly suggests.

"Win him back? Is that possible? Do you think it could work?" I ask.

"Totally. I can help you. Look, I know Nate is for sure Blink, CARAT, and ARMY. Oh, and he's obsessed with Son Ye-Jin. He tried to get the drama department to do *Crash Landing on You* for the school musical next year. So those are good places to start. Get to know the things he likes, Hannah. If he doesn't want to date you because you don't have anything in common, change his mind by, you know, having things in common."

Her words are gibberish to me. And why do I feel defensive at being schooled by Shelly Sanders, of all people? But maybe she's right. Maybe I can win him back.

"Uh, thanks," I manage to get out. "I've got a lot to think about." And a lot to google.

"Anyways, a bunch of us are gonna try out that new rolled ice cream place so I gotta run." And she's gone before I can even close my mouth or ask if I can come along. Wait, did I lose my friend group in the breakup, too?

"Bye," I say to no one. I wipe the chocolate smear off the phone screen with the cuff of my sweatshirt. I stare at the mark on the fabric and consider licking it. Maybe later.

I throw myself prostrate back onto my bed.

My mom barges into my room and throws the curtains open, blinding me with sunlight. My eyes, my eyes. "Okay, Hannah. Time to get up. Why are the curtains all closed? It smells bad in here. Did you take a shower yet today?"

"Mom, please, can't you see I want to be alone right now? I need time to heal," I whine.

"Yah, wallowing in the dark, eating chocolate, and being dirty is not the way to move on, Hannah."

"Mother, this is my process."

"Process for what? For wasting your life? Hannah, you and Nate dated for not much time. The batch of kimchi I made isn't even igeosseo yet." Leave it to my mother to compare a relationship's validity to the fermentation time of kimchi. "Now, get up and clean your room. We need to get to church so you can sign up to be a VBS teacher this summer."

My mother cannot think that just because Nate and I broke up, I'm suddenly free all summer to teach Vacation Bible School to a bunch of screaming elementary school kids. I hated elementary school.

"Um, no, not interested. I have other plans," I lie. I mean, I *could* still go to lifeguard camp after all. Although seeing Nate in board shorts, tanned muscles on display, and knowing he doesn't want me might be the end of me.

But teaching VBS may actually be a more painful way to my grave.

"Hannah, it's either VBS, or you sign up for hagwan to prepare for college."

"But I have my internship," I say. I've used this internship as an excuse to get out of things on more than one occasion. And even though it's only one day a week for two hours, because it's working for an immunologist, my mother thinks it's basically my surefire way into medical school. She may not be wrong.

"You can do both. VBS is only in the mornings, and isn't your internship only on Monday afternoons?"

Busted.

I bury my face into my pillow. "Go away, please," I beg.

I feel the bed lower as Mom comes to sit down beside me. The light touch of her hand pats me on the back. "Hannah, you are better than this non-Christian, American boy." Her voice is suspiciously kind.

"You don't understand, Mom." *He liked me*, I want to tell her. Me. But maybe now he doesn't anymore. I knew I should've jumped on the BTS train when everyone else was hopping on. It's just that K-pop and K-dramas were things I thought "they" enjoyed, *they* being Korean Koreans, not Korean Americans, and definitely not American Americans. Where was I when the tide shifted so quickly? Now I'm on the outside looking in. And Nate is definitely in.

"What's to understand? Hannah, you should want a boy who likes that you are smart and talented and appreciates your strong calves. What you need is a good Korean boy."

Here we go.

I sit up and brace myself for my mother's attempt to fix me up with the latest "good Christian boy" from our Korean church. Will it be Timothy Chung because he's perfect and plays the violin? Or will it be Joshua Lee because he's perfect and drives a BMW? No, no, it's gotta be Elliot Park, because he's perfect and got an early acceptance to UCLA.

"But let's not worry about boyfriends right now. I have really good news, and then we go to church."

Wait, that's it? No résumé of some new Korean kid to present to me for my consideration? Is this a trap? Something is not right here. I brace myself for the other shoe to drop.

"Um, what kind of good news, Mom?" I turn my head slowly and face my mother, my brows drawn together, inspecting her face. Her makeup is perfectly done, eyebrows filled in over her microblading, her complexion appropriately dewy from the latest Korean cushion, and lips stained two shades darker than millennial pink. She could be my sister.

"Well, with your dad and sister gone, we have so much extra space..."

With my dad being transferred to Singapore for his job and my sister leaving for Boston for hers, the house has been emptier and emptier. Not to mention it feels like my mom is at church more often than she is at home.

But we've always had summers together. Summers are family time. "They'll be here for the Fourth of July at least," I say, trying not to punctuate my words with a question mark.

"Sure," she says unconvincingly. "But we still have room for guests."

"What guests?"

"Well, I was talking to my friend the other day..."

This is not sounding good at all. "Mother?" I say slowly. "What did you do?"

"Guess who is coming to town all the way from Korea to spend the summer with us?" she exclaims, clasping her hands together.

Oh no.

"My best friend, Mrs. Kim. And her family!"

No, no, no.

I gasp.

Jacob Kim.

After all these years.

I open my mouth to scream in horror, but my mom grabs me, pulls me up off the bed, and envelops me in a celebratory hug. "My best friend is coming, and she's bringing her wonderful son, Jacob, and her beautiful daughter, Jin-Hee, with her. Our house will be full of laughter and joy!"

It's not like it's a hospital around here. I laugh. I joy.

"I can cook Korean food, and we'll all eat together," she says.

She makes it sound like I don't ever eat her cooking. So I don't like Korean food every meal of the day, and she doesn't make anything else.

She releases me from the hug but grabs my arms and gives me a shake. I'm limp with shock and am thrown around like a doll. "You remember Jacob! You two were as close as can be growing up. Best friends through elementary and middle school."

Oh, I remember Jacob alright.

Our mothers never let us forget that we were friends

"even before you were born" just because they were friends and preggers at the same time.

Heat creeps up my neck, and a tightness squeezes my chest, but I ignore it. I've stopped having any emotions when it comes to Jacob Kim. I'm not starting again now.

"It's a perfect time to have friendship like when you were little," she says wistfully.

"That was a long time ago," I remind her. We *had* a friendship, a best friendship. He threw it away. He traded me in for a life of fame in Korea. "I'm not interested," I say, pushing away from my mom.

Mom's brows rise in shock. "But this is Jacob, Jacob Kim," she says. Like repeating the name suddenly takes away what he did.

"Fine, but if he comes here, he'd better stay out of my way. I have plans this summer," I say.

"But you and Nate broke up. You have no plans now." Damn, Mom, way to go for the jugular. "You can teach Vacation Bible School in the daytime. And then you can have fun with Jacob the rest of the day. It will be a perfect summer."

"Mom." I drop my shoulders, stopping short of stomping my foot. This can't be happening.

"Hannah," she says in warning.

We stare at each other. I won't look away. It's a battle of wills at this point. She won't win this one. I won't give in.

I blink.

"Anyways," she singsongs like a victory chant, "there's so much preparation to do." She hustles away whistling a church hymn.

Wait, there was dust in my eye! I want a rematch.

I swear I see her skipping down the stairs. Great, my mom now has more exciting summer plans than I do.

And that's when I make up my mind. Everyone else is gonna be living it up this summer, doing whatever they want. So why shouldn't I? Forget Vacation Bible School. Forget guests from Korea. And definitely forget Jacob Kim.

I've only got one thing on my mind now—Operation Win Back Nate.

Step one: google Blink, CARAT, and Son Ye-Jin.

CHAPTER 2: Jacob

"Don't go, please," she sobs, voice trembling in desperation. She grabs my arm with a force I wasn't expecting, pulling me back from the door.

I drop my head, barely looking over my shoulder back at her. "I have to. I have to do this for myself, for my family. I don't want to hurt you, but we have to break up." My voice cracks, and I'm surprised by the tear that escapes down my cheek.

"What am I going to do?" she wails in agony, heart shattered.

Dramatic pause.

"And…cut," the director says, the ringing of a young woman's cries still in my ear.

I snap out of the scene, out of my character, back onto set in a posh high-rise apartment under stage lights, a floor-to-ceiling view of the Han River in the background. I wipe the tear away.

"Very good, everybody," the director says. "We're done for today."

A flurry of activity happens around me as everyone starts cleaning up the set. It doesn't take me as long to come down from an emotional scene as it used to, but I'm still amazed at how quickly people can just move on.

"Here." Two small wipes are placed into my hands to remove my eye makeup, followed by a packet of papers. "The car will be here in ten minutes," my manager, Hae-Jin, says to me, and she promptly leaves to follow my co-star. Warm and fuzzy, she is not.

I flip through the sheets, the script for the season finale, a brief summary of what season two will look like, and some very official-looking legal documents. My contract renewal. I still can't believe we're getting a second season, which is not the norm in Korean television.

I like acting. Getting to play characters so unlike myself is cathartic. I like the paycheck even more. But thinking of a second season with this character and this cast makes me exhausted already.

I walk to the window and peek down at the size of the crowd today. Even up on the thirty-second floor, I can see, or maybe just feel, their excitement. The number of people is bigger than it was yesterday and seems to be growing every day we shoot here.

This isn't where I live. I may be Kim Jin-Suk, the rising star of the K-drama world and SKY Entertainment's big bet. But I'm nowhere near rich enough to live in Gangnam's Hyundai Tower West. Yet. The real me, Jacob Kim, a young actor just starting out, lives with his mom and sister in a decent-sized, two-bedroom villa apartment a couple dongnaes over.

But it wasn't too long ago that we weren't even sure we'd have a place to live at all. So I am not complaining by any means. I'm just thankful we're not on the street and starving. The familiar panic starts to bubble in my gut and threatens to grow inside me, consuming me, pulling me into the shadows. When you've grown up always worried about money, it's hard to get rid of that anxiety. Even now.

"Time to go," the deep voice of Eddie, the SKY staff member assigned to me, says. He directs me down the hall and into the elevator. Two floors down we stop and as the doors open, I'm immediately slapped with the overwhelming scent of jasmine. It's the unmistakable perfume worn by my costar, Shin Min-Kyung. My nose hairs are singed.

She's changed her clothes and her hair from the shoot that ended what feels like just minutes ago. Her makeup is flawless, and she looks like she's stepped straight out of a magazine. The pound of cover-up over this morning's zit on my chin starts to crack under the pressure of her perfection. She's stunning.

She's also the meanest person I've ever met.

She steps into the elevator with her own entourage pushing me and my one handler into the corner. I watch her eyes spare me the tiniest of glances as her lip curls slightly.

"Annyeong haseyo," I greet her in honorific, bowing slightly to her back.

"I told you to stop eating chocolate. Your skin is a mess," she says.

I've found it's safer to just nod and not respond when she's in a mood to throw jabs my way. I know my place. And yet…

"The scene went really well today, don't you think?" I ask.

The air is sucked out of the elevator, and all of us collapse to the floor, suffocating to our deaths. Or at least, that's how it feels when she lets out an insufferable sigh. Damn it. I should've gone with the original strategy of keeping my mouth shut.

She doesn't answer me.

When the elevator doors open, we're shuffled through the lobby and out the front door of the building. The screaming is loud out here, and I'm blinded momentarily by all the flashbulbs going off.

"MinJin! MinJin!" The fans scream our ship name. Min-Kyung leans in closer to me as we walk. She tucks her hair behind her ear in an award-winning show of shyness and modesty. I put my hand on her back.

I want to stop and thank every single person who took the time and waited out here to see me today. It's really cool of them to be here. But that's not allowed. Every fan interaction has to be carefully choreographed. Instead, Min-Kyung and I smile and bow politely in greeting to the group as a whole and keep moving.

As we wait for the car to pull up to meet us, Hae-Jin gives me the nod, my cue for one last bread crumb to give the fans. I look back and wave my hand to the crowd, then run my fingers through my too-long bangs, garnering more screams. I look over the group, wink, and cross my thumb and forefinger into a mini-heart. They all go nuts.

Mixed in with the enthusiastic shouting, a painful wail cuts through the air. "Oppa! I love you," a girl cries, reaching out her hand, desperately trying to touch me. The crowd pushes forward as they notice my attention drawn towards the crying fan. The girl in front is being smashed into the guardrails, a look of panic on her face. I race over to try and help her, pushing people back. But my foot gets stuck between two railings, and my ankle twists awkwardly. My face scrunches as I scream out in pain.

I feel two hands grab me, lifting me off the ground. "Out of the way," I hear Eddie shout as he removes me from the crowd and shuffles me quickly into our car. He barely gets the door shut before we speed away, the fans a blur in the rear window.

"What were you thinking?" Hae-Jin hisses at me.

Hae-Jin is meticulously put together in her signature Armani black pantsuit and white silk blouse. Not a hair is out of place in her sleek pulled-back bun. But it's clear she's frazzled.

"They were crushing her," I say. "I'm sorry." I am a chronic apologizer. It doesn't matter if I think I've done something wrong or not.

"You put everyone, including that fan, in danger," Hae-Jin says. "And what if you were photographed with that awkward look on your face? You know the rules."

I close my eyes and swallow down the boulder of irritation stuck in my throat. I don't know if I'm more annoyed at her or at myself. Because she's right. I do know the rules, and I messed up. I let out a silent sigh and try to drown out the noise in my head. And ignore the pain I'm feeling in my ankle.

I take in a deep breath. The car is new, and the smell

of leather floods my nose. The family car I grew up with had dingy upholstery, stained and ripped, with a faint sour smell that could never be washed out no matter how hard my mom tried.

When I first came to Korea, I was a poor, sickly kid. Three grueling years in the company's Training Program, basically the farm system to find new talent to make the next huge K-pop or K-drama stars, helped me perfect what Koreans call my "charms." And now I'm the male lead in *Heart and Seoul*, the much-anticipated series about star-crossed teen lovers. Now that Netflix has picked it up, our viewership has skyrocketed. We've gone international.

I can't take it for granted. And I can't fuck it up.

"We're heading to the interview with the German magazine, and then you will be with *Entertainment News Canada*. Minky will be in the floral Gucci dress and change to the lavender Celine. Jin-Suk will wear the red Supreme sweater and then change into the white Balenciaga button-down shirt. Looks like your popularity indexes highest when you wear white with the North American crowd."

"How is that even a thing that you guys pay attention to?" I ask. It's crazy the stats that the company tracks. It totally blows my mind that fans even care what I wear, let alone think I'm hot in it.

Fans. I have fans. I couldn't even get a second glance before I moved to Korea. I was always the small, nervous Asian kid with severe allergies growing up in San Diego. Who knew that a bowl cut on a tall, scrawny guy would make the girls go wild one day?

"Stop asking stupid questions. I'm so tired of working

with an amateur. And what was that stunt you pulled back there? Why can't you just follow the rules? I never want to work with an undisciplined *American* actor again." Min-Kyung's sharp comments cut like a knife, slashing one of my most sensitive areas—not being Korean enough for this career.

"Minky." Hae-Jin's voice carries a warning. *Stop being a diva and cooperate.* Truth is, Min-Kyung can't afford to have another male costar unhappy with her. She'll soon be uncastable in any romantic shows if no actors want to work with her.

"Tomorrow we go to Busan for the photo shoot for *Vogue Korea*," Hae-Jin continues.

"Ooh, cool. Do you think we can hang out at the beach?" I've missed the beach so much since we moved. "Or will we have time to check out Gamcheon Culture Village? I've seen pictures..."

"There is no time for that," Hae-Jin cuts me off.

"This isn't a vacation. This is work," Min-Kyung says, not even trying to hide her disgust with me.

"Sorry," I say for maybe the one-hundredth time today. It's still early.

I let out a sigh and try to hide my disappointment. I never get the chance to do or see anything, even when the job takes me to fun places. No rides at Lotte World, no staying for the guard change at Gyeongbokgung Palace, nothing. Not to sound like I'm having a midlife crisis or anything, but I feel like my entire youth is wasting away.

"And, Jin-Suk." The sternness in Hae-Jin's voice pulls me from my thoughts and gets my full attention. "During the interviews and in the photos, try harder to sell your feelings for Minky. No jokes. No sarcasm. Sell the emotion between you two."

Make the world believe I'm in love with Min-Kyung in real life to raise the emotional stakes in the hearts of our fans for our on-screen relationship. When Hae-Jin first told me this was an expectation, I thought for sure she was kidding. I quickly remembered that she doesn't have a sense of humor. And I don't miss the threat in her tone. Give a believable performance or risk losing this second season, this paying job. I must be one hell of an actor if people actually believe I like this girl.

I look over at Min-Kyung, eyes closed, earbuds in. I'm still new to all this, but she's been doing this a long time. Is that why she's so miserable? When the shine of stardom dulls, will I end up jaded and mean like her?

Nope, I'm not gonna let that happen. This job is demanding, sure, but people recognize my face. They scream my name. Plus, it pays the bills. And at this point in my life, that's all that really matters.

"Well that was a disaster."

My little sister, Jin-Hee, has a way with words.

"Shhh." My mom tries to silence her as if that's ever worked before. We all sit in the doctor's office, waiting for him to come back and deliver the news.

The entire day, from the time I tried to help that fan, has only gone downhill. The stylist put me in incredibly stiff ankle boots, and every time I winced in pain, she kept telling me, "It's okay, they're Dior." To which my ankle screamed back, "Fuck Dior!"

I could barely walk onto the set where we were having the interviews, and my face grimaced in pain the entire time. Hae-Jin stood behind camera one with her own grimace, though hers looked more pissed off.

And to make matters worse, during the live Q and A, someone asked about my life leading up to my debut. Why that would be of interest to anyone, I have no clue. And I was speechless. I still am.

But of course, ever the professional, Min-Kyung jumped in. She saw an opportunity and she grabbed it.

She had the entire audience eating out of her hand. They awww'd when she talked about loving to work with me on the show. They ohhh'd when she mentioned how much she enjoys how close we've become. And then she had them all crying as she told them the story of how I was sick as a child. How my dad died suddenly and left us in financial hardship. How we came to Korea begging his family for help, and they turned their backs on us. And how I overcame it all to make myself who I am today. She outed my whole life story in embarrassing detail without my consent.

Min-Kyung grew up healthy and wealthy. But that story doesn't gain popularity and fans. Tying herself to me and using my history to win fans' hearts is her new strategy. Showing herself as a caring girl in love with her costar is how she solidifies her place in this partnership and for our future. I should be thankful. I should be in awe at the mastery of how she sells us and the show. I should take notes, because this is what the studio wants from us.

Instead, I feel sick. She revealed personal things she had no right to say, that people don't have the right to even know, and I just sat there and let her spew it.

The doctor enters the room with my manager. Grim looks on their faces tell me everything I need to know. It's not good. Shit. My heartbeat picks up just as it always does when I think I'm in trouble.

"Jin-Suk," the doctor addresses me in a voice that immediately makes me nervous. "Your ankle is not broken, which is a relief. It's just a bad sprain. You won't need surgery, but you will need to wear a boot, and I do suggest at least four to six weeks minimum off of the ankle to give it time to heal."

I let out a deep sigh. It's not as bad as it could have been, though not gonna lie, it still hurts like hell.

"Well, it's a relief you won't need surgery," my mother says.

"Doctor, can you give us some privacy?" Hae-Jin asks.

The doctor nods and closes the door behind him.

Hae-Jin releases a breath, and her nostrils flare like a wild bull's. I gulp.

"This is just one of a number of unfortunate events today," she says, jaw clenched.

"Why, what else happened?" I ask.

"We received a call from a gentleman named Kim Byung-Woo."

A gasp comes from behind me. I look over my shoulder and see my mother's hand covering her mouth, eyes wide in shock.

"Mom?" I ask.

"Who's Kim Byung-Woo?" my sister asks.

"He's your keun ahbuhji, your father's older brother," my mother explains. I don't have the warmest feelings towards my dad's family. When he passed, they insisted he be buried in Korea. So our entire family had to fly out here when we barely had enough money to pay rent. And when we asked for some help, some support, we got nothing.

"Why is he calling the company?" I ask. My voice sounds panicked to my ears.

"Apparently, he saw the interview today. He wants to clear the air about what happened when your father died. He's willing to give an exclusive interview…for a cost. The network reached out to us first to confirm his identity," Hae-Jin says.

"How's he gonna do a tell-all interview when he knows nothing about us? And he wants to get paid for it?" I'm shaking, and my voice is too loud for this small exam room.

Hae-Jin examines me closely and then turns her eyes to my mother. "Unless you disagree, the company will take care of it." Take care of it. It all sounds so sinister, and I wonder how the hell I got here. My life has become its own K-drama.

"This isn't my fault. Min-Kyung is the one who shared my family's personal information in the interview. I didn't ask her to. I don't even know how she knew any of it." I'm so busted. I'm so busted.

Mom's hand rests on my shoulder and she squeezes. "No one's blaming you, Jacob," she says calmly. "Let's just let the company take care of it."

"We've discussed it, and we think the best idea right

now is for you to be out of the spotlight for a short while. With your ankle hurt, it's a good excuse. We'll cancel the photo shoot in Busan tomorrow and work around the injury for filming the finale. Then we'll issue a statement, and you and your family will go away for a couple months for the summer, maybe to Jeju-do. Weren't you complaining about not getting to see the beach? We'll take care of the errant family member."

Hae-Jin is all business. She sounds like a mafia consigliere. *We'll take care of the errant family member.* I imagine her with a scratchy voice, barely moving her mouth as she speaks in a raspy whisper. I fold my fingers to my thumb and hit the air a few times. *We'll lay low, boss*, I say in my head.

I look up, and all eyes are on me. I might have said it out loud. I clearly have seen a few too many mob movies in my day.

My mom and Jin-Hee giggle.

Hae-Jin just rolls her eyes and shakes her head. "I'll call you later when I have more information," she says over her shoulder as she leaves the room.

"Well, a few weeks off doesn't sound so bad," my mom says.

"It actually sounds like exactly what I need, to be honest," I say.

"Where should we go? It will be busy in Jeju right now. Yuck, so many crowds," Jin-Hee says.

"No, I don't think Jeju. And I don't think Busan. In fact, I have another idea," Mom says. She pulls out her phone, puts it to her ear, and steps outside, leaving Jin-Hee and me staring at each other, confused.

I can hear my mom's loud voice through the door but can't make out what she's saying or who she's talking to.

"I don't care where we go. It will just be fun not to have fans screaming for you all the time. Ew," Jin-Hee says, scrunching her nose.

"Hey, I can't help it that people love me," I say.

"You're gross."

"Well, after today, people will probably hate me. I looked so bad on-screen and god, all that stuff Min-Kyung said in the interview." I pull my hand down my face and shake my head, reminded of the interview, embarrassed.

Jin-Hee turns her phone towards me. "Look, the comments aren't that bad. Most people noticed you didn't seem yourself from your facial expressions. But they seem more worried than annoyed. And as far as MinJin goes, the opinions are mixed so far. Not everyone thinks that you and Minky should be a couple off-screen, too. She has a…reputation."

I raise an eyebrow at my little sister as I take the phone from her. What does she know about Min-Kyung's reputation? "Haven't I told you already to never read the comments?"

Still, I look at the page my sister has pulled up and scroll through hundreds of comments about the interview. Some are excited that we might be dating in real life. Lots of MinJin hashtags. Others say I'm too good for her because of her rumored past relationships. A few say I looked like I'd eaten a sour lemon.

"You know, you could solve this all by dating someone

else. The studio couldn't force you to date Minky if you already have a girlfriend."

"No more K-dramas or webtoons for you, understood? Where do you get these ideas? It's not that easy. The studio would never allow it. Plus, how am I supposed to even meet anyone and build an attraction, exchange witty banter, and escalate the emotions until we get to define the relationship? It's not like I have a lot of interaction with young women these days."

"Uh, wow, you really *are* a dork, huh? A true romantic," she says, shaking her head and rolling her eyes. "Real life isn't a K-drama, Oppa. Just find a girl you like and ask her out."

"Yeah, just like that." As if it was that easy.

"Well, you could at least make it seem like you're interested in other girls so they can't force you into dating Minky. I mean really, Oppa, you're just rolling over and letting them make you miserable. They even control all your logins. That's pretty much an invitation for them to tell whatever story they want online."

I rub my face with both hands, trying to erase this conversation. My ankle is throbbing, and I'm craving hoddeuk. I don't care that the studio controls my social media accounts. It's not like I have anything to post myself. I don't even have friends. The truth echoes through the hollows in my heart, reminding me of how lonely I really am.

Mom comes back into the exam room, a wide smile on her face as she finishes the conversation on the phone. "I am so excited, too. It's been so long. We can't wait to see you." I stare at her, wondering what she's up to. I wait for her to say goodbye to whoever is on the line.

"Well, I have some very good news," she announces as she hugs the phone to her chest. My mom's eyes sparkle, and the ever-present lines on her face seem to melt away. "Pack your bags, kids. We're heading to the land of sun, surf, fish tacos, and dear old friends."

No.

"Oh my god, we're going to San Diego?" Jin-Hee squeals with excitement.

"Yes! We leave tomorrow right after shooting the finale," Mom exclaims. "I've set it all up for us."

"But how?" I ask. The studio would never allow us to go all the way to America, would they?

"Don't you worry. They were worried about you flying with your injury, but we'll spring for business class seats," Mom says.

We have some money saved now. But I never feel comfortable with us spending recklessly. "Mom, I don't think that's a good idea."

"Well, we'll be saving money on everything else, because—" she clasps her hands together "—we'll be staying with the Chos." Her voice rises high with delight.

I freeze.

Exactly what I was afraid of.

Hannah.

My throat constricts tightly with a mixture of sadness, worry, regret...and anger.

It's been three years. I've always wondered if I'd ever see her again and what that reunion would look like.

Brutal. A bloodbath, that's what.

For a brief second I wonder what's worse: Staying in

Korea and being forced to fake feelings for someone I can't stand? Or going back home and facing the person I cared about the most, but left behind?

So much for time off.

The cameras and the studio may not be following me, but my past definitely is.

CHAPTER 3: *Hannah*

Mom has been bustling around trying to get the place ready for our guests. I, too, am getting the place ready…by hiding candy wrappers, trash, and dirty socks while making the guest room bed. Jacob and I both grew up neat freaks, which makes messing up Jacob's space so satisfying.

When my mom got off the phone yesterday with Mrs. Kim, her expression grew even brighter. Which meant my doom grew even greater. Jacob had some accident at work, probably an unfortunate pimple on his nose or something. I had hoped it meant he wouldn't be coming. But apparently, it means their trip will happen sooner than later. They'll be here today.

My heart threatens to Usain Bolt itself out of my chest. But I reprimand it for even pretending to care.

Because I don't. Care. About Jacob.

I'll be busy. I've got my internship and lifeguard camp and other important business to do. I have Nate to win back, and that requires my full focus. I won't even be around enough to see Jacob.

But that doesn't mean I can't do a little something to make his stay a bit less pleasant.

Our house has two rooms open at the moment, my sister's old bedroom and my old playroom, now called the guest room. The guest room is adjacent to mine, but there's more in there to sabotage. I've assigned it to Jacob and have been getting it ready for the unwelcome visitor. Thoughts of Jacob in the tiny children's bed and too-short sheets have the evil genius in me cackling inside.

I look at the clock. One thirty, almost time for them to arrive. One last thing. I shove a banana down my mouth and hide the peel underneath the bed. The ants are brutal during the warmer months. Let's set out a little welcome mat for them. I take one last look around. Perfect.

I hustle to my room and shut myself in. I turn on the *Hamilton* soundtrack and turn up the volume to drown out everything outside my door. I grab my television remote control and turn it on as well. The Food Network is on, and the sound of The Pioneer Woman making another one-pot wonder makes for some additional noise cancellation. And then I sit on my bed and wait.

I drown out the opening and closing of the front door. I drown out the call from my mother that they're home. I drown out the apologies she makes to our guests for my behavior. I drown out her calling to me one more time from downstairs. I drown out her footsteps as they make their way up to the second floor and my room. And I drown out her knock on my door.

What I can't drown out is her face inside my bedroom and the very irritated expression she's sporting.

"Hannah, didn't you hear me calling you?" she asks.

"Huh?" The duet of Lin-Manuel Miranda taking his shot and Ree Drummond mispronouncing every ingredient she's using is on full volume, but my mom is not having it. She doesn't even raise her voice or turn off the noise. She speaks with the authority of someone expecting to be listened to, and somehow, every single one of her words is heard over the commotion.

"We have guests downstairs. Do not make me ask you to come join us again." With a raise of her perfectly shaped, microbladed left eyebrow, she punctuates her point and walks away. My mom is no joke when it comes to hosting guests.

I let out a deep, tortured sigh, slump my shoulders, and drag my feet out of my room, down the stairs, and around the corner into the kitchen.

Standing there are three semi-familiar faces that all slowly turn my way when I walk in. Like a heat-seeking missile, my eyes betray me and focus on only one. My heart braces for a second and forgets to beat as I look at the young man in my kitchen. My eyes widen as I take in Jacob, my childhood best friend, standing in front of me. Gone is the small, scrawny, sickly boy. He's so much taller than he was, broader, his face more angular. He's handsome, 'ish, I guess. I mean, if you're into that type.

He's different. But also, the same somehow.

His eyes lock on mine. Light brown, a kindness that makes you feel like the sun is shining down on you whenever he looks your way. A flood of memories from the past scroll through my mind…a little boy and little girl, laughter, scraped knees, whispers and promises. Memories of betrayal, a best friend not coming home, fear, crippling loneliness.

He drops his eyes, and his cheeks flush pink, like he's watching the same highlight reel of our past.

Maybe he doesn't want to be here, either. Actually, I know he doesn't. He said so three years ago. He doesn't want to see me just like I don't want to see him. My feet itch to turn around and run away.

"Hannah unnie!" Lanky arms come and wrap around my waist as the head of a sweet young girl lands on my shoulder.

"How can you possibly be this big already?" I say to Jin-Hee, my voice not as shaky as I would have thought. I pull back and look at her face. "Holy cow, you are so gorgeous."

Her sweet smile grows even larger. Jin-Hee's face at twelve years old reminds me so much of Jacob's at that age, it jabs at my heart. Her smile is completely free, and her eyes sparkle.

"Hannah-ya, look how pretty you are," Mrs. Kim says in greeting.

"Annyeong haseyo," I say, bowing slightly. "Mrs. Kim, it's good to see you again." I go up and give my mom's best friend, and basically an aunt to me growing up, a hug. I try not to blush at her compliment. All Korean aunties tell young girls how pretty they are. They butter you up before they then start asking if you've gained weight and comment on how your hair is too long and criticize other details of your appearance.

"You still do not speak good Korean? Oh, Hannah. It is

important that you keep Korean in your heart." Her voice is kind, but her words are laced with an all-too-familiar judgment, and I bristle at the sentiment.

"Umma, leave her alone," Jacob says to his mom under his breath in Korean. I bet he thinks I don't understand him. But I do. I'm not as helpless with Korean as they assume just because I live in America. My accent may be off, but I do know the words.

I force a smile and walk to the refrigerator, grabbing a coconut water.

"Jacob, please take a seat. You have to rest your ankle," my mom says.

I look over my shoulder to see what she's talking about. Jacob's left foot is in a boot, the kind you get at the hospital. He hobbles to the table and takes a seat. A slight wince betrays his attempt to convince everyone he's fine. So he really was injured.

"Hannah, please offer some drinks for our guests," Mom chides me.

Mrs. Kim is already drinking out of a teacup, so I grab two more of the coconut water cartons, tucking my own under my arm. I put one down, none too gently, on the table in front of where Jacob is sitting. I barely spare a glance his way, but I catch him straighten slightly out of the corner of my eye. I try to ignore the heat I feel coming from his direction. He was always a human furnace.

A quick memory of Jacob and me sitting shoulder to shoulder, watching Fourth of July fireworks on a breezy summer night, flashes in my mind. The chill coming off Mission Bay feels so real from my memories. Goose bumps pepper my arms even now as I think of it. His natural body warmth cuts my shiver as he leans against me, unspoken, just noticing my discomfort and attempting to warm me up, both sets of our eyes never leaving the colorful lit-up sky.

I force myself back to the present, refusing myself any more strolls down memory lane. It won't do me any good. I am not that same girl, and he is not that same boy. He is not my friend. And I'm not into Korean things, or people.

Except I might pretend to be in order to win Nate back. TBD.

I grab the other carton and put it down in front of Jin-Hee, tousling her hair with my now-free hands, shaking my head, still unable to believe how much she's grown.

She giggles in response.

I swallow back the lump forming in my throat. I haven't allowed myself to miss him in the past. And now with him right in front of me, my heart is strangled with emotion, mourning over everything we let be forgotten when we grew apart, and struggling with the betrayal that took its place. Jacob's betrayal.

"Jin-Hee, you and your mom are in Helen's room. Jacob, you're in the playroom." Saying it out loud doesn't bring me as much satisfaction as I thought it might. Maybe I can have a laugh later when I picture him lying in a too-short kid's bed.

"Oh cool, thanks," she says. "I guess I just thought Jacob would sleep in your bed drawer like he used to."

I got rid of my twin bed and its roll-out trundle the summer the Kims moved to Korea and left us. I didn't plan on having anyone else ever sleep over, and no one has since then. "Got rid of that old thing years ago," I say.

"I'll take all our bags upstairs," I hear the deep voice say. Jacob's voice is completely different, but there's not even a tinge of a Korean accent in his English. I don't know why I notice that.

I shrug and say more nonchalantly than I'm feeling, "You know where you're going."

"I've spent more years in this house than I have away from it," he says under his breath.

"What's that supposed to mean?"

"You're treating us like we're strangers who've rented out rooms for the summer."

"Well, you *are* a stranger," I snark back, not bothering to lower my voice.

"You two, still always competing to be the one who is right. I'm so happy to have everyone here. It's just like the past, my favorite times with my favorite people," my mom says. Her voice is happier than I've heard in a long time. She means it. I can see the joy all over her face. Mom is happiest when she's taking care of anyone and everyone other than herself. And since it's just the two of us, I don't think it's been enough. It's why she's always at church. But now, in her mind, she has family here again.

"It's not like the past, Mom. We're not kids anymore. And I don't even know these people, really," I say.

"Well, we have the entire summer to make up for lost time," Mrs. Kim says. She nudges Jacob to translate for me.

"She said..." he starts.

"I understood her," I say sharply to Jacob. "I'm not completely useless in Korean," I say under my breath.

"Sorry," he says. "You used to hate having to speak Korean before," he adds.

"So did you," I remind him. "But I guess a lot has changed. Now you're taking a paycheck to be on a Korean show. I never would have called that one." My voice is sharp and bitter.

I let out a huff and angle my way past him, heading upstairs to my room, suddenly craving the comfort of my bed. Being angry is so exhausting. Straddling the past of knowing someone so entirely, and the present of not knowing them at all, is putting me off balance.

"Jacob, you can't take the bags with your ankle," Jin-Hee cries out.

"I'm fine," he says back.

But I know he's not. I see it. We all do.

"No. I'll take mine and Mom can take hers. And…"

"And I'll take yours," I say. But I don't look at him. He'll fight me if I give him the chance. So I reach and grab the handle of his very heavy bag. What the heck did he pack in here? Jacob used to have three T-shirts to his name. It feels like there are enough clothes in here for him to wear a new outfit every day. For some reason, even Jacob's wardrobe makes me feel betrayed.

I reluctantly start to drag the bag up the stairs.

I hear him hobbling right behind me.

I look back down the stairs just as he looks up and catches my eye. He narrows his own eyes and tilts his head slightly, trying to figure me out. Still no smile. I have the urge to look at him for hours, inspect each and every thing that's changed about him. I want to find out everything that's happened in three years.

No, I don't.

I shake my head, trying to loosen the hold he has on my mind right now. I remind myself that Jacob Kim, my best friend since birth, abandoned me. And he can say it's because there was something for him and his family in Korea. But he can't deny how much he wanted to leave.

We made plans for our lives here. We were supposed to be each other's sidekicks, the rock for each other as we entered high school. No one was gonna give us shit, and we'd never be alone.

But I've been exactly that, alone without a best friend, for three years, and probably even longer.

Because the entire time, he was looking for a way to escape.

Korea was too strong a draw, a reason to leave. A short summer trip turned into years. They never even came back for the rest of their stuff. Fourteen years old and abandoned by my best friend. And I didn't hear from him again.

I didn't even really get to say goodbye.

How do I forgive someone who just ghosted me, never mind my best friend? I don't. And I haven't. And I won't. Just watch me.

I leave the bag in front of his door without a word and turn the corner to walk into my room. I need to put some space between us. This is all too much.

Just as I shut my door, I hear a low laugh coming from

the guest room. "Of course she did," I hear Jacob say to himself.

I tried to piss him off, punish him by sabotaging the guest room, make it messy, leave zingers everywhere. But instead of getting mad, he inserted himself into my inside joke. He got it.

"Of course he did," I say quietly. I close my eyes and lean against my door. Nope, we're not playing this game. Inside jokes are for my entertainment only.

As far as I'm concerned, I can share a roof with Jacob Kim for a summer, but I won't be sharing anything else.

CHAPTER 4: *Jacob*

Of course she did.

I stare at the bed with the too-small, kid-sized mattress and the Pokémon bedding and can't fight the smile that breaks out. Exhaustion pulls at me so I can barely stand, I could really use a shower right now, and the tense reunion scene downstairs only adds to my fatigue. But staring at that bed and being one hundred percent certain Hannah did this to me on purpose makes me laugh.

This is some form of punishment, but I can't help but be amused by her effort. And that probably pisses her off even more. I laugh to myself.

She is such a nut.

I want to go next door and talk to her for hours. I want to break down and overanalyze together the interactions we had in the kitchen earlier, high-fiving when one of us guesses the other's unspoken intentions correctly. I want to make fun of our moms and belly laugh until we can't breathe. I want to sit in silence and feel completely at ease.

But instead, I remind myself of the black hole that was

Hannah's side of our friendship, trying to reach out to her only to have my messages return undeliverable, and all the times I really could have used a friend.

Fear. Hurt. Anger. She's probably the only one that can incite these strong feelings in me. And I won't let her. I don't have the energy.

I unstrap the boot to let my ankle free. My pain meds are in my mom's purse, and there is no way I'm hobbling back down those stairs.

I collapse onto the bed and sprawl myself out, feet hanging off the too-short frame. Relief floods through my muscles, and despite hearing the voices of my mom and Mrs. Cho laughing and gossiping downstairs, it feels so quiet, so peaceful here.

No screaming girls outside.

No cruel costar cutting me down at every turn.

No demanding manager watching my every move.

I don't even recognize that life and the person living it from my spot on this bed.

I have weeks of time all to myself. I can do whatever I want. I can… My mind does the thing it always does when I accidentally let it start to wander and think of silly things I want to do, to try, to eat, to explore. It blocks itself. I never have the time and most definitely don't have the freedom, so I rarely let myself even dream of such things. Of normal things.

But I'm here. And for the first time in a long time, I can. I should make a list.

I grab my backpack and pull out a sketchbook. It's blank. All the ideas of everything I want to draw in my head, but

I'm never given time to create them on the page. I'm going to fill it up with sketches this summer, I decide. My hands itch to create something beautiful.

"You look happy."

I turn my head, and my not-so-little-anymore sister stands in the doorway. Hannah was right. When *did* Jin-Hee get so big?

"I'm just glad to get away for a beat, ya know?" I wonder if she does know. She's a smart kid, and though my acting skills include irresistible teen love interest, I don't know if they're good enough to cover how stressed I've been lately.

"Me, too. I mean, San Diego feels way more like home than Seoul does," she says. "And Hannah is so cool and so pretty. Oh my gosh, she makes girls like Min-Kyung look like clones. She's awesome," Jin-Hee says.

I have also noticed how gorgeous Hannah has become. There's something that's always set her apart, a confidence, a badassness. She's really grown into herself. My heart stretches with some kind of pride. I'm glad one of us is confident in their own skin.

I live off of chicken breasts and steamed vegetables. I get an occasional treat like ice cream or patbingsu if my mom can talk me into it. It's all mind games from my trainee days, when my weight was strictly monitored and any possibility of a debut was threatened by bad skin or bloat. I look in the mirror, and all I see are reasons for me to lose my job or not get booked for the next one.

"You done fangirling?" I tease my little sister.

"Whatever," Jin-Hee says. "I'm gonna unpack. Wanna go exploring later?"

"I don't have a license. And San Diego is not like Seoul. You can't just walk anywhere or take the train."

"We can ask Hannah," she says.

"Uh, good luck with that," I say.

Jin-Hee shrugs like asking Hannah to drive us around will be the easiest thing ever. She leaves to go back to the room she's sharing with my mom.

I grab the flat pillow under my head and hug it close to my chest. Something sticks to my hand, and I pick up the candy bar wrapper hidden under the pillow. Wow, Hannah is in top form already. I throw the used wrapper aside and pull the pillow up to my face, taking a deep breath in. Yup, same laundry detergent they've always used. I smile at the familiarity. This smell, clean ocean and clear sky, wraps itself around me like I'm being swaddled in a blanket. I'm five years old again, seven years old, twelve years old, and now eighteen years old, and the smell is exactly the same.

Home.

I'm safe here. I don't have to put on a show here.

"Are you smelling the pillow?"

My head turns towards the open door where Hannah is standing, looking at me like I'm the creepiest person she's ever seen. "Kirkland brand laundry detergent from Costco," I say. She narrows her eyes. She still thinks I'm a creep. "I miss the hot dogs there. And the pizza." My mouth waters at the memory.

"They have brisket and acai bowls now," she says matter-of-factly.

"What? Why overcomplicate a good thing?" I ask. I'm

genuinely disappointed at the direction the Costco food menu has taken.

She shrugs one shoulder. "I know, right? Pretentious foodies and health nuts always ruin it for everyone else."

I try to stop myself from smiling but don't catch it in time. I feel the left corner of my mouth lift as a tiny bit of my delight in our conversation escapes. The familiarity is comforting in a way I hadn't realized I craved. I watch as Hannah's attention is drawn to my mouth. Her eyes betray her. She has a mask of pissed-off on her face, but her eyes dance with satisfaction knowing she made me laugh.

I know this game like I know the back of my own hand. It's a duel between us, a long-standing matchup that has defined our relationship over the years: fighting to hide the emotions, but knowing exactly what the other is feeling, and battling to not be the first to break. I've missed it.

"It's good to be back," I say. It's a moment of weakness, and I regret it immediately.

"Huh, funny. Last time we talked, you said you hated it here. Why did you even come?"

I should have been ready for it. The accusation. The hatred. The bite. I should have expected it, but instead, it finds a hole in my armor, and the words reopen three-year-old wounds.

How dare she throw that in my face like she has more reason to be mad than I do?

"My mom made me." The words are out of my mouth before I can stop them. "Trust me, it was hard to leave. Everything is amazing in Korea. You wouldn't believe the apartment I live in. The fans wait outside for me to come and go. It's crazy. I just had a top Korean designer send over a rack of clothes for free, just to have me wear them." I sell the words with every bit of acting skill I've built over the years. For some reason, I need her to believe this. I don't want her to think I've ever regretted the choice to go. And I want her to see that my life turned out better than hers. Because maybe then I'll believe it, too.

She narrows her eyes and bites down the corner of her mouth. Probably thinking of the next shot to hurl at me. But instead, she just rolls her eyes at me and turns to walk away.

"Hannah," I call out. There's so much I want to say to her. My best friend for my entire life and we can barely talk to each other now. It's too hard not being close to her. It's been hard for three years and six thousand miles apart, but it's an impossible struggle being this physically close, face-to-face again. One of us has to extend the olive branch first. One of us has to reach out so that we can each say we're sorry, right?

She stops but doesn't even turn around or look at me over her shoulder. Tension radiates off of her and smacks me in the face. Have we grown this far apart that we can't find our way back?

"What's a guy gotta do to get a McDonald's soft serve cone around here?" I ask. It's risky, bringing up past inside jokes. Our Sunday afternoons were always marked by counting up change and getting McDonald's soft serve ice cream cones across the street from church. She has to remember. But maybe it's too soon for nostalgia.

I hold my breath.

She turns her head slightly towards me. Even with her long hair lightened and her full lips painted red, I still see the girl I grew up with. She's taller now and has lost some of the soft curves in her cheeks, but it's a face I've looked at a thousand times and could paint by memory if I had the talent.

She takes a second and then shrugs off whatever she was about to say. "I wouldn't know. I don't eat that shit anymore," she says as she walks away.

Ouch.

I see not everything's changed. Even when we were kids, that girl could hold a grudge.

Fine. But she doesn't get to ruin this for me. I won't let her.

I lie back down and cross my arms behind my head. I'm free to do what I want, and I don't need Hannah for any of it. She can stay out of my way, and I'll stay out of hers.

My phone rings, and anything resembling a happy thought is zapped away.

"Hi, Hae-Jin," I answer.

"Are you staying off your ankle?" Not even a greeting. All business.

"Yup. I'm lying down as we speak. Hey, did you talk to my uncle? Is he, um, cooperating?"

"We're taking care of it," she says, leaving no room for discussion.

"Can you keep my mom in the loop at least?" I ask.

"Obviously. Listen, Jin, I didn't agree with the company's decision to let you go all the way to America for your break. It's made a lot of people's jobs tougher to do, just so you know."

Her voice is tight and so are my lungs, strangled with guilt. "We're looking into some publicity opportunities for when you're in California. I'm going to see if we can maybe get you and Minky some press time at the Teen Choice Awards in Los Angeles in August. Netflix may help make this happen."

My heart drops. So much for laying low. I'm not in California to work, to be recognized, to get press time. I'm here to get a break. I don't want them coming here to ruin everything. But Hae-Jin doesn't care about any of that. My desires are none of her concern.

Hae-Jin continues on with her one-sided conversation, and I barely listen. I close my eyes and take a deep breath and wonder what it is I'd choose to do if I had no other demands on my time. What would life be like if I wasn't a K-drama star?

"And I have some surprising news."

Hae-Jin's words grab me from my thoughts.

"Seems you've been nominated for Best Newcomer at the Baeksang Awards."

"What? Are you serious? Wow, that's amazing. Really? I'm nominated?" I take a second to allow myself to be happy about this. I've worked hard on my acting, and to be recognized for that feels good.

"I mean, it's unfortunate that you won't be at the awards ceremony." This is what I mean when I say I always feel like I'm in trouble. Wasn't it *her* suggestion that I leave town and stay out of the spotlight? "In any case, seeing the list of other nominees, you're likely not a favorite to win anyways."

Ouch. Direct hit to my ego.

Hae-Jin doesn't even stop to acknowledge the carnage.

"Check your email within the hour for the possible schedule from the publicity department. You'll have to post to your social media on your own at the designated times with the approved content. They will work on ways to connect you and Minky over the summer. You've made this very difficult on them, but since you can't be in Seoul, then we'll have to figure out a way to keep the fans engaged with your love affair."

"Love affair? That's a bit much, don't you think?" I say.

She ignores me and continues on. "And Jin, you and I will need to check in daily to ensure your progress and success."

"Daily seems excessive."

"Check your email and I'll call you tomorrow," she says and hangs up.

Why did I even bother flying across the world? There is no getting away from the demands of my life. And all the hopes I had for the summer feel like their own distant memories.

I hear the music coming from Hannah's room and wonder what she would think of all of this, my life. Three years ago, I'd have told her everything, and she would have helped me come up with a plan to be free. But now, I'm starting to feel stuck in a cage of my own choosing, and getting out is not an option.

CHAPTER 5: *Hannah*

Lifeguard camp is the worst.

There's so much…swimming. And practice pulling other students to the pool's edge. And pretending to be drowning in three feet of water so someone else can practice pulling me to the edge. My muscles hurt in places I didn't even know existed. Why did I think this would be a good idea, again? Oh yeah, because Nate is here.

I need to make him understand that having things in common can be acquired. We're both budding lifeguards now. Check. And I can learn to love K-pop. Some of the songs are bops! Check. I need him to see that we're good for each other. We didn't go through all that history to not see our futures together.

Plus, we had a plan. Be each other's person through all of senior year, and since we're both hoping to stay in San Diego for college, see if a freeway relationship between UCSD and San Diego State is doable. "No one loves this city like we do," he said. "We're meant to be," he waxed poetic.

I just have to remind him of all of this.

An odd pang of guilt hits me. Jacob used to be my person when we were kids. Thinking of Nate as my person now feels like betrayal. But why does it suddenly matter to me? I haven't had these notions in three years. The Kims staying in my house is messing with my head and getting in the way of my plans. I try to push all thoughts of Jacob out of my mind and press on.

I've got on my new red-and-white-striped bikini. And though it's technically not regulation for lifeguarding, it's my not-so-subtle way of trying to be noticed. I have to up my game to win Nate back. I'm not giving up on us so easily. I can remind him what he likes about me. And if all else fails, I can rewatch *Riverdale* and try not to laugh during the musical episode.

Jacob would laugh at the absurdity that is *Riverdale*.

Stop, I tell myself. No more.

"Hey, I know you don't really care about this or anything, but..."

Shit. When Shelly starts a sentence with that, she very well *does* know I care about whatever it is she's about to say to me. And it's likely to be a bomb. She honestly can't help herself.

But before Shelly says another word, I hear it. I hear a wonderfully melodic, high-pitched feminine giggle, something akin to tinkling bells. Not anything like my own hyena laugh. I slowly turn my head towards the hypnotic sound and am hit with the coldest reality I could ever imagine.

She's tiny, lucky if she's even five feet tall. Her ivory skin is pale and smooth, without a blemish, not even a single freckle. Though if she did have one, it would probably be symmetrical and perfectly placed, no doubt. She's wearing a modest one-piece with a skirt ruffle and manages to make it look attractive, for god's sake. Perky ass. Long, black, silky hair, so dark it looks almost blue.

Her hand covers her mouth as she laughs, and her eyes dance in delight.

She looks like the flawless girls I see on my mom's TV when I walk past her bedroom. The ones that are either singing and dancing on a variety show or crying and screaming on some K-drama. She's the prototype of every Grace, Esther, and Jeannie at any neighborhood Korean church east of the Pacific Ocean.

The blistering San Diego sun shines behind her, creating a perfect halo effect. Of course it does.

And Nate is staring at her like she's a prized jewel.

"Who is she?" I ask. I've never seen her around campus. I mean, I'm not the only Korean person at our school, obviously. But I am the only Korean girl in our friend group. And I've tried very hard to make sure I fit in despite being so different. If she's here, talking to Nate, she's trying to infiltrate my turf. Oh god, Hannah, do not break into some song and dance number about being a Jet. Get a hold of yourself.

My throat closes in on itself, and my nose tickles with the ghost-scent of the very expensive hair dye my stylist used on me to give me the just-right butterscotch-colored highlights. What's it all for if not to fit in, to impress Nate, to show him that I'm perfect girlfriend material?

"That's what I was about to tell you. I heard that Nate might be seeing someone new." Shelly's voice calls me back to reality.

"What?" I whip my head around to face hers, checking for any sign of a lie or overexaggerated gossip. I see none. "It hasn't even been a week since we broke up."

"Technically, the party was eight days ago, but I know what you're saying. The corpse isn't even cold yet."

I have two choices right this second. I can push Shelly into the pool and refuse to listen to her water-gurgled next words. I mean, it would be so easy. She's *right there.* Or, I can take a deep breath and go find out more information about this new complication.

My heart is pounding. She's not local, I'm sure of it. Based on the way she looks and acts, my guess is she just moved here from Korea. No SPF is high enough to keep you that perfectly pale. I can't stop my feet from dragging me closer towards her. Please let her breath stink like kimchi. Please let her hair smell like mothballs. Please let her have short, stumpy eyelashes.

"She just moved here. Her parents own that new store at the mall that sells all that cool streetwear," Shelly informs me.

Damn. I like that store. It's unfortunate that I now have to get every person I know to boycott it.

Shelly and I reach the shallow end of the pool, where That Girl sits at the edge, feet dangling daintily in the water. Nate sits down next to her, looking huge and smitten.

"Do you like BTS? BTS is my ult. I'm Taehyung bias,

OT7 wrecker," she says to Nate. "I also really like BLACK-PINK. Lots of people say I look like Jisoo." Her voice has a slight lilt to it that reminds me of my cousin who grew up in Busan and only moved to the States a couple years ago.

"I've been getting into fourth-gen groups like Ateez and Stray Kids lately," Nate responds. "Soo-Yun, you really do look like you could be Lead Visual in a K-pop group."

What is this secret code they're talking in? Is it K-pop? Great. They have something in common. But still, that's only one…

"Do you watch K-dramas? My new favorite is *Heart and Seoul…*"

…make that two things they share.

"Kim Jin-Suk is so handsome and talented. He has dimples like Jungkook!"

My steps come to a halt as soon as the name leaves her lips. Kim Jin-Suk. I know that name. It's Jacob Kim's Korean name. Is she talking about the same guy? My childhood bestie that abandoned me? The one likely sitting in my home sweating in his room since I only left him the small fan that works but half of the time? She's fangirling as if he's a big deal. She's definitely from Korea. It's not like anyone else here would know him.

"I love *Heart and Seoul*," one of my classmates calls out. "Kim Jin-Suk is so hot."

"Ohmigod, right? I'm dying over that show," says yet another. "I'm so glad there's gonna be a second season."

Everyone starts to gather around her, eager to take part in this apparently riveting conversation about my childhood best friend and some lame TV show he's on. I reminisce about the good ol' days when those shows were only popular in Korea and I didn't have to worry about the mindfuck that is going on in my head right now.

And has everyone lost their minds? Jacob is not "so hot." I mean, I guess I could see why someone might find him just hot, but adding a "so" in front is a little much.

No. No. No. This isn't happening. Worlds colliding in some weird alternate reality. I've spent my entire life compartmentalizing my Korean home life and my American school life and keeping them very, very separate. None of my school friends have even met my family. This is all just too weird, and all because of Jacob Kim. Curses!

I hold my breath for a moment, waiting for Nate to see me, for his eyes to meet mine. He should know how confusing this is for me. He gets me, I think.

But he doesn't stop staring at the new girl, the shiny, more authentically Korean version of me, listening to her talk about my ex–best friend. My cheeks heat as rage builds inside me. Jacob left San Diego and didn't look back. It's not fair that he suddenly gets all this attention. It's not fair that it's suddenly "in" to be Korean, and it's throwing my world upside down. And this new Korean girl gets Nate's attention when I've been here all along.

"You're way hotter," Shelly says out of the blue. "I mean, I didn't even know he was into Asian girls."

I stop and direct a stare at her.

She shakes her head. "I mean, like *real* Asian girls. You're American Asian, ya know?"

"Uh, thanks, Shelly. But, I'm Korean… Korean American. I mean, I guess there is a difference between someone who's, I don't know, directly from Korea or something. But…"

"Yeah, that's what I meant," she says. "Anyways, I'm gonna go say hi to Lizzie. Laters."

Great. I didn't want to have to explain this to Shelly anyways. I'm not even sure I understand it myself. But I've spent my entire life trying to be an "Americanized" Korean, finding a perfect balance in my identity to fit in with everyone around me, without seeming to be trying too hard. And here comes a "Koreanized" girl who is everything I looked down on about my heritage, and she wins the hearts. Is that what Nate wants? Apparently, all the world wants this now. It's suddenly hip to be Korean. And it's clear I'm just not Korean enough. In fact, I feel like the least Korean person here.

"Hannah, come here. I want to introduce you to someone." Why is our swim coach calling me over? I walk to where the group is gathered, dragging my feet in protest. "Hannah, this is Soo-Yun. She recently moved here from Korea. Soo-Yun, this is Hannah Cho."

Why our coach felt it important for me specifically to meet the new kid is obvious. But I don't even have it in me to call him out on it.

"Annyeong haseyo, Hannah-ssi," Soo-Yun says, quickly standing up and bowing. What the heck? Why is she acting like I'm her mother or something?

"Daebak," one of the other students says.

I turn and shoot my classmate a death glare. He can enjoy Korean stuff all he wants. But don't start speaking Korean slang to me like we're bros.

I'll never be able to wrap my head around all of this.

I turn back to Soo-Yun. "Hey," I say, raising a limp hand. "Nice to meet you."

I can't take any more. I turn and look for my escape route. I could just run and not look back. Be free from this madness.

"Alright, guards, let's warm up with ten laps, freestyle," the coach calls out. "Group one, in the water."

Plans foiled. Great. Just what I was hoping for...more swimming. Well, it's either swimming, surrounded by my confusing present, or going home to face my tortured past. I take a deep breath, hold it, and jump in.

As soon as practice is done, I take off. I don't even say goodbye to anyone. It's not like they'd even notice I was gone. Not with Soo-Yun in the picture now.

All the emotions of the past couple days catch up to me, and I'm suddenly feeling trapped. I need to get away.

I didn't anticipate how hard it would hit me seeing Jacob and his family again. It shouldn't matter. Why does it matter? He's history, the past, and I've had all these years to make my childhood friend a distant memory.

But the moment I saw him, memories consumed me, flooding every one of my senses. Kind eyes, sounds of crickets on warm summer nights, the smell of strawberry-and-lychee boba, all so familiar it felt like a warm hug and a punch to the face at the same time. What's not familiar are the angles of his face now, the deep timbre of his voice, evidence of the years lost between us.

Problem is, the moment I opened up this once-locked

box of childhood good times, I also allowed all the pain of being deserted, alone, and friendless out, too. And I'm not loving that so much, I gotta say.

And then to have it thrown into my face while at lifeguard camp? There's just no reprieve.

I grab my keys and squeeze them tight in my hand, pressing harder until the jagged edges start to sting. I have to get out of here. I run to my car and jump in. The black leather front seat is hot as hell, and pain lances the bottom of my legs, but I can't be bothered. I'm willing to wear maxi dresses and jeans to cover first-degree burns for the rest of the summer in order to avoid the risk of being stopped from my escape.

"Ouch, damn it!" The steering wheel, however, has other plans. I shake my scalded hands out. There's no way I can hold on to this thing.

I mentally fall to my knees, pounding the ground. Weather is so unfair! Damn you, San Diego summers.

I start the car, turn on the AC, and back out of my spot in the parking lot. I don't even have to think about it. My car heads west towards the water.

As I pull onto the crowded Torrey Pines Road, all the tension releases from my body. It's really hard to be upset when the blue water of the Pacific Ocean is laid out before you. Despite the crowds walking the beach path, and the cars stopping in the middle of the road, hoping for a parking spot near the ocean, my face spreads into a smile. I turn the air conditioner off and roll down all my windows, soaking in the sun and the ocean breeze.

My dad loved living in San Diego because of the ocean.

In his mind, it was a symbol of success, having made it in life. Maybe that's why he moved to Singapore. It's all about success symbols, with being an international commuter the next step up towards the top of the corporate ladder.

A deep ache fills my chest. I really miss my dad. I haven't seen him in six months. He's missed the last two Skype calls we were supposed to have. I wonder for a second what it will be like the next time he comes to San Diego, a visitor in his own home. Will he be happy to see me? Or will jet lag and exhaustion render him out-for-the-count for most the trip until it's time for him to pack and leave? That's the problem with too-long distances and too-short trips. There's barely any time to connect, to remind us we're family.

When he left me, left us, to take a job in Singapore, he swore it was temporary. He promised we'd see each other often. He hugged my mom, gave my sister a kiss on the cheek, and then picked me up. I wrapped my legs around him and held on to his neck. I was too old and too big to be doing this. But he didn't care, and neither did I.

"Don't go, Daddy," I said, twelve years old and crying for my dad to stay.

"I won't be long, Hannah-ya," he whispered into my ear.

And then he was gone.

Five years later and he's the president of the company now. And I see him three times a year, if I'm lucky.

I slam on my brakes just in time to avoid hitting a car who suddenly stopped in front of me with their turn blinker on. Mutherfucker thought he found a potential parking space. I shake my head. That one's a fire zone...every newbie falls for it. Rookie.

At least I'm brought back from woe-is-me'ing about Dad.

I'm at the end of Torrey Pines Road and the end of my escape route. Time to head home.

Just as I merge back onto the freeway, the ringing of an incoming call fills my car. A quick check of the screen on my dash and I press the accept button.

"Hey," I answer in a resigned sigh.

"Uh-oh. What's going on?" My sister's familiar voice, on the other hand, is both kind and a jab to my heart, a reminder that she's three thousand miles away.

"Well, the Kims are here," I say.

"Did you get everything ready at the house?" Helen asks me from the other side of the phone.

"Yeah, I set it up perfectly, used the Pokémon sheets and everything. That comforter is for a ten-year-old. It's way too short for him," I say. "And I also put that crazy clock back up on the wall. You know, the one where the bird flies out and cuckoos every forty-two minutes?" Just thinking about Jacob being driven mad by these crazy cuckoos raises my spirits a little.

"Remind me never to get on your bad side. Oh wait, I moved to Boston and sealed my fate. My bad."

She jokes about it, but it still stings. I laugh into the phone, but it sounds bitter. "It will never not be too soon," I say.

Helen and I were always close. She and Jacob were the two people I trusted the most. After college she was supposed to stay in San Diego for a job offer. But after "just a quick trip" to Boston, she met a guy, fell in love, and ended up staying, working for a firm that offered her more money and better growth opportunities. As if love, money, and success are all that important. Sheesh.

"Oh, Hannah," she says, "sounds like you really rolled out the welcome mat. Listen, I know you're feeling a little raw right now after the breakup, but try not to take it all out on poor Jacob. He hasn't been back in America for three years, and who knows how out of place he'll be. Don't just leave him somewhere to fend for himself, okay? At least try and remember that he's basically family."

"It was so weird and awkward. Like seeing strangers in your house. Oh yeah, because there are strangers in my house."

"Stop being so dramatic. Okay, now tell me. What's Jacob like? What was it like seeing him again? Does he seem like a TV star? Is he as cute in person as he is on-screen?"

"I don't know. I didn't pay attention. I'm nursing a broken heart over Nate, remember? I need to figure out how to get him back. I'm pretty sure he wasn't thinking straight when he broke up with me, and now there's this new Korean girl, Soo-Yun," I say. "He's not replacing me with her, is he? God, how badly would that suck? Dumped and replaced. Should I start going by my Korean name, too, you know, to be more authentic?"

"I'll remind you that your Korean name is Ha-Na. Don't know if that's gonna make that big of a difference to people. Listen, you're irreplaceable, and don't you forget it. Nate's a fool. Now tell me what I want to know."

"Helen, I don't have time or energy to think of anyone

else but Nate. I barely glanced at Jacob for more than a second, and he hasn't crossed my mind since."

"Uh-huh..." she draws out.

"Hey, if someone wanted a crash course on all things K-pop and maybe an entry-level K-drama to watch, where would one start? I need to have something in common with Nate, and quick."

"Well, you've got a K-drama star sleeping in your house. That might be a good place."

"I don't acknowledge his presence," I say.

"C'mon. Throw me a bone. Is he hot?"

"Ew." I cannot listen to my sister fangirl over Jacob. "He's tall."

I hear her laugh on the other end of the phone. "You like tall," she says.

What the heck does that mean? Who doesn't like tall? That doesn't mean anything. "And...he's skinny. Tall and skinny. And he has a ridiculous bowl haircut like all those trendy K-pop boys."

She keeps laughing, and my face really heats now. I close the windows and crank the air-conditioning. The 56 freeway is uncharacteristically empty of cars, and I press the gas to go a little faster. Maybe I'll get pulled over and taken to jail and can avoid Jacob for the rest of the summer. They give you three square meals a day, right?

"You just told me you want to be a fan of those trendy K-pop boys," she reminds me. Ruthless.

"That's for Nate. I need to share his passions."

"I still can't believe Nate Anderson, of all people, is a Koreaboo now. Anyways, Jacob really works that look."

How dare she defend Jacob's bowl haircut? It's indefensible. And why does she keep bringing the conversation back to him?

"I mean, if the rumors are true," she continues, "he's super in-demand for the upcoming shows being produced. And apparently, he managed to snag the hottest Korean actress right now. Though I don't quite believe it. There's something off about her. That last interview of theirs was just wrong, if you ask me."

I pull into the driveway at home but keep the car running.

"What do you mean? Who is she? What interview?" I ask. "You know what? Forget it. I don't want to know."

"Oh yeah, I forgot how you hate all things Korean. You really should broaden your horizons and embrace your culture, little sister. K-pop, K-dramas, Korean snacks, Korean makeup are all the rage right now. But don't just do it for Nate."

"I don't hate Korean things. I just won't jump on the bandwagon. You will not see me crying over some K-drama with a sheet mask on, eating uncooked ramen noodles they've packaged to pawn off as a snack. No way."

"Hey, that was my weekend! Why are you calling me out like this?" Helen chuckles at her own joke. "Anyways, you might want to check out Jacob's show, *Heart and Seoul*. It's on Netflix now. It's awesome. Promise me you'll at least take a look, okay?"

I let out a groan, as if being asked to do the most miserable thing in the world. Close enough.

"Hannah, listen. I know you felt hurt. And boy do I

know you can hold a grudge. But give Jacob a chance to be your friend again. It's been three years," she reminds me. "Don't you think it's time..."

"No, it's not time. It never will be time," I say definitively. "Plus, I don't have time for any long-lost friendships. I have to focus on winning Nate back."

"Why can't you do both? Why can't you spend time with both Jacob and Nate this summer?"

I freeze at the thought of the two of them in the same space. That would not go well.

"And why do you have to try so hard? If Nate likes you and wants to be with you, he should be fighting to get you back. If he doesn't, he's not worth your time. You don't have to change anything about yourself for him or for anyone."

I let out a deep, long-suffering sigh that turns into a raspberry. If only it was that easy. "That may be how it works in K-dramas. But in real life, I don't exactly have a lot of guys asking me out."

"You don't need a lot. You just need the right one."

"And that's why I want to fight for Nate. There's something special about knowing someone your whole life. You know, two kids growing up together, starting as enemies and blossoming into more."

"I get the whole soul mate appeal. But are you sure it's Nate who's your destiny?"

"There is no such thing as soul mates or destiny. I'm just saying that Nate is a good guy who was there for me when everyone else in my life was leaving." My sister can be Team Jacob over Nate, but there's no denying that Nate was the one out of everyone who stuck around and is still here.

Well, that is, before he broke up with me.

"Look, I'm at home now, so gotta go before Mom loses it," I say. "Talk later. Bye."

I hang up before she can keep nagging me. She really is her mother's daughter.

I turn off the car and get out, taking a deep breath before going back inside. I catch movement out of the side of my eye and look at the window of the guest bedroom. The blinds are pulled up, and Jacob's standing there. I still can't get over how tall he is now. He was a small boy growing up. And maybe he's not as skinny as I described to my sister. He's filled the entire window.

I force myself to look away.

The memory of the fateful day three years ago that Jacob and I Skyped, him in Korea for the summer with his family, me at home, bored and waiting for him to come back, flashes through my mind. He told me that something crazy happened that I'll never believe and that they would be staying in Seoul for longer than expected. He was going to miss the first day of high school. He didn't know how long they'd stay there. Please don't be mad.

I broke down and cried.

I was furious. I was heartbroken. I had a bad feeling.

He broke down and cried.

He was scared. He was alone. He seemed uncertain.

His last words forever seared into my brain were the greatest betrayal of all. "I hate my life in San Diego." Most of the other words feel like a fuzzy memory. But those words screamed at me loud and clear.

I was the biggest part of his life in San Diego.

I waited.

I waited for his next call. I waited for news he was coming back home. I waited weeks, months, and with no word.

The tightness in my chest is as fresh as it was that day. I'm tired of caring about people who end up leaving me.

And I've never been good at giving second chances.

CHAPTER 6: Jacob

I am going stir-crazy.

In a completely unexpected turn of events, my ankle is starting to feel better. I can actually put some weight on it now. That could be because I've been stuck in this house for a week with nothing to do. A few weeks away from Korea, away from my regimented schedule, should be freeing, relaxing, fun. Instead, I've been sitting on the couch watching SEVENTEEN and TXT dance practice videos on YouTube with my sister while listening to my mother and her best friend talk about Korean recipes and reminiscing for hours about their younger years. We've only been to the church, H Mart, and Target.

The only upside is that I've had time to work on my sketches. Drawing wasn't anything I'd ever done as a kid. But one of the other trainees gave me a sketchbook and some pens, and I got hooked. For someone self-taught and who doesn't have a whole lotta time to practice, I'm better than I thought I'd be. I've finished three sketches this week alone and I…don't hate them? I have that much time on my hands. But there's only so much inspiration I can get from inside this house.

I need out. There are things I want to do, places I want to see. I want to take in every detail of the ocean, palm trees, little kids building sandcastles. And I want to stretch my drawing skills, putting it all on the page if I can.

And mostly, I just want to do things that regular people my age do, but I haven't had the time or liberty to experience since I was a kid.

Other than the one time she made a big deal about leaving for some internship, Hannah has been locked inside her bedroom most days. At least that's what she wants us all to think. Honestly, I suspect she's been sneaking out. Her music plays way too loudly and on a constant loop for hours on end. And even when I do see her around the house, she barely says a word. I want to ask her what she's doing all day long "in her room." But she never gives me the chance.

At least that's still consistent. Hannah will shut you out if she doesn't want to hear what you have to say. I know this firsthand. Three years ago I hurt her. And not one to be outdone, she cut off all communication and hurt me back.

I overheard Hannah and her mom arguing about teaching Vacation Bible School at the church, but she flat-out refused. Her mom yelled something about taking me around town. She wouldn't be my first choice. But it's been a week, and no other options have presented themselves. So at this point, I'd suffer time with Hannah and her attitude just to get out of the house and actually do something.

Right now, I'm craving carne asada and fish tacos. Drooling for In-N-Out burgers and fries. I'd kill for a Jersey Mike's Italian sub.

No offense, because Mrs. Cho is a really good cook, but I'm sick of Korean food. I suspect we eat in most of the time because everyone's still afraid of everything I'm allergic to, and we're not as familiar with places out here. But I've done my research. Restaurants in America actually are much more aware and careful of food allergies than those in Korea. And my allergies really have become less severe over the years with the medication I've been receiving in the clinical trial. Thinking about how this medication works and will be available for other little kids growing up with severe allergies makes me feel like maybe being in Korea is worth it, even with as demanding and unforgiving as my job can be.

I look down at my phone's notes app and add two more things to the list I'm building. The way things are going, this is all probably just a pipe dream. My "Things to Do in San Diego" list, places I want to go to, things I want to eat, things I want to experience while I'm here, feels out of reach. It's all stuff I miss from when I lived here growing up or stuff I've missed out on since I've been in Korea. And I need someone to take me.

I need Hannah.

It's hot in the room, and I'm starting to get uncomfortable. I notice the small room fan in the corner and go to turn it on. It's not plugged in, so I grab the cord and get down on all fours, looking for the nearest outlet. I reach under the bed to try and get the prongs to match up with the holes.

My hand brushes against something slimy. I pull out a very overripe, almost black banana peel. Wow, that's low even for Hannah.

I wipe my hand on my shorts and reach back to find the plug.

"Ow, fuck," I hear as I'm on the ground.

It's Hannah. And she's up to something on the other side of the wall. For some reason, I can hear so much clearer down here through the outlet. Her music must be playing from a speaker projecting higher up.

I hear her window slide open, and my suspicions are confirmed. She's sneaking out.

I get up and look both ways outside my room. The coast is clear, and I hustle down to the front door. My ankle smarts a little, but I ignore it and power on. I open the door slightly, making sure she doesn't see me from outside, and I go out, checking around the porch corner to see which way she's going.

Hannah's in short denim cutoffs that make her tanned legs look so much longer. It's kinda odd seeing a Korean girl this tan. Most of the girls back home preserve their pale skin. She's got a tank top on, and I can see the straps to her red bathing suit tied at her neck. And her hair is...blond. She must have gotten it lightened during all that time she avoids me. It reminds me of when Rosé from BLACKPINK went blond. I can barely recognize her from behind. But I know that walk anywhere.

She can't walk to the beach from here, so where the heck is she going?

I follow her a couple blocks, and we're heading towards

the high school pool. I recall an argument Hannah and her mom had about lifeguard camp. Her mom saying no, she can't go. And Hannah storming out of the room saying something about her social life being ruined.

Looks like she's sneaking away to claim that social life of hers.

I can't help myself. I keep following her. I'm slowed down by my ankle and have a slight limp. But curiosity fires all the neurons in my brain, making me forget about the pain. I wonder what Hannah is like now. Who are her friends? Is she the same smart-ass, hilarious, strong-willed, incredibly loyal, and kind girl I knew growing up?

There's a weird feeling in my chest, a tightness. I miss her. Anger mixed with regret made me accept the years without her in my life. But being right here with her, face-to-face, it's hard not to think of the friendship and bond we once had.

I'm overdressed in my skinny jeans and oversized Off-White T-shirt, and sweat is dripping down my back. I wipe away the errant bead on my forehead. Damn hair sticking to my face. I look over the fence and check out all the kids hanging around in their bathing suits. All the guys are wearing baggy board shorts down to their knees, haircuts buzzed and short for the most part. I make a note to get a longer pair of swim trunks for the summer. In Korea, we wear them shorter and tighter. I have the feeling I'm asking to be made fun of if I stick to what I've packed.

I'm bigger than I was when I was a kid. But I'm not looking to get picked on by these local guys.

The girls are all in two-piece bathing suits, pretty skimpy, too small, and impractical for lifeguarding if you ask me. But I get the sense that saving lives isn't exactly why they're all here. Everyone's fit, and tan, and talking and laughing too loud.

I'm not used to being around groups of kids hanging out together. I hate that it feels foreign, and not just because I'm in America. It's an irritating reminder that I actually have no friends.

Hanging out in the group but off a bit to the side is Hannah. She's laughing at all the right times, just as everyone else does. I'm so used to Hannah being the one telling the jokes that make me laugh. I'm thrown off watching her within this group. She's trying way too hard to fit in.

Both frustration and sadness battle within me.

Why is she trying so hard to hide? She's never been a follower.

An instructor blows a whistle, and all the kids start pairing up for a drill. Hannah rushes over to stand next to a tall, built, tan guy sure to be named something like Chad. He looks at her with a small smile and drops his eyes down to her chest.

I'm surprised by how much I want to fucking punch him.

I ball my hand into a fist and clench my jaw. I take a closer look at the face so I can imagine clocking him in his perfectly whitened teeth.

My blood turns cold as recognition punches me first.

I'm suddenly ten years old again. Nate Anderson holds my EpiPen above his head and I jump to try and reach it. I'm surrounded by his laughing friends, and I'm four inches too short, freaking out that I'll never get it back.

I'm eleven years old again. Nate Anderson has me pinned against a wall at school, threatening to break my arm if I don't let him cheat off my math test. My shoulder is on fire, and tears threaten to fall. I beg myself not to cry.

I'm twelve years old again. Nate Anderson grabs my GameStop bag with the video game I saved up all summer to buy. I pretend to be brave, and yell at him to give it back, and he laughs at me. They're all laughing at me. I don't scare him.

And then Hannah steps in front of his face. She tells him to fucking give the bag back or she'll tell his mother how he smoked cigarettes behind the lockers. I've never heard Hannah cuss before. And then she leans in and whispers that she'll tell all his friends how he got sick afterwards.

Nate's smug face is a forced expression. There's fear in his eyes. He's afraid of Hannah. But he laughs it off and throws my bag to the ground. Hannah picks it up and plays it off like nothing happened. She walks home, and I follow her. She starts talking about fan fiction she wants to write in the *Star Wars* universe. And she asks me what universe I'd write about.

Eighteen-year-old me bends over and wants to throw up. It's the heat, that's all. I'm not that scrawny, small, weak kid anymore. And Nate Anderson means nothing to me.

But he clearly means something to Hannah.

I can't watch anymore. I turn around and limp back the way I came.

Two things I've figured out during my rise to fame over the last few years. One, people will use me to get what they want. And two, in order to get what I want, I need to start using people right back. What's it gotten me so far being the nice guy? I'm definitely overworked and underpaid for what I do for the company. I bend over backwards for them, basically on call to step into the role of Kim Jin-Suk whenever they need me, 24/7. And I have zero friends to show for it, no life outside my job. I get tutored on set for school. I'm treated like dirt by my costar and my manager.

But this summer, I have Hannah. And if I'm gonna do all the stuff I planned to get done while I'm in San Diego, it's time I get off my ass and make it happen. And if in turn I can buy myself a little more time away from the demands of the studio, all the better. I won't let myself feel guilty about my plan.

"Mutherfucker! You scared the crap out of me," she whisper-screams as she climbs back through her window and catches me sitting on her bed. She's rubbing the top of her head, having banged it on the way in.

"You've got quite the mouth on you," I say. My voice is calm, cool, collected. I've got this. It's my turn to get what I want.

Her tan cheeks turn a slight shade of pink, and I want to smile, knowing I've gotten to her. But I don't. I hold my face in check. I'm a pretty good actor, damn it. At least, that's what I'm told. It's what I get paid for. Let's earn that cheddar.

She stands and throws her hand on her hip. "What are you doing in my room?" And there's that attitude I've been waiting for.

"Waiting for you," I say. "Good day at lifeguard camp?"

Her eyes grow huge. "You—you—you followed me?" she hisses.

"You bet I did," I say back calmly.

Her nostrils flare, and irritation rolls like waves off of her skin, aiming their break right at me.

"How dare you? What kind of creep are you? Those years in Korea turned you into a real weirdo. I don't know how you guys do stuff out there, but that's not okay here in America."

"Oh, I remember how it's done here in America," I say, standing up, putting most of the weight on my good ankle so as not to show any weakness. Hannah tilts her head back to look at me. "Guys like Nate Anderson pick on and steal from and bully the little kid. And apparently, girls all fall head over heels for that shit. Isn't that right, Hannah?"

Her mouth drops open, and I'm not quite sure if she's gonna try and deny it, or apologize, or tell me to fuck off. But I keep going before she can say anything at all.

"Look, I don't care who you hang out with or make a fool of yourself over. But I bet your mom would care that you're sneaking out of the house when she told you not to go to lifeguard camp. I don't know what's going on between you two, but I have a suspicion she's about as big of a Nate Anderson fan as I am. I always did love and respect your mom."

Her fists ball up at her sides, and I keep going, poking at the bear. I can't stop myself.

"What I do care about is having some fun this summer. And I have a full list of things I'd like to do, places I'd like to go, things I'd like to eat. I don't get a ton of time off, and I'm gonna make the most of it. Think of it as a summer bucket list for everyday teenagers, things I'd do if I wasn't a famous actor in Korea." I nearly roll my eyes at my own words but stop myself. I'm almost there. "But I need a ride to do it all. So, Hannah." I step even closer to her, mere inches separating us. She smells like chlorine, coconuts, and sunshine. I stare down into her eyes and hold her glare, daring her to look away. "You're going to be my chauffeur this summer."

"No way. I have things to do, too. And your needs mean nothing to me. Just as history has proven that my needs mean nothing to you."

I jerk back a tiny bit and close my eyes for a second, defending myself from her direct hit. The pure vitriol in her voice poisons my resolve. I look back at her, searching her face for any sign that my once best friend is still in there. But I can't let up now. I'm too close to getting her to agree to help me, and I need her to make this happen. I straighten up, standing even a little taller, and press on.

"Look, it's the perfect cover. You can go to lifeguard camp during the day and say you're taking me out. We hit up a few of the things on my list after camp and come back home. Our moms are none the wiser. We both win."

Her eyes narrow, and her mouth is curled up into a snarl. She looks about to bite. I can almost see the thoughts running through her head. But then she stomps her foot in frustrated surrender.

She opens her mouth to say something, but I cut her off. "It's not that hard, Hannah. Take me around San Diego.

And your mom doesn't have to know about your other, not as interesting, if I must say, summer plans."

Her lips jut out into her signature pucker.

"How dare you come back to San Diego without so much as a word in three years and blackmail me to be your servant. Who do you think you are?"

I swallow my anger, but I can't help the heat rising up my neck. She wants to yell at *me* for us not talking in three years?

"I wasn't the one who never responded," I say.

"You disappeared..."

"I was in training..."

She holds her hand up in my face. "I don't care. I'm not doing this. I don't want to hear your excuses. I won't."

I'm so close to getting what I need, what I want. I can't let her say no. Self-loathing creeps into my head, accusing me of being an awful person, of pushing Hannah too hard. But I ignore the taunts and keep going.

I shrug my shoulder and turn to walk out. "Wonder if our moms are back from church yet. I think it's time for a little chat. Being grounded during summer break would really suck. Start practicing those fun camp songs for kids, Hannah. I always did think you'd make a great VBS teacher."

A frustrated growl comes from behind me. "One hour a day, two days a week," she says. How cute. She thinks this is a negotiation.

"Three hours a day, five days a week," I offer.

Her jaw drops open and then closes as her face puffs up in fury.

"And I'll pay for gas," I throw in.

"Two hours a day, three days a week," she shoots back reluctantly. It hurt her to give that much up, I can tell.

"Three hours, five days," I say, "and I get you out of teaching VBS."

Her eyes widen. She lets out a deep breath. I think I have her.

"I control the music," she demands. "And I won't participate in any of these things you want to do. I just drive. I wait in the car. And—" she stops to think of what else to demand "—we don't have to talk to each other."

"Sounds like fun, the perfect summer companion," I say sarcastically. I hold out my hand.

She stares down at it and then moves her eyes back up to mine. Her full mouth is twisted into a frustrated knot.

"Shake my hand, Hannah," I say.

She lets out another frustrated growl, this one even higher-pitched than the last. I wait for her to stomp her foot again, but she manages to hold back. "Fine," she hisses and grabs my hand. Hers is tiny in mine, but I envelop it and shake for us both. "But let's just be clear, I'm doing this in protest. We are *not* friends. I am a hostage to your twisted plan, and I will not enjoy even one minute of it."

I let go of her hand and turn to leave, playing as nonchalant as I can. The walk out of her room is painful, but I do it with a sense of victory and without another word. I close the door behind me.

I'm getting what I want. I don't have any regrets blackmailing Hannah to get it, either. I mean, she said it herself: she's not my best friend anymore. Shit, she's basically a stranger. I win.

I close my eyes, take a deep breath, and force away the feeling of dread. Why do I get the feeling I'm gonna end up the loser after all?

CHAPTER 7: Hannah

I have two options today. I can either eat the expired turkey meat in the fridge, hoping it will cause me illness so great that no one can deny my need to visit the emergency room, or at the very least, stay home in bed. Or I can suck it up and go on this first outing with Jacob. Rancid turkey meat. Jerkface, blackmailing abandoner. Tough call.

I close the refrigerator door and drop my head to my chest, defeated.

"Ready?"

"What the..." I scream as I jump back. "Don't sneak up on me like that. You scared the crap out of me."

"Sorry. Just asking if you're ready to go."

There's something wrong. Jacob is not looking like himself today, and his voice is missing any emotion. The dark circles under his eyes are new. For someone willing to blackmail an old friend to get out of the house for some fun, he looks miserable. Has he changed his mind? Is it me...has he changed his mind about me?

I try not to think about how this bothers me. Maybe I'm

not worth the energy to even blackmail anymore? Or the thought of spending time with me, even as just a chauffeur, is so dreadful?

"Um, yeah, I'm ready. Do we need to bring anything with us to prepare? Water bottles? Sunscreen? Snacks?"

A small smile breaks from the corner of Jacob's mouth, transforming him instantly back to himself. Apparently, I amuse him. Sheesh. Whatever. My mom raised me to always bring snacks, okay?

"We don't need anything. We can just go." He grabs my keys off the console table and hands them to me, then opens and holds the door, putting his hand out, inviting me to walk through. So what? Lots of guys our age have good manners. Just because I haven't met any of them yet doesn't mean that Jacob is something special. I walk past him without a glance, bracing myself for what he has in store for the day.

"Are you ready for our first date?" Jacob asks me as he grabs the seat belt of my passenger seat. That one doesn't click that well, and I force back the giggle as I watch him try a few times to get the belt to stick. It's the little things that bring me joy.

"Do not call it a date," I say. "Where are we going?"

He looks straight ahead out the windshield and smiles. I stare at his profile and watch his entire face transform. His is a face made for smiling. His eyes flick to mine, and I quickly look away.

Now, where was that pack of gum I had in here last time?

"Okay, so I've got this list, right?" There's an energy coursing through him as he bounces his knee. Seriously, what could be this exciting? I'm actually starting to worry that I can't deliver on whatever amazing things he wants to do.

Shades of what he looked like as a kid, full of joy and wonder, warm my cold, dead heart a tiny bit. A pang of guilt hits me. He's been stuck at home for a week already because I've been unwilling to take him out. We may no longer be friends, but I'm willing to give him this. I'm not a complete monster.

Plus, he is blackmailing me after all.

"I thought I'd ease us into it. So today should be pretty chill," he says. He grabs his phone and passes it over to me. I look at the notes on the screen.

`Day 1: Find the best California burrito.`

I look back over to Jacob. I try to keep my expression blank, but this is literally my dream come true. I thought this bucket list would suck.

"Okay, this won't be too awful," I say, trying not to let my excitement show. "How many are you thinking of comparing before choosing a winner? I mean, I clearly have thoughts on the matter. But this is your list."

"I think four will suffice," he says. His face is completely focused, and I get it, this is serious business. Finding the best California burrito in San Diego is not a joke. But, still...

I tuck my lips under my teeth and press down, trying not to laugh.

"What? This is no laughing matter."

I lift my hands up. "No, no, I agree. In these parts, one does not joke about a California burrito."

He looks down at his phone, a small smile forming. "It's just one of those things that I've always wondered about. I mean, french fries…in a burrito."

I can't even blame him for the awe and wonder. "I know. It's genius. So, what's the criteria you're judging on?" I ask.

Jacob nods once and then turns to me, complete determination on his face. "I've been doing some research, reading reviews, watching YouTube videos. And I've decided that the perfect California burrito has about a two-to-one distribution of carne asada to fries. It has to be thick but can't be overstuffed. Not too much sour cream, and the fries inside have to be crispy, not soggy, but still soft on the inside. Extra points if the guacamole is fresh and has a kick."

I give him a nod of impressed appreciation. I don't let myself think about how he spent time researching all of this from afar, never having eaten one as a kid. "Not bad. I know where we should start."

A California burrito virgin. I imagine that first bite and the expression of wonder when he gets a taste of what's in store. It suddenly dawns on me that Jacob never would have had a California burrito growing up because he couldn't eat out. The risk of cross-contamination was too great. But…how can he do it now? I pass him back his phone and grab mine from the center console. "Just let me check something before we go." I do a quick Google search and pump my fist in the air when I find what I'm looking for.

"Uh…do I even want to know what you're looking at? Did you figure out how to secretly poison me?"

He's teasing, but it hurts, surprisingly. Jacob's EpiPen had been a constant in everything we ever did and everywhere we ever went as kids. I worried about him all the time. I hated that he had to go through that.

Nuts are basically his poison. And I don't want to even joke about what they'll do to him.

His gentle touch on my arm startles me.

"Hey, I was kidding, okay? Don't worry about me. I've dealt with this shit my whole life. And—" he shrugs "—it's getting kinda better."

What does he mean that it's getting better? There have been quite a few clinical trials on how to combat even the most sensitive of allergic reactions, fascinating studies with scientists approaching it almost like they would a virus. I'm learning a lot about those while interning for the immunologist.

I raise an eyebrow in question.

"Oh, well, my company helped pull some strings and got me into a special experimental treatment program for allergy sufferers. And over the course of a year, well, I'm not healed, but I'm a lot less susceptible to an attack. Guess I built some tolerance to nuts or something. See?" he says, patting himself at his pockets. "No EpiPen today. I figured I wouldn't need it."

My head pops up, and I look at him in surprise. "Really?" I reach over and teasingly tap his chest, searching for his EpiPen hidden somewhere under his pocketless shirt. He squirms trying to avoid me. Jacob is the most ticklish person I know. When his high-pitched squeal begs me to stop, I lean back into the driver's seat, holding my stomach, trying to catch a breath from my own laughing.

"That's amazing." Both of us are still smiling as we come down from our tickling high. "That must be such a relief for you. A game changer," I say. And I mean it. I've never wanted Jacob to feel debilitated by his allergies. I don't admit to him that my goal is to go to medical school and become an immunologist myself. It's too sappy for this moment.

"Plus, it's second nature to ask about the risks no matter where I eat. And I know with—" he pauses "—eighty-nine percent certainty that you're not trying to poison me." His smile is kind, and my heart, which I didn't even know had taken off, starts to calm down.

"Honestly, that percentage is way high," I say with a straight face. "Don't give me that much credit. But in this case, I actually was making sure the Mexican place was nut-free. They've confirmed on their website that they are." I give him a wry twist of my mouth. "Today is not your day to die, not by my hand."

"This is morbid," he says. "Speaking of morbid death, how's lifeguard camp going? Any chance you were unable to save Nate Anderson from a tragic drowning?"

"Damn, that's cruel," I say.

"He doesn't deserve it?" Jacob asks. I start to wonder if he might not be kidding.

"I'm surprised you even remember Nate Anderson."

"I'm supposed to forget the guy who made my life hell growing up? Some of us may be able to forgive that kind of torment, but it's not that easy for me." His eyes slide to mine, and I shrink in my seat. This is not a conversation I'm ready to have right now.

"I saw a skateboard park on that list of yours," I say, changing the subject. "There are some really cool parks nearby. But, your ankle. There's no way you can ride with that injury."

"I know. I just thought I'd go and watch. I've never actually ridden a skateboard." He turns to look out the window, so I can't see his expression.

"It's not big in Korea?" I ask.

"It is," he says. "But I don't ever get free time to do stuff like that."

I stare at the back of his head and wonder, not for the first time, what life in Korea is like for Jacob. I just don't really have the guts to ask.

"I can't imagine you doing it for some reason," I say as I start the car and back out of the driveway. "Riding a skateboard, that is." Jacob was small as a kid, and he wasn't the most coordinated person. He's a lot bigger now, obviously. But I've been surprised at the grace with which he handles himself. He walks and talks and stands and breathes like he's so much more comfortable in his skin, even with the big ankle boot on. So much has changed, and not just physically.

The thought hurts like a punch in the gut. The shock of not being best friends anymore should subside eventually, right? The desire to hear more about "the work and life and stuff" that made him who he is today gnaws at me.

I look over my right shoulder to make sure the road is clear, and I catch Jacob looking at me. But he quickly turns his eyes back to the front.

"Yeah, well, I was kinda wimpy back in the day," he says with a laugh. It doesn't sound like he finds anything about it funny, though.

I open my mouth to make a comment, but before I can, Jacob reaches a finger out and covers my mouth. "Don't say it."

"What?" I murmur through closed lips.

He removes his finger and we both laugh.

I try to shake all the feelings of familiarity and nostalgia off. I don't want to like doing this, spending time with Jacob. It's too confusing. I decided in my head a long time ago that this friendship was over. So my heart had better get with the program. I am unwilling to not be mad at him. This is Jacob, the one who hurt me.

This is Jacob, my once best friend.

"So, you not-so-subtly tried to change the topic away from lifeguard camp. Look, I promise I won't delight in the thought of Nate Anderson drowning, okay? I'm just curious how things are going for you." Jacob's voice is deep and surprises me anytime it cuts through the silence when I'm not ready for it. He sounds like a grown man. It's interesting to me that he doesn't have an accent at all. I figured years in Korea might do that. In fact, the way he talks is so polished. I know his acting gig is all in Korean, so when does he even get a chance to speak English in Korea?

Korea. Koreans. That Girl. Urgh.

I groan. "I thought our deal was no talking."

He laughs. He runs his hand through his long hair and grabs it into his fist at the back of his head. If he asks for a hair tie to do a man-pony, he's officially kicked out of my car.

"You don't have to tell me. But you can if you want to. Or if you need to."

The offer is like a magical key turning in an old, rusty lock. Click and the floodgates open.

"There's a new girl, Soo-Yun. And she covers her mouth when she laughs. And doesn't remotely smell like mothballs. I don't want to be compared to her."

I see Jacob tilt his head and purse his lips out of the corner of my eye, but he doesn't say anything. I slow the car down to a stop at the red light and turn to see if he heard me.

He nods his head a couple times. "So, there's a Korean girl that you want to hate but she's not awful? And what, is Nate making the moves on her? Are you worried he was just dating you because he's got, like, a Korean fetish?"

My jaw is officially on the floor mat of my car. How did he do that?

Jacob looks over at me and starts cracking up at the expression on my face. "Look, it's been a while. But I became pretty fluent in translating Hannah-speak throughout my life. I haven't forgotten it all."

"But I barely said anything, and you got all of that from it?" I'm still in awe.

"It's a gift. Plus, you're not as mysterious as you think you are, Hannah." He stops, looks down, eyes moving all around like he's trying to find something. When he looks back up again, he raises an eyebrow. His voice drops lower. "To me, you're an open book. And my favorite kind of reading."

The words hang awkwardly in the air just as the light turns green. I press a little too hard on the gas, and we both jerk forward but level out when the car catches up.

"That's a pretty slick line there, Jacob. Did you borrow it from one of your scripts?" I didn't intend for it to come out so sharp, but I can almost see the words cut through any good feelings we'd managed to build up.

Jacob rubs the back of his neck, looking embarrassed. He takes a second and then clears his throat. "Hey, so, fun fact, I'm, um, just not that great socially. I think I slipped into actor mode right then. Sorry."

"Huh." I don't know why that surprises me, but it does. "Do I need to worry about that happening a lot? How will I know if it's you or if you're acting?"

"Well, you can call me out on it like you just did. You know me well enough..."

"Do I? It's been a long time. I don't really know you at all anymore."

I glance over, but Jacob's head is turned, looking out the side window.

I'm trying to pick a fight, and he isn't biting.

"Can I ask you something?" he asks, still not looking at me. "Why Nate Anderson?"

I wasn't ready for that one. Especially not from Jacob. A cloud of shame actually hovers over me. I can justify dating Nate to myself. I've seen the good parts of him. But it's harder to do to Jacob, especially considering our past. I never thought I'd have to explain it to the one person who would never understand.

"I had no friends freshman year, for obvious reasons, and

planned to keep it that way through high school. But then Nate and I had some classes together the first couple years, and he started to show interest. Turned out he wasn't who we thought he was. He's actually really nice." There's no accusation in my voice. I keep it steady, so Jacob understands that it's a nonissue. Life moves on.

"I'm sorry," he says anyways. He drops his head, eyes on his hands, fingers intertwined in his lap.

"Look, it happened. You and I are both different people now, so it is what it is." I don't feel anything near as nonchalant as I'm trying to sound. A tornado of emotions swirls inside of me, and at the center of it all is the hurt of an abandoned young girl.

"Well, if you're hoping to win him back, our agreement," he says, pointing between the two of us, "may actually make him jealous. Guys like Nate want to win. If he thinks you're spending time with someone else, especially someone he sees as a potential threat, and if he thinks that you've moved on, he'll likely want to get you back. We could post some pictures on Instagram and stuff, dropping hints."

I hadn't thought of it that way, but it makes sense. I guess I can use this to my advantage with Nate. I mean, if I'm gonna be stuck hanging out with Jacob, might as well see if Nate will take the bait. Something to think about. Problem is, I'm not sure if Nate would be more jealous of me spending time with Jacob, or the other way around. Great.

"So, now that you know how pathetic I am, let's change the subject. My life clearly isn't as interesting as yours. Tell me more about this fabulous life in Korea." Do I really want to know? Do I run the risk of being open to what Jacob's life is like today? I hate that life, the one that replaced what we had.

"You're not pathetic. I envy how normal your life is. And I don't mean that to sound condescending," he adds quickly. "It's just, well, I wouldn't mind dealing with the kind of stuff that other kids our age do—dating, relationships, real-life situations. I only get the fake stuff I read about in scripts."

"So, you're saying you *want* drama in your life?"

"I want something real. I know earlier I said stuff was awesome back in Korea. But actually, it's hard. Life is far from perfect, not even close," he says. "I'm always on a strict schedule. And I'm constantly under a microscope, no mistake going unnoticed." He looks down at his ankle boot, and I wonder why anyone would give him shit for an accident. "And, I, well, I don't have many friends. I actually don't have any friends, to be honest. There aren't a lot of people I can trust to like me without wanting something from me. It fucks with my head."

"Whoa, that sucks. I'm sorry to hear that." I may be bitter about how our friendship ended. But I'd never wish for what Jacob is telling me.

He shrugs. "Just the nature of the beast, I guess. The show is getting pretty popular. Life is really fast-paced, no time to build real connections. And it makes it hard to know if someone wants to be friends with me for me or because of the fame thing. And people I work with just aren't very nice."

I want to blame him for his life today and for mine. I have

people around me, but I don't have any real friends, either. No one even close to as important as Jacob was to me. I want to throw it in his face that he chose a life in Korea instead of here, thinking it would be better, that he'd be happier. And look what it did. It ruined us.

But I don't blame him.

Everything inside of me feels heavy, the weight of a years-long grudge dragging me down. I'm so tired of holding on to it so tightly. I just don't know that I can let it go, though.

I pull into the parking spot just outside Roberto's Taco Shop. Before I kill the engine, Jacob turns in his seat to face me. "I'm sorry, Hannah. Life got really crazy, and then, when I finally came up for breath, you never gave me the chance to explain. I said some harsh, horrible things. If I had known those would be the last words I'd get to say to you, I would have never..." He hesitates, shaking his head. He lets out a deep breath. "And then the divide between us became so big so fast..."

I hear his words, but I don't understand how we went from being the closest friends to complete strangers with one conversation. And I don't think we can go back to where we started with just this one now. What I do know is that I can't handle the answer right at this moment.

I nod. It's all I've got to give.

We stare at each other, but as always, when I look in Jacob's eyes, I see everything he can't say aloud, and it's just too much. I turn off the engine, unbuckle my seat belt, open the door, and get out of the car.

The summer heat hits me in the face, reminding me of where I am. San Diego. Home.

The scent of tortillas frying and meat grilling wafts in the air, making my mouth water. I'll share this with Jacob today, but I can't let myself forget that he's only here for a few short weeks and will leave again, just like the rest.

But at least I'll always have California burritos.

CHAPTER 8: Jacob

It's twenty-four hours later and I'm still stuffed.

I selected a winner out of four different burritos we tried, all of them so delicious, the choice was not easy. The portrait shot of the winning California burrito from Cotija's, cut perfectly in half, stacked at an angle, steam rising up from the freshly made french fries, was food-influencer-worthy. Hannah went through the trouble of arranging the entire scene to make it look picture-perfect.

I pull that one up for my Instagram with the caption, "The Winner—San Diego's best California burrito." I add the trophy emoji and tag Cotija's Taquería in the post. Done. That wasn't too hard. It's a small act of defiance. But if I'm gonna have a "normal" summer, posting online is a good start, right?

When I scroll through my profile, I see a picture of me and Min-Kyung taken a few weeks back but posted on my account yesterday. "Going to miss this one for the summer. Hopefully won't be apart for long." That doesn't even sound like me. Whoever's handling social media for the company is likely forty years old and hates his job.

I switch to my pictures app and look through the rest of the shots from yesterday. I scroll to the one I snuck of Hannah, holding her burrito with two hands, stuffing it into her mouth. She has no idea I took it. Her eyes are closed as she's biting, and it's pure magic.

I laugh and shake my head. Young Hannah would have been proud to show how she could stuff this whole thing in her mouth and not drop even one piece of meat. Would seventeen-year-old Hannah be pissed I didn't catch her at her best angle? Min-Kyung once bit my head off when I took a picture of us for a fan. She was livid I hadn't captured the light.

My smile fades. Yesterday I let go of thinking about the stress of work for half a day. That might be a record. The packet with my script and contract renewal taunts me from my closed book bag in the corner. *You can't see me, but you know I'm here.* I usually like opening up a new script and digging into the scene. But this one is the first episode of season two. Sixteen more episodes of this ahead of me. I don't know why I'm avoiding it, but it's the last thing I want to do right now.

I look back down at the picture of Hannah. It would be fun to post this one, too, but putting her in the crosshairs of the studio, and possibly worse, the fans, would not be a good idea.

"Jacob, Mrs. Cho and I are going to church to help organize the clothing drive. Do you want to come with us?" my mom shouts from downstairs. That little woman can pack a punch with her voice. It amazes me how at home my mom has made herself so quickly. It's like we never left.

"No thanks, Umma. I'm going out with Hannah today," I respond.

I hear a giggle of glee and some happy whispers between my mom and Mrs. Cho. "Yes, yes, this is a very good development," Mrs. Cho says.

"Yes, yes, fortuitous indeed," my mom replies.

I roll my eyes and shake my head. Moms are so weird. They think Hannah and I are soul mates. I don't even know if we're friends again. I hope we can be, though.

A tortured whirring from the wall starts and picks up speed and volume. Quickly following the buildup, a small plastic bird juts out from a broken window on a clock hung crookedly from the wall.

Cookoo. Cookooooooo. Coooook… It stops.

It dies as quickly as it began.

At least I figured out how to get it to stop announcing itself every forty-two minutes. Now it just scares the crap out of me at completely random times, three times per day.

I'd destroy the damn thing if I didn't recognize it as the clock Hannah's dad bought for her at the Saturday swap meet we used to go to the first weekend of every month. He always let her buy one "treasure." When she saw it, her entire face lit up and as if it was waiting for her, that damn plastic bird escaped its house just as Hannah picked it up and cuckooed its way into her heart. It was broken, and she could not have loved it more.

Kinda like me, when we were growing up.

Shit.

The clock mocks me. 12:13. I'm supposed to meet Hannah at the school parking lot by twelve thirty for our next outing.

I grab a ball cap and my wallet. Looking at the EpiPen, I decide to leave it. I won't need it where we're going. In fact, I decide to leave my ankle boot behind, too. I jam my feet into my seullippos and take off towards the school.

As a kid, my short little legs and wimpy heart made this walk feel like miles.

Now, with my much longer legs, I cover the distance in less than ten minutes, walking up to the fence around the pool just in time to watch Hannah, I mean, er, to watch lifeguards at camp, in training, to save lives, and stuff.

I scan the faces looking for Hannah like I always do, like I always have for as long as I can remember. She's been my best friend, a rock in my early life, and pretty much my favorite person to be around. It made sense I always looked for her. It makes sense for me to look for her now. Nostalgia, and all that. And she's my ride. And, yeah.

Prickling heat crawls up my neck first. Then a deeper anger slowly starts to build from my stomach. But by the time the rage hits my throat, threatening to choke me, I recognize the source of my ferocity. Hannah is standing next to Nate Anderson and another girl, and he's looking between the both of them and laughing. The other girl covers her mouth as she giggles back at Nate. Hannah laughs, too, but it doesn't reach her eyes.

Her attention suddenly shifts, and she looks in my direction. I raise an eyebrow, wanting her to know I see her. She gives me a barely noticeable lift of the side of her mouth in return. It may have been a tiny gesture, but that *did* reach her eyes. Nate notices her gaze and shifts his attention my way, too, lifting his hand to block the sun so he can see me better.

I freeze. My heart starts to race. My fingers tingle, and breathing has ceased being a thing I do. I'm that little kid again. And I'm no longer angry. I'm afraid.

Hannah looks my way again, and like a heat-seeking missile, her attention locks on me. I'm not sure what she sees, but her eyes widen at first and then narrow into a steely determination.

Suddenly, in a show of arms and legs flailing and a scream so dramatic she'd give Min-Kyung a run for her money, Hannah jumps into the pool. Well, it's more like she flops into the pool, taking a dramatic breath as she resurfaces before going back under. It takes a second for people to make sense of what's going on. Hell, I can't figure out what's going on. Either Hannah is pretending to be drowning, or she's doing an epically bad solo synchronized swimming routine. And now ten kids and two instructors are all frantically trying to pull her out of the pool.

Frozen to my spot for only a second, I run through the gate and head towards Hannah, now lying like a wet dog on the concrete at the four-foot depth marker. Hannah is over five feet tall. Truth be told, the whole thing looked so ridiculously staged, I am more worried about her emotional state than her physical one.

"I'm fine, I swear," she says to the crowd gathered around her. "I lost my balance, that's all."

"It came out of nowhere," someone says.

"Right? One second she was standing, and the next she was falling into the pool. I didn't even see her move," another says.

"I'm just clumsy, uh, so so clumsy," Hannah stutters as if this explains everything. Thing is, Hannah isn't clumsy at all. I've always been the clumsy one that is more likely to trip over air. She's so in control of her body and the space it occupies, it's actually impressive how agile she is.

I push a guy in red shorts aside, and do my own check to make sure she's okay. I look down at her, and she looks back up at me, squinting. I move a tiny bit to my right to block the sun from her face. All the confused voices die out, and nobody else exists at this moment, not until I can make sure she's actually not hurt at all. I scan her body from head to toe. I don't see any blood or bones jutting out, nothing twisted the wrong way.

The real test is in her eyes.

God, there's an entire novel basically explaining the situation in those eyes, and I start reading all of it.

"I fell in," she says matter-of-factly.

"I noticed," I say back.

I keep reading.

She caught me freezing up when Nate looked my way. She saw me fall back into my scared elementary school–aged self. And she did what she always has. She rescued me.

Her fake fall into the pool was one hundred percent a way to get everyone's attention, including Nate's. She lies here wet and soggy because she wanted to give me the moment I needed to find myself again.

"You walked all the way here in your Korean house slippers?" she asks.

I look down at my feet. "Seullippos aren't just for indoors," I explain.

"They should be," she says back.

I smile and shake my head as I find myself so often doing when engaging with Hannah. Too much fun.

I reach my hand down, and she grabs it, letting me pull her up to her feet.

I see the towel hanging off one of the other kid's shoulders. "Hey, can we borrow this?" I ask. He nods and hands it to me as I wrap it around her. Her hair is soaked and hangs down around her face. I grab my ball cap and put it on her backwards. And just for the hell of it, I touch her nose with my finger. I may be pushing it. She might bite it off. But she just presses her lips together and tries to shoot an irritated look my way. She can't hide the sparkle in her eyes, though.

"How'd you get this?" I ask. I notice a small scar about an inch long on her shoulder. I don't know why it surprises me to see it. As kids, I would have known about every one of Hannah's scars. Heck, I would have been present each time she got hurt.

My finger runs the length of it slowly and back up again, as if trying to memorize what it looks and feels like. Her skin is so soft, even as goose bumps rise on the surface.

"A guinea pig scratched me," she says, watching as I touch her scar and then finding my eyes. God, it's good to see the trust from her again.

"I'm sorry, what?"

"My freshman English teacher had a pet guinea pig in my class. It didn't like me."

The corner of my mouth lifts up, and I shake my head. The scriptwriters I work with can't even make up this kind of stuff.

A loud gasp behind me breaks us out of our bubble.

"Oh my god, is it..." someone says in response.

"No way, are you..." another voice chimes in.

I look over my shoulder and then over the other, trying to figure out what's going on.

Before I know it, three girls surround me, one touching my arm, another standing in front of me, staring with her mouth open. More start joining.

"Kim Jin-Suk! It's Kim Jin-Suk!"

The name sounds foreign, coming from these mouths, here in what is supposed to be a safe place. It takes me a second to register. It never occurred to me that kids here in my old hometown watch my show. I should be more surprised no one recognizes me from when we were kids.

But just like the Winter Soldier programmed back into his trained reaction when hearing the code, I hunch myself a bit into my casual "all is cool" stance. I shake my head so my hair falls a little bit into my face. And then I let them have it, Jin-Suk's signature smile. I haven't had to use it in a couple weeks. It feels like when I'm at the dentist and he's had my mouth propped open for so long, it no longer feels like it's mine, like someone else's ill-fitting mouth has taken its place on my face.

Hannah sees me and scrunches her nose like she's smelled something bad.

"Oh my god, it *is* you!"

"Oppa!" Um, even these American girls call me that?

Hannah's eyes dart from squealing girl to squealing girl. It hits me that Hannah, the girl who always shunned Korean stuff growing up, has sheltered herself from it all just enough that she has no idea how big Kim Jin-Suk has become. And honestly, until this moment, neither did I. Fans in Korea, I can understand. A few fans in Europe and Canada, okay. But here, in San Diego, where I grew up as a nobody, suddenly everyone is looking at me like I'm Kim Taehyung or Park Bo-Gum standing in front of them.

"Hi," I say, bowing my head slightly. "Nice to meet you."

The girls all talk at me at the same time. I can't understand anything being said. It's a jumble of words and squeals. I raise my hand and shake it. "I'm sorry, I wish I could stay to talk, but I need to get Hannah home so she can recover from the trauma of her near-death experience."

All eyes turn to her. A chorus of "yes, please take care of yourself, Hannah" and "I'm so glad you're okay, Hannah" and "you must have been so scared, Hannah" fills the air. Followed by the whispers of, "How do you know Kim Jin-Suk, Hannah?"

"Jin-Suk oppa, annyeonghaseyo." A small Korean girl comes and stands in front of me, hands clasped at her heart, barely holding herself back from jumping in for a hug. "I'm Lee Soo-Yun. I'm such a big fan. Oh, where is my phone when I need it? My family will never believe it. You're here in America, too." She takes her hand and slaps my arm playfully, lowering her face down towards her shoulder, acting shy.

Hannah's nostrils flare, and daggers shoot out aimed at Soo-Yun. She is clearly not happy.

"Wait, what's going on here?" The question shouted from the crowd silences everyone, the voice deep, strong, and clearly pissed off.

Nate Anderson muscles his way through the group that gathered, separating him from me and Hannah, until his huge bulk blocks the entire sun and the sky darkens to the shade of the end days. God, I hate this guy. Someone else is the center of attention, and he can't handle it.

"Nate." Hannah stands between me and Nate, facing him with her hand on his chest.

He looks down at Hannah. "Are you okay? Did you get hurt when you fell in?"

Hey, King of Lifeguard Camp, where were you when Hannah was fake-drowning?

"I'm fine. Don't worry," she says.

"Who is this guy? Is he bothering you?" Nate looks me over, all caveman-like, head cocked, trying to figure out how he knows me. His eyes widen in recognition.

Shit. He's gonna beat me up.

"Wait. Holy shit, you're Kim Jin-Suk from…from…from *Heart and Seoul*. What's up, man? It's an honor to meet you." He holds his hand out to shake mine.

Oh god, Nate Anderson is…a fan.

Hannah's head drops to her chest as she shakes it back and forth in disbelief. Same, Hannah, same.

"Yeah, uh, man, nice to meet you," I stutter, meeting his hand and having mine shaken vigorously to the point of nerve damage. I quickly turn to Hannah. "Uh, Hannah, we should go. Let's get you out of these wet clothes," I say.

Hannah's eyebrows shoot up to her hairline.

My cheeks heat immediately.

"…privately, I mean, erm, out and then in…into dry ones so you don't, uh, catch a nasty cold, and…"

"No way, man, you know Hannah?" Nate says, sidling up to her, wrapping an arm around her shoulders. "Hannah, I thought you weren't into K-dramas. And here you're friends with a big star. That's so cool."

Words race through my head, but I can't find my voice. Three years of training, and I can't project my emotions when it matters. *I know you, too, Nate Anderson. And I don't like you using Hannah to get friendly with me.*

Hannah's glare at him makes it clear she doesn't like it, either. She observes Nate, probably wondering exactly what I'm wondering: *Don't you recognize me as Jacob Kim as well?*

But like suddenly snapping out of a spell, Hannah shakes her head and paints on a smile. "Yeah, we're old family friends. *Jin-Suk* is staying with me for the summer," she says, her voice sweet and cavity-inducing. She almost chokes on calling me by my Korean name. Huh, maybe she doesn't mind being used after all. I guess if it wins her points with Nate Anderson, it's okay.

I'm gonna be sick.

I reach out to grab Hannah's hand and start towards the exit. We need to get out of here.

"Don't," she says, breaking free from my grip as she storms past me.

"What did I do?" I ask after her. We're going in the same direction. And why does she get to be mad? I'm the one who's mad!

"Is Kim Jin-Suk dating that American girl?" the Korean girl asks Nate.

"Oh my god, I'm KOREAN AMERICAN," Hannah shouts back over her shoulder, not slowing down, not stopping.

I hustle to follow her. The crowd follows me.

"Hey, Hannah, wait up." Nate runs past me to get to Hannah, slightly bumping my shoulder along the way. Asshole. No way that was an accident. He may be a fan of my acting. But he is clearly not a fan of the prospect of losing Hannah to me.

Don't stop, Hannah. Don't turn around.

Hannah stops and turns around. That girl never was good at following directions.

"You sure you're okay? I'll call you later to check in on you, yeah?" Nate glances over his shoulder at me and turns back to Hannah.

I want to break his perfectly pointy nose.

I swallow hard. I can barely register the chirping of fans talking to me, asking me questions, wondering if Minky is in town with me or if I'm here by myself, asking how I know Hannah. The only thing that matters in this moment is how Hannah answers Nate.

Like it always has been with us, like magnets, her gaze finds mine.

She hates the attention from these other students. She hates the position Nate's put her in. She hates that I've suddenly inserted myself into her life.

I open my mouth to say something, but I can't do it here, not with all this attention on us. We can't have this conversation here for it to show up on the internet later. The studio has ingrained in me the importance of controlling every public interaction. I struggle but manage to put the actor smile firmly back in place.

Hannah holds my focus and then shakes her head slightly, closing her eyes, slowly breaking our connection.

She opens them back up and looks to Nate. She throws her head casually to the side, puckers her lips, and says, "Sure, give me a call," in a voice way too perky to be genuine.

She glares at me in challenge and then turns around and heads out to the car, not giving me another thought.

I follow closely behind, my seullippo-clad feet dragging. I'm not sure what I did wrong, but I'm certain that I'm off to meet my doom.

CHAPTER 9: Hannah

One minute it's a completely normal day at lifeguard camp with me begging for Nate's crumbs as he falls deeper in infatuation with Soo-Yun. And the next, I'm faking a drowning, my classmates are all fangirling over Jacob, and Nate, within the span of minutes, goes into take-care-of-Hannah mode again.

Jacob mentioned that Nate might want me back if he thought I was hanging out with someone else. But I didn't expect it to happen the very next day. I'm not ready for this level of drama and emotional manipulation.

I'm a hostage to Jacob's plan, blackmail, nice and simple. It's not supposed to invade my own reality. Is this one of those portals that leads me to an alternate universe? Did I step into a fan fiction life of my own making? It's the only explanation. I'll just write my way out of it.

The knock on the passenger window startles me out of my freak-out.

Jacob's face leans to look in the window. I think of that fake actor smile he gave to everyone. It scared me. It was too perfect, too practiced. And the lines he fed me yesterday. Truth is, I have no idea what Jacob's been up to the last three years and who he's become. He's an actor on a Korean TV show, and he tells me it's hard. But he has fans, for goodness' sake. My school friends, even Nate, are his fans. They screamed his name like he was Timothée Chalamet or something.

But the Jacob looking at me now is as familiar as my own family. This face I know. Which is the real one, though, and which is acting? Has fame changed him? Is slick Jacob the real version and this familiar, kind, earnest face the facade?

And the real question I have to ask myself is...why does it matter to me now?

I click the doors unlocked and let out a deep breath. I turn the battery so I can crank the air-conditioning because if we're gonna have some kind of fight, I refuse to let him see me sweat.

But I don't want to fight, I realize as my shoulders slump. It's just too exhausting. Being mad *all the time* is too heavy a burden to carry. I'm no longer feeling like hanging on to hurts of the past when doing so just keeps perpetuating the pain.

He gets into the car, and I sneak a look at his face. He's looking back at me, eyes soft, worried. He doesn't want to fight, either.

Okay.

I take a deep breath and let it out.

"Start from the beginning?" I ask, though really, it's more of a plea. "I need to know what happened to you in Korea. And I need to know what happened to us."

He searches my face, eyes taking it all in. I don't know what he sees, but he ends up giving me a quick nod and then turns to face forward. "We went to Korea that summer to put my dad to rest. And afterwards, my mom swallowed her pride and asked his family for some financial help. They didn't even want to see us after the burial. They've iced us out the entire time, for years. They blame my mom for my dad's death, always saying if she had fed him better, he wouldn't have died of stomach cancer. It was crazy." He shrugs his shoulder and takes a deep breath. "I never knew them, and my dad never really talked about them when he was alive, so I just wanted to get out of there. But where would we go? It's not like life was easy for us here, either. Dad died quicker than we expected, and nothing was really in order. My mom didn't even have a job."

"I never realized you guys were struggling so much," I admit.

"Yeah, it was your mother who lent us the money for plane tickets for my dad's funeral, actually." He turns his head slightly, his eyes sneaking a peek at me.

My mom. I never knew.

My hand automatically goes and touches Jacob's arm. His eyes follow the gesture along with a small, sad smile. I remember how hard Jacob, his whole family, took the loss of his dad. He puts his hand on top of mine and squeezes before letting go. I draw my hand back and place it in my lap.

"And then one day, we're at the market, and some lady comes up to me and starts touching my hair and my face. I'm about to scream for help. Then two other people walk up, and I'm super confused and more than slightly freaked out. My mom comes over, and they start talking really fast to her, and she looks at me, and then we're all whisked off to some studio with cameras. They take my picture, and the next thing I know, I'm part of a new trainee class at SKY Entertainment."

"Trainee class? What, like an internship?"

Jacob's hand covers his mouth. But his eyes crinkle at the sides. He's trying not to laugh, and I'm pretty sure that's why he won't turn to look at me. I have a feeling I'm about to get schooled on some Korean cultural thing I've never heard of or known about.

"In Korea, there are these entertainment companies. They basically discover, prepare, launch, and manage new talent in the country. Almost all K-pop bands are tied to them, as are some up-and-coming actors. Young talent is put through an Idol Training Program, basically a school to make K-pop Idols."

"Wait, I'm confused. You started in K-pop?" I think back to when we were kids. Jacob was never allowed to hold a mic in our church holiday programs because he was so off-key. Unless a miracle happened, I can't imagine anyone wanting him to be a singer.

The bark of laughter pulls me from my memory. "You've heard me sing. No. I mean, I did start as an Idol trainee, but only because they wanted me to train on how to perform, how to project my voice, how to take direction, how to build confidence, how to do interviews. A lot of the new batch of Korean actors are put through a year or two of Idol training. It's grueling and merciless and all-consuming. But totally worth it."

"So, what happened after training?"

"I was cast as a secondary character in my first show." This time the smile blooms over his whole face. Pride.

"That's crazy you were just picked out at a market to eventually be on-screen. And you barely spoke Korean back then," I say, amazed.

"I've always been fluent in Korean. I just never told you."

"No," I say, shaking my head, "we ditched Korean school every Saturday together. We hated it because we didn't understand it."

"I hated it because I would rather be hanging out with you than be stuck at Korean school on the weekends." He shrugs. "I swear I never lied to you. I just never spoke Korean around you."

The sudden quiet fills the car, and I wonder if I'll eventually drown in it. I thought I knew everything about Jacob, and I'm finding, even when we were friends, that maybe I didn't.

"And so, I took the job, which required me to stay in Korea. Then we had the video chat..." he goes on.

"You didn't tell me any of this then. I had to find out from my mom that you were suddenly working as an *actor*. I didn't even know you wanted to do that." My voice reminds me of when I was fourteen. I'm accusing him. I'm blaming him. "I wanted to be there for you after your dad died. But you didn't come back. You told me you hated your life here," I whisper. If I say it too loud, the words will take life again in my heart. And it will hurt.

"I told you I'd share more details later. We hadn't signed the contract yet, and I wasn't allowed to tell anyone anything. Two days later, I moved away from my mom and sister into a dorm with other trainees. I didn't have any time to myself and could barely even talk to my family. It's why I couldn't contact you those first months." Jacob's voice sounds like he's fifteen again. He's trying to explain. He's begging me to listen. "Hannah, I did hate my life here. It was hard. The only highlight was our friendship."

"I thought you were saying you hated me, too," I admit.

"I was hurt and scared and dealing with a lot of shit. We needed the money. My mom got a job at a restaurant near my dorm, and we'd get to see each other maybe thirty minutes total a week. But I hoped that if I worked my ass off, maybe I could make it. And I could finally take care of my family."

My eyes don't leave the windshield. But I nod my head, processing, understanding, acknowledging. That day, I made the whole thing about my feelings and didn't stop to consider how Jacob was feeling at that moment. I'm a terrible human, and an even worse friend.

"It was hard, and I felt so out of place. The other trainees all dreamed of doing this. They were raised to. I had no idea what I was doing. I wished every day that I had you there to talk to, to share it with. But by the time I was able to finally contact you, my email came back undeliverable. You deleted all your accounts. I figured, well, I knew you probably blocked me or changed your email address because of me. I guess it hit me that I'd lost my best friend in the world without even getting to talk it out. Why wouldn't you talk to me, give me a chance to explain? Didn't our friendship mean enough to you? You just...cut me out of your life."

After Jacob gave me the news that he wasn't coming home, I was so hurt and disappointed. But when he just disappeared and didn't contact me? My mom kept telling me he was so busy. But too busy to even contact me? To make sure I was okay? I was devastated. I deleted my email account because I was sick of checking it every ten minutes, hoping for a message. I drop my head on the steering wheel.

"I waited," I say. It's barely a whisper. It's all I can get out.

"I needed you," he admits.

"I'm sorry, Jacob," I say. Tears form in my eyes, but I won't let them fall.

"Yeah, I'm sorry, too, Hannah."

"Jesus, we took emotions and decisions made as kids and fueled our separation for three years." Even as I say it, I can hardly believe it.

"Talking about it now makes it sound bonkers, to be honest," he says.

I let out a deep sigh. It doesn't loosen the tightness in my chest, though. I want to keep talking. I want to ask him for more details. I want to figure out where we go from here. But we both look like we've run a marathon. Emotionally spent.

"Anything on that list of yours require sunlight and a long drive?" I ask, changing the subject as my lifeline.

He thinks for a second while a smile spreads slowly over his face. "Absolutely," he says, his eyes dancing with excitement.

"Where am I heading?" I ask.

"Coronado," he says.

I start the car, roll down the windows, and drive west.

"You know, I've never been to Coronado, even when I was a kid?"

I take my time driving over the long bridge connecting downtown San Diego to Coronado Island. It's not busy this time of day, and I want Jacob to see the views as we ride.

"Yeah, it's its own world over here."

We drive down the quiet streets, past small shops on one side, and the world-famous Hotel del Coronado on the other. Jacob's eyes are wide and his mouth opens in awe as he takes in the mix of old-fashioned and rich-and-new that makes up this tourist hub. The beaches here are white sand with crystal clear blue waters, and I hear Jacob say "wow" and "whoa" and "oh" a few times.

I smile as I drive on with the windows down, ocean breeze blowing through the car, enjoying Jacob's excitement experiencing this. I find us a parking spot on the main road, and we walk over to the beach.

"This beach is huge. I've never seen or felt sand this soft," Jacob says. He reaches down and grabs a handful of the superfine sand and lets it blow through his fingers.

He really must not get the chance to get out much in Korea. I want to give him this, a carefree day at the beach. Today I'll forget that he's blackmailing me. Today, I'll let him be an old friend who needs to have some fun.

Because I think I need it, too.

I hand him the two beach towels from my trunk and start running towards the water. I weave my way between families and couples and umbrellas and sandcastles. Right where the dry sand meets wet, I stop to kick off my sandals, peel off my tank top, and climb out of my shorts. I drop everything there and run into the water. I still have Jacob's hat on from earlier, and when I turn to throw it to the shore, I see Jacob.

He's running right behind me, favoring his injured ankle a bit. He kicks off his slippers and then grabs the hem of his shirt, pulling it over his head.

I freeze.

Oh no. This is not good.

"Nooooo," I yell, but everything is in slow motion, and the waves swallow my warning.

Jacob Kim, K-drama star extraordinaire, stands at the water's edge, pulling off his top to reveal the *worst* farmer's tan in the history of all farmer's tans. Worse than real farmers. Under that T-shirt, he has on a skin T-shirt, the color of the palest skin tone I've ever seen.

And in less than two minutes, that kid is gonna fry.

He tosses his shirt aside, a wide, goofy grin on his face as his eyes find me in the water and he comes towards me.

"Jacob," I scream again, trying to warn him to cover himself to prevent turning a painful shade of lobster red. I head towards him, but a wave hits me from behind.

I lose my footing. I'm going under.

An arm wraps around my waist, lifting me up, keeping me from falling into the water. Jacob's arms are strong, and he stabilizes me. At least, my balance is stabilized—my heart, however, is off to the races. Having Jacob hold me does weird things to my insides.

He looks down at me, face smiling, two-toned, color-blocked upper body heaving. His chest is more built than it seems when it's hidden under clothes. But his shoulders are as broad as I hoped, I mean, thought. He doesn't have any chest hair. Trust me, I'd see it against that whiteness.

Jacob's eyes dance with joy as we both look back at another wave and jump together over it.

"We forgot sunscreen. We've gotta get this—" I point my finger at him and circle in the vicinity of his chest "—situation covered up."

"Don't worry. I'm not gonna burn. We're in the water, and the sun isn't even fully out right now," he says.

"Uh, are you new? You're *from* San Diego. You should know that the sun reflects off the water, and you burn the most in the ocean. And UV rays are stronger through cloud cover than direct sunlight," I preach.

"Whoa, whoa, okay," he says, hands up, face fallen.

I hate myself a little, but he'll thank me later. I look back at his sad puppy face and, well, a few more minutes won't hurt, right?

The next wave swell prepares to break, and I take his hat off and put it back on his head. I turn out of his arms and dive under the break.

I scream when he pulls me out of the water, lifts me up, and throws me back over the next wave. His laugh is swallowed up by the wave as I dive under. When I come back up, Jacob emerges from under the wave as well, hat gone, and he flips his hair to the side.

"Your hat!" I look around us to see if it's floating anywhere. I take a deep breath in, about to dive under in this mass expanse of salt water, a futile attempt, but I have to try.

Jacob throws his head back and laughs, the full, life-giving sound stopping me from my descent. His face is unguarded and painted of pure joy. It's possibly the single most beautiful thing I've seen.

"This is amazing," he says. Watching Jacob makes me really appreciate how awesome it is to be able to experience this, the beach, the San Diego summer. I let myself look at his smile for one more second. I've missed our friendship. I can admit to myself that spending time with him makes me want it back.

We jump a few more waves and finally swim and ride one back into shore.

I lay our beach towels next to each other and plop down onto my stomach, putting my cheek on my crossed arms, and look to Jacob. Jacob sprawls himself out on his back, droplets of water running down his face, his chest, his legs. He slowly turns his head to look at me, and our eyes connect. I hold his gaze.

Tightness begins to grow in my chest, and I swallow back the lump of emotion in my throat. Jacob's eyes widen as he watches.

"I meant it when I said it, Hannah. I'm so sorry. I'm sorry I left. I'm sorry I didn't keep our promises," he says. His voice is thick and his heart so freaking open. His words pierce me with their understanding of my hurt, but the pain brings healing with it, too.

I turn my head, forehead on my arms cocooning myself, looking down at the sand, prepared to make my confession. "You're right. I changed my email account and blocked your number from my phone. I wouldn't even let my mom try and pass me her phone when your mom called and I knew you were on the line. After you said you weren't coming back, I was so mad. But when you disappeared afterwards, I was so hurt. I just removed you from my head, my life." And my heart.

Silence.

Jacob lets out a deep breath. "Yeah, I figured you were pulling a Hannah. You know, holding a grudge so tightly you'd cut off all communication. I just didn't think you'd hold out for three years." He chuckles, but it's more of a sad sound, mourning time and friendship lost.

"I don't recall getting any messages from you, even after the first few months. You gave up pretty easily," I say. I feel the sting of bitterness again.

"We were young. I was old enough to know you were my best friend and the most important person to me. Old enough to worry that the news would hurt you. Old enough to hate that it was happening but making the choice anyways. But I wasn't old enough to handle what losing my best friend would do."

He's right. We were just kids. I let out a sad sigh.

"It's my turn to apologize, Jacob." I sit up and face him, crossing my legs into a tight pretzel.

I catch his eyes travel the intricate pattern my legs have twisted into. His eyes lift back up to mine. I shiver.

"I cried the hardest I've ever cried those first days," I confess.

"Harder than when you rode Jimmy Shen's BMX bike

down the hill, only to find it didn't have any brakes?" Jacob asks.

"That bush had thorns, Jacob! It wasn't a soft landing, as you kept insisting. To this day, the words *soft landing* traumatize me," I say. "And stop doing that thing, that Jacob thing that you do."

"What thing?"

"Saving me, saving me from my feelings and having to say or do the uncomfortable thing. You were always saving me," I remind him.

"No, no, no, as I remember it, you were always saving me from getting my ass kicked," he reminds me back.

I look down at the sand, trying to hide my smile. Falling back into such a natural rhythm with Jacob starts to heal wounds I let fester for years.

"Anyways," I drag out, "I forced myself to stop crying after one week. Then I cursed you and our friendship. Blocked you, and never shed a tear again. Drama queen, huh?" I sneak a peek at his expression.

It's soft, thoughtful.

Jacob rolls onto his side, rising up to lean on one elbow. The move tempts me to look at his shoulders and chest again. The pale skin over the well-sculpted muscles is definitely looking pinker. I should look a little bit longer just to make sure.

"Wait, you haven't cried in three years?"

I shake my head, drops of water falling onto my crossed legs. "Nope."

"Dang, that's harsh," he says, a twinge of awe in his voice.

"I'm basically dead inside." I laugh. He doesn't laugh back. I roll my eyes, a habit my dad hates, and that I picked up in full force when he moved to Singapore. "Anyways, I think maybe, if you're down, we can agree that we both made mistakes. And it sucks that it took three years, but we can at least agree to be civil to each other this summer, and maybe, eventually, even be friends again."

He reaches over and wipes a droplet of water from my shoulder, gently tracing my scar again. Goose bumps break out all over my arm, and his eyes move their way down as he tracks their appearance. I hold my breath the entire time. "Yeah, that's exactly what I was hoping for, too."

I quickly grab my phone to distract us from what is getting to be a little too heavy. I turn so the sun is behind the camera. I snap a picture and look down. A perfect sun flare, and Jacob with a minor squint making him look serene. My eyes are closed. I crop myself out of the picture except for my shoulder and some of my bathing suit and hair. "Cute," I say.

I turn the phone to show Jacob. He doesn't look, his eyes still on me.

I look back down and open up my Instagram app.

"Wait." Jacob quickly reaches a long arm out for my phone.

"What? It's a cute picture, don't worry," I say.

"It's just that, well, my company has to approve anything that's posted about me," he says.

I furrow my brow, questioning the logic.

"Yeah, they control pretty much everything about my life."

"That's harsh. I've never even heard of anything like that. Maybe that's why child stars are so messed up here in the States—they need more supervision."

"I'd give anything to have a little bit of that freedom, freedom to make my own choices and learn from them," he says.

"You sound like an old man in an eighteen-year-old's body."

"I feel like one," he says.

"So I shouldn't post this?" I ask.

"It's just, well, I'm so programmed to be careful what's posted about me online. Some of my sasaeng fans can be brutal in the comments. If anyone finds their way to your account and sees my picture, it could turn ugly for you. I don't want that to happen."

"What's sasaeng?"

Jacob sits up and turns around to look out at the ocean. Do the miles between him and Korea right now help him feel removed from his hard life there?

"Sasaeng fans are, well, the more obsessive fans, sometimes borderline stalkers, always trying to find out personal information about their favorites."

I sit up immediately and grab his hand. "Are they dangerous?"

"They can be, I suppose. For some bigger stars, it's why they have security. I don't really have any dangerous ones that I know of. But I do have a few very, um, enthusiastic fans that I see around a lot, both online and in person. I'm okay, don't worry. I just don't want to expose you to it."

"Don't worry about me. I'm more worried about you," I admit.

"If it was just the acting, I think it would be okay. But they can get crazy. The fans, the lifestyle, it's all…a lot. It's not like in the States where it's enough for fans to catch a glimpse of their favorite actors coming to and from big events. In Korea, you have to give access to yourself, your personal life and time, make fans feel like they know you. It's the way stars are made. We do more press events and variety shows than actual filming of the drama." He drops his head to his chest, running his hands through his hair. "And the studio expects me to act like I'm in love with my costar, Min-Kyung. But, Hannah, she's awful. She's so mean, and she treats me like shit."

"What the heck? Why is she mean to you? What's her problem?"

He shakes his head. "She's just a miserable person, I think. She's been doing this too long, maybe beat down by the system? I'm afraid I'm going to become like her if I have to continue on with this growing pressure. Anyways, I don't want to talk about her. She's pretty much the worst part of all of it."

"So, you can't stand her but you have to pretend to be in love with her? Wow, you must really be a good actor."

Jacob lets out a soft laugh. "I'm decent," he says modestly. "Good enough to make decent money, too. We're more financially stable now. I'm able to support my mom and Jin-Hee."

"That's amazing, Jacob."

He nods towards the phone. "It *is* a cute picture."

I shrug a shoulder. "I only have like thirty followers on here, don't worry. Plus, I never read the comments," I say. I pick up my phone and post the picture.

Jacob rubs his arm to wipe the dried sand off of him. A handprint is white against his pink skin.

"That looks like a sign that it's time for us to leave," I say.

Jacob pulls his shirt back on and stands up, offering me his hand to pull me to my feet.

"Thanks for today, Hannah," he says. "Thanks for listening. And thanks for bringing me here to get away and just have some fun. I'm glad we cleared the air…finally."

"Hey, it's either this or VBS, so I think I should be thanking you for blackmailing me." I put out my fist for a bump, and he meets mine with his.

It didn't kill me being nice to Jacob Kim. I don't know how I feel about being friends again, but at this point, I just might be willing to give it a try.

CHAPTER 10: Jacob

"Ow, ow, owwwww."

"Hold still, Oppa," Jin-Hee says.

"You told me this sticky stuff was gonna help," I whine.

"Yes, aloe vera is what you need for a sunburn. So just chama and let me put it on."

"I could chama if you'd be a little gentler."

"You're such a baby. Really, why would you go to the beach without sunscreen on? And how are you gonna win Hannah over if you're this big of a wimp?"

My entire body stiffens. "What do you mean 'win Hannah over'?" I ask.

"Oh please, you're gonna make me spell it out for you? Boys are so lame," she says. The eye roll is key punctuation, apparently. "You like Hannah. Hannah likes you. There's unresolved tension there. It's classic romance material. Hannah's mom, Mom, and I were all talking about it. It's kinda like the storyline of *True Beauty*, but you guys are a little bit more tortured and slower to realize. But still cute."

"You watch too much TV," I say. "And how are you

twelve? Mom really shouldn't let you watch this stuff. For one, the content is too mature for you. And for two, it makes you delusional. Hannah and I do not like each other like that. We're just friends."

I mean, I like Hannah. Of course I do. And I feel relieved that we've broken the ice. It feels like we might just be able to be friends again. And yeah, I mean, she's super cute, and there's nothing wrong with me thinking so. My mind takes off down a path of its own, thinking about Hannah's full lips, and her hard-earned smiles, the tiniest dimple on her right cheek that only sometimes makes an appearance, and her tan skin that is so unbearably soft.

I clear my throat. And shift my thoughts to her very strong kneecaps and capable, um, elbows.

"When I suggested you get a girlfriend to solve your problems, I will admit that I was definitely hoping for someone like Hannah unnie. She's perfect."

"Not an option," I say, laying down the law.

"Sadly, your potential ship names are awful. I mean, HanJa is the best I could come up with, and that's not gonna cut it. But the way I see it, you don't need a ship name because, well, what you guys have is real."

"Jin-Hee." I try to put a warning in my tone.

"Whatever, Oppa," Jin-Hee says, sassiness punctuating each syllable. She rears her hand back and slaps my sunburn, hard. "Good luck fighting it." Her parting shot as she walks out of the bathroom stings not only my back, but my ego as well.

I grab my T-shirt, gingerly pull it on, and head downstairs.

The talking stops, and four sets of eyes turn to me the moment I walk into the kitchen. "Um, good morning?"

Four suspicious smiles look back my way.

"Sit down and eat some breakfast. You need your energy today," Mrs. Cho says as she gets up to scoop me a bowl of rice.

"I do?" I ask. I turn to Hannah, but her head is down, finding way too much interest in her bowl. "And why's that?"

I clearly did not inherit the acting gene from my mom if her exaggerated shrug and effort to put on an innocent face are anything to go by. I don't know if I should be excited or terrified at the expressions around the table. I'm leaning towards the latter.

"Hey, so I thought maybe I'd take you somewhere today that might not be on your list, but trust me?" Hannah asks.

I can't wait. "Sure, sounds good. I trust you." I always have.

Jin-Hee claps excitedly.

"It's one of my favorite things to do in San Diego, and I'm pretty sure you've never done it before."

"Oh, he definitely hasn't," Jin-Hee confirms. "We were gonna go once but..."

"Yah," my mom says, cutting Jin-Hee off. Jin-Hee's cheeks pinken.

"I wasn't gonna tell him," she mumbles.

"Good, good," my mom says, smiling, with a piece of seaweed stuck between her teeth.

"But, it's so daebak, Oppa."

My sister tends to think everything is daebak, but the

excitement in her voice makes me think she really, really does think this is gonna be awesome. I'm intrigued.

I sit down and dig into breakfast. I'm going to need my energy today after all.

"LEGOLAND?" My voice pitches as we take the exit off the freeway towards the amusement park nestled by the flower fields.

"Yeah, I mean, we always talked about going when we were kids. And I checked with your mom, and she says you've never been here. I thought it could be fun." Hannah's voice lowers with uncertainty, eyes focused straight ahead on the road. "Unless you want to do something from the list today instead?"

"No way," I whisper in awe as I look towards the park. It's massive. And the colors shine bright in the sun. "This is so awesome."

"Jin-Hee wanted to come with us so badly. Your mom wouldn't let her, says she has to help the moms organize donations over at the church. Poor kid. We need to do something fun for her. It's her summer break, too," Hannah says.

My heart does a weird triple jump thing as I hear Hannah talking about my sister. I'm just touched she's looking out for her, that's all.

"Remember that *Star Wars* LEGO set you got for Christmas?"

"I loved that so much," I say, remembering the generous gift Hannah and her mother gave me when I was six. No way we could have afforded it, and I'm sure Hannah saved up half the year to make sure she could give it to me.

"I—I didn't bring it with me to Korea." I drop my head, wondering where the set ended up. We took so little with us when we moved, because the original plan was to only be there for a short visit. I start cataloging all the things I ended up leaving behind.

But the list always ends with Hannah. I left Hannah behind. I decide then and there that today, I'm buying Hannah a LEGO set. She'll pretend like it's lame. She's gonna love it.

We park the car, and Hannah takes a quick picture of the signpost where we're parked.

Smart.

"Remember when we went to Disneyland and our moms packed up gimbap and saewoo kkang for lunch?" I smile at the memory. "We had to walk three hundred miles back to the car to get the cooler but couldn't find it..."

"It was E10," Hannah says. "I told you all along."

"No, we walked to E10 and it wasn't there, remember? It was F14, like I was telling you," I say.

Hannah shakes her head. "Definitely E10."

"Nope, pretty sure it was F14," I say.

"Whatever," Hannah says. "E10," she whispers under her breath.

I laugh. She always has to get in the last word.

"But ohmigod, we smelled like fish the rest of the day! Dang, that shrimp flavoring in saewoo kkang is no joke," Hannah says.

"I was so embarrassed," I say.

"Hey, the food costs at amusement parks are highway robbery. Our moms were resourceful."

"Since when did you become a Korean ajumma?" I ask, giving her a small push in the arm.

"Cockroaches and Korean ajummas will be the only ones who survive when the world is destroyed," she says, giving me a harder shove back. The ankle boot has zero give, so I lose my balance and stumble a little.

"Are you okay?" she asks as she reaches out and grabs my arm.

My ankle screams at me a little. I can put more pressure on it now, and it's definitely getting better. But I haven't been staying off of it the way I should be. "Yeah, I'm good," I say.

"We can rent a wheelchair if you want," she says. The twinkle in her eye betrays her.

"Ha ha, thanks, but I'm good."

We stop in front of the huge LEGOLAND sign, and Hannah lifts her phone. "Picture?" she asks.

"Sure," I say, leaning in.

She snaps the shot and looks down at the screen. "Cute," she says, like she always does after a picture, and shows me the screen.

I look at the photo, Hannah's head cocked to the side with a playful smile, and my practiced PR pose next to her. Something about the picture irritates me. It's me. I irritate myself. Why can't I just take a normal picture and not a press-ready photo?

Hannah reaches for her phone, her left eyebrow lifting in question.

"Can we try another one instead?" I ask.

She shrugs and puts the phone back up. This time, I lean

in and put my arm around her. It feels right, and I smile thinking about how much fun today will be.

She takes the shot and shows me the results.

I nod in appreciation.

She reads aloud as she's typing. "LEGOLAND with J, confetti emoji, post." Dang, she's good at this.

Her phone pings a second after. Hannah's eyes widen at the screen. She looks up at me. "Nate liked the post. I think it's working."

Yay. Great. What an asshole.

From the moment we enter the park, my senses come alive. LEGOLAND is amazing. My eyes move from vibrant color to color, attractions and rides calling to me.

We hit up the Ninjago ride, and I have way too much fun trying to slash the bad guys through my VR headgear. Hannah is super competitive, and while I'm laughing my head off, her steely focus has her scoring higher than me. I pretend that I let her.

The LEGO Technic Coaster is scarier than it looks, and though we're in a car with a bunch of kids, I can't help but scream. Hannah throws me a wicked side-eye, but her mouth wrinkles up as she tries to force back her smile.

"Hands up," I say as we take the last climb to the final drop. She rolls her eyes at me but follows suit. We both hoot and holler on the last curves until the ride slows to a stop.

We walk on through the park, finding rides and playing games as we go. Everything is a smaller, less aggressive version of what you'd find at other amusement parks like Lotte World in Seoul, from the pictures I've seen. But it's perfect for me. I don't tell her I'm a bit of a wimp, and she doesn't comment on it either way.

A big pirate ship ride comes into sight. "Oh look, it's your ride," I say, pointing to the sign that reads, "Captain Cranky's Challenge."

"Har har har," she says. Her smile breaks through, as does that elusive dimple of hers. She stands and watches the pirate ship as it rocks back and forth and then turns and undulates. The kids inside are screaming, but there's uncertainty in her eyes. Maybe I'm not the only wimp. The thought settles me.

"Whaddaya think? Wanna try?" I ask.

"Yeah, let's do it," she says. She's putting on a brave front.

We sit down and strap in. As the ride starts to slowly move, I grab her hand and hold on tight. I don't look at her. I just want her to know that we're in this twisty, turny ride together. She shifts her hand a quarter turn and interlocks our fingers. Something about the small change in how we're holding each other's hands makes my heart start to beat faster.

I sneak a peek at her sitting next to me, just as she looks back at me. We hold the gaze for a second, smiling the entire time.

"Ready?" I ask.

"You know it," she says.

The ship begins to turn, swaying Hannah into my body. Our joined hands twist at a weird angle, so I release hers and put my arm around her shoulders instead. She freezes up for a second, but before she can pull away, the ride shifts suddenly and spins in the other direction. The momentum sends me leaning, and before I know it, my head is in Hannah's lap. My cheeks heat. I scramble to get up just as the ship spins in a new direction, and my hand lands squarely on Hannah's chest.

I turn to face her, her eyes wide with shock.

"Uh, sorry," I say, quickly righting myself. "I didn't mean to feel you up."

We stare at each other for a brief second and then both start to laugh just as the ride swings, sending us both towards the man sitting on my other side.

"Sorry," I say to him this time.

Hannah's hair is flying with the air, and the expression on her face is soft and lit up with joy.

My heart expands almost painfully as I watch her laugh while our bodies are flung from side to side. She is so beautiful I can barely breathe.

She turns and catches me staring...again.

This time Hannah grabs my hand and says in a barely audible voice, "I got ya."

I know that she does. Suddenly the waves of movement don't make me feel so imbalanced anymore, and neither does the motion of my heart. Here, where the world feels like just us, she's got me. And I've got her.

"Feeling pretty good about yourself, are you?" Hannah asks.

"I just beat you and everyone else at Dune Raiders," I shout. I look over my shoulder at the six lanes of slides I just conquered. I puff my chest out with pride.

"You have fifty pounds on me, and everyone else is six years old," Hannah points out. My chest deflates in shame.

"So, you ready to trade bags now?" I ask.

Hannah and I separated for fifteen minutes while we each went into the gift shop. She said her bag is for me. Funny, because my bag is for her.

She holds hers out, and I grab it as I pass mine over. We look inside at the same time.

"Holy shit," I say.

"Oh my god," she says.

I pull out a LEGO set of the Millennium Falcon. It's not exactly like the *Star Wars* set I had as a kid, but it's incredible. It's possibly the coolest thing I've ever seen.

I look up and catch Hannah's eyes widening in wonder. She's pulled out the *Sailor Moon* LEGO set I found for her at the store. She slowly lifts her eyes to mine. "This is the most awesome thing in the entire world, and I mean that with my whole heart," she whispers in awe. The innocence and pure wonder in her voice are so beautiful I can't stop myself. I wrap an arm around her, and give her a peck on the top of her head.

"I'm glad you like it."

"I love it. Do you like yours?"

"Best gift I've ever gotten," I answer.

Hannah lifts her chin towards something behind me.

"What?" I ask, looking back over my shoulder. "Do you know them?" A group of girls stands staring at us.

"Nope, but I get the feeling that they know you," she says.

My phone buzzes. It's not even four in the morning in Korea. So, likely not my manager or the company.

Another buzz. Another message.

I look down to see the message just as I hear the gasp and a squeal.

"I think that's him."

"He *is* here."

"He really *did* injure himself. Look at his ankle."

"Who is the girl he's with?"

"I wonder what happened with Minky."

Voices surround us, and the growing crowd draws closer.

Hannah turns to me, eyes wide in shock.

I shrug, because I have no idea how everyone knows I'm here. Except… Hannah posted a picture of us at the LEGOLAND entrance earlier.

"Well, that was quick," Hannah says, looking down at her phone. "Reposted twenty-seven times. What the heck? And they found you within, what, an hour?"

"I'm sorry to bother you, but can I get your autograph?" The first of the crowd reaches us, and the rest start to circle. The pretty blonde gives me a starry-eyed stare broken only briefly by a death glare thrown Hannah's way.

I take her pen and sign my name on her LEGOLAND map. Three more are shoved in my face. The continuous buzzing of my phone finally stops, only to be replaced by the ominous ringtone of Darth Vader's entrance music.

Hae-Jin.

"Excuse me for one second," I say to the crowd, putting the phone to my ear. I take a quick sweep of the group of girls and find Hannah off to the side. I reach out my hand, and she grabs it as I pull her behind me, just to be safe.

"Hey," I say into the phone, "can I call you back?"

"Jin-Suk, explain to me why there is a picture of you with a girl who is not Minky floating around the internet. Do you really just disregard everything I advise you to do and not do? What about 'stay out of the spotlight' do you not understand?" she asks. To the amateur ear, she sounds completely normal. But I know better. The extra sharp hit on the *K* of my name rings of frustration and disappointment.

I'm just in too good of a mood to be brought down. "Hae-Jin, explain to me why you're glued to Google Alerts right now. Shouldn't you be sleeping at this hour? Listen, I have a group of fans, American fans, standing here asking for autographs. I'm sure you'd want me to thank them for watching," I tell her. "I'll call you back later. Get some sleep, Hae-Jin." I disconnect. I'm going to pay for that later, I'm sure.

"Everything okay?" Hannah asks. Her voice is worried, and a tiny bit freaked out. She's never had to go through this circling of the fans before. There's at least thirty people here, and the crowd seems to be growing. And I can already tell that American fans are a little more forward, more aggressive.

I look down at her and then look up at all the fans waiting for their autographs. I try and swallow down the frustration swirling, gaining steam like a tornado inside me. The panic starts in my lower belly, and it's building. Pretty soon it'll circle around my lungs, and I won't be able to breathe.

I knew this day was too good to be true.

Hannah squeezes my hand, and the pressure brings my attention back to her. *I got ya*, I remember her telling me on the pirate ride. She rubs her thumb over the inside of my wrist. Her eyes focus on the crowd at hand, and her expression is determined. It's the same expression I saw when we were kids and I was getting picked on. The same look I saw at the pool when the panic attack threatened to take over.

She wants to rescue me.

She positions her body slightly in front of mine, a position of control. And she stands up straighter to convey power and authority. She's tiny, but even I take notice.

"Hey, everyone. I'm so sorry, but do you mind just giving Jacob, um, I mean, Jin-Suk some privacy? He doesn't have much time here today, and Jin really wants to get as many rides in as possible." She takes out her phone and taps on it a few times. "Jin, you have a couple hours left, and then I need to get you to the private event tonight in Del Mar."

I just stand there, tongue-tied, watching the master at work. Damn, she's good. Maybe Hannah should give acting a try. Even I'm convinced that she's working as my manager or personal assistant or something.

She turns and meets my eyes. Hers speak to me, and then they widen, repeating themselves until I get the message. *Take the baton, Jacob*, they say.

"Oh, yes, thanks everyone. But I can only sign a few more autographs really quick, and then I gotta go," I chime in. I step up and sign the slips of paper and pens shoved my way. I don't agree to any selfies, but pictures are still snapped of me and some of Hannah.

"Okay." She turns back to the crowd. "I'm sorry, but Jin has to go. But he really wants to thank you, his American fans, for showing such enthusiasm."

I wave my hand to the small crowd and smile and bow a few times. And then Hannah pulls me away towards the exit.

"That was…something," she says. She's out of breath even though we barely walked fifty feet. Adrenaline. "So that's what it's like?"

"Yeah." I nod. "Pretty much. Wanna explain to me when you became such a good actress?"

She shakes her head. "I'm no actress. Just someone who wants to help."

"Thanks for that," I say. "So, you just got a taste of it. My fans can be, well, enthusiastic to say the least. There might be comments—no, there will definitely be comments—people who wonder who you are and what your role is in my life. I know you said you don't read them, but I don't want you getting hurt. I blackmailed you into doing my bucket list with me. But if you want out, say the word. I won't tell your mom about lifeguard camp or anything. I promise."

She shrugs like it's no big deal. "Naw, I'm good. I just worry about you and all this attention and pressure. I can only imagine how much worse it is in Korea."

"And Singapore. I'm most popular in Singapore for some reason."

"Impressive," she says. "Wonder if my dad is a fan." Her mouth drops into a frown.

It makes me wonder when Hannah last saw her dad. She was devastated when he moved, and it took me weeks to even get her to break the smallest smile back then. God, I hate seeing her sad like this. I quickly change the subject.

My phone rings again. Hae-Jin. I look back at Hannah, but she's lost in thought. I press the red button and send the call to voice mail.

"Hannah?"

"Yeah," she says, looking back at me.

"I feel like I'm going to be saying this a lot, but thanks for everything today. I know I was kind of a dick to blackmail you into this. But I haven't had this much fun since…well, I guess the beach yesterday." Truthfully, every new moment with Hannah, whether we're doing something or not even saying a word, has been more fun that I've had in three years.

"Me, too," she says, dimple on full display.

And for a moment, I stop worrying about calls from Hae-Jin, fanservice with Min-Kyung, contract negotiations, money, my future. All I care about is that I think I've got my friend back. For right now, this is all I need.

CHAPTER 11: *Hannah*

I've seen the look on Jacob's face each time his phone dings with a notification, anytime he talks about his life in Korea and the stress. It's the face of someone broken down by the pressure, holding back the anxiety about to take over. Guilt grabs hold of me and squeezes, hard. It's like my insides are shaking a finger at me. "You should have been a better friend," they taunt. "He needed you and you blocked him," they remind me.

I don't quite understand his reality, strangers wanting to know everything about him, people looking for any small evidence online of where he is and then *going* there, hoping to run into him, fear of being fired by a studio asking more than they should for the job you're doing, being the sole source of income for your family.

He's only eighteen.

But what matters is that I have the power to do something for him now. I have some time to make up for. And I'm dead set on helping Jacob have the best summer of his life.

My phone buzzes with a new message.

Shelly: Party at Liz's tonight. Bring Jin-Suk if you can.

Shelly: Also, Nate is asking if you'll be there.

I stare at the screen, emotions a complicated swirl. It's been a couple days since I've even thought of Nate. Jacob will be gone at the end of summer, and I'll have to pick my life back up where I left it. I can't put off my plan to win Nate back, because what if he's dating Soo-Yun by then? But I've got three years of lost time to start to make up for with Jacob. How can I give both Jacob and Nate the time and attention needed?

This is summer, damn it. Angst and drama are supposed to be on vacation. *I'm* on vacation. I shake my fist into the air. Curses, world. How dare!

I send off a thumbs-up emoji to Shelly and head down to the kitchen.

Mom and Mrs. Kim are squatting over large buckets of cabbage covered in chili paste. It looks like a crime scene. It smells like heaven. Spicy, pungent, home.

I lean over them and let out a contented sigh. "I can't wait until this is ready to eat," I say.

"You eat kimchi now?" Mrs. Kim asks.

"It took seventeen years, but I finally got her to try it and like it," my mom answers.

They share a laugh, and the hairs on the back of my neck stand, fists up, ready to fight. I'm annoyed. Look, maybe I shunned a lot of Korean shit growing up, but I'm not some punch line to a joke. So, I'm not fluent. I don't listen to K-pop or watch K-dramas. I don't live to eat Korean food. I'm easily susceptible to heartburn, okay?

I hate that I've been getting so defensive. My hair-trigger reaction to any perceived question of my "Koreanness" isn't healthy, and I've gotta stop playing the victim. I am who I am.

"You okay?" Jacob walks into the kitchen, his voice kind and concerned. My identity crisis must show all over my face.

"Yeah, I'm good. Hey, didn't you have something about a house party on your bucket list?" Quickly changing the subject to avoid talking about my emotions is my MO. I hold my breath, hoping it works on Jacob.

"Yeah." That's all he gives me. But his eyes linger, not quite ready to let me off the hook.

"That's right. I think it read, and I quote, 'go to an epic summer party,'" I tease. It's exactly what it said on his list, but I've already made fun of him a few times about it because it's just impossible not to.

He shakes his head at me and smiles. He can take my teasing.

"Okay, be ready by eight," I say and head to my room. There's something I've been wanting to do.

I grab my laptop and spread out across my bed. It's time. I open up Netflix and type *Heart and Seoul* into the search bar. Up pops the handsome face of the boy I just left standing downstairs. And he's looking seriously into the eyes of a gorgeous Korean girl. I hover over the play button. Time to see what all the fuss is about.

Three episodes later and my eyes are already red from my crying. The tears won't stop. I never cry. Haven't in years, not a single drop. And now it's waterworks.

But really, how can life be so cruel and unfair to these two? They're just a young couple trying to be in love. What more can they take? I sneak a peek at the clock, doing the math to see if I can watch just one more episode before getting ready for the party. Shit, it's already seven thirty.

The knock on the door catches me by surprise, but not as much as seeing the face on the other side. I look at him, dressed in black trousers, a white button-down, and a black skinny tie loosely hanging from his neck. He's holding a suit jacket. It's him.

My face crumbles, and I break down into tears.

"Hannah?" Jacob's arms wrap around me, and he pulls me close, his chin resting on my head. "What's wrong?"

What's wrong? Won-Jin's mother just got in a car crash, and she was on her way to tell him the lie she made up to keep him and Sun-Hee apart. He still doesn't realize that Sun-Hee never betrayed him, and he can't fight the conflicting feelings. She has no idea why he's turned on her. And it's raining but she left her umbrella at school. It's all too much.

And...why is Jacob dressed in a freaking suit for a party?

I pull back from his embrace.

He looks down into my eyes, and the expression on his face is different from the one I was watching on Won-Jin, his character. So *that's* what good acting looks like.

Jacob's thumb wipes away a stray tear rolling down my cheek.

"You can't wear that to the party," I inform him. "Oh, and I started watching *Heart and Seoul*."

Two-point-four seconds pass until Jacob finally nods, turns around, and heads back to his room. "Lose the tie?" he asks at the doorway.

"Yeah, and the jacket," I say. "And the button-down," I add. "And maybe the..."

"Alright, alright," he says with a smile. "Oh, and what episode are you on?" he asks.

"Um, I just finished episode three."

He nods, pushing his lips out in thought. "You're in for a ride. Brace yourself. It only gets worse from here," he says as he walks into the room and closes the door.

My heart cracks.

I stumble back into my room in a daze. But Jacob's muffled voice grabs my attention. He sounds frustrated. Is he mad that I told him to change? I walk closer to our shared wall and put my ear against it to listen closer. I feel slightly guilty for eavesdropping, but it doesn't stop me from leaning in.

"She can't do this," he grumbles. "I won't let her get away with it."

My heart seizes. Oh no, he *is* mad at me. I should have given him a heads-up on appropriate teenage summer party dress code. He clearly thought that a perfectly tailored suit, hella-sexy I can't deny, is what actors are supposed to wear to things like this. I didn't mean to embarrass him.

His heavy footsteps walk out of the room, and I hear him pound down the stairs.

I hurry up and pull on some jeans, ripped at my knees,

and a pink sleeveless blouse. I do a quick swipe on my lips with a plum-colored gloss and hastily give my lashes a few jabs with the mascara wand. This will have to do. There's nothing I can do about my puffy eyes now.

I hustle down the stairs to try and smooth things over with Jacob.

He's standing in the living room, back to me, looking down at his phone. I feel the tension radiating from him clear across the room. He's changed, but still has on his black trousers, fitted and cropped slightly shorter at the ankle. He's wearing a white V-neck T-shirt that fits him perfectly. And he has on Chucks. He doesn't look like any of the other guys at my school. He looks like a star. A star with a nice butt.

Oh my.

My mouth waters.

A tiny *meep* escapes my lips.

Jacob turns around and pockets his phone. His eyes catch mine before making their way down, examining every inch of me. I've never been looked at this way. I can't quite make out the expression. So I file away the memory to obsess over later.

His stern face softens, and he smiles.

"Everything okay?" I ask. I fist both my hands at my sides, waiting. "You seem, um, upset, a little."

He closes his eyes slowly and takes a deep breath, letting it out evenly.

He opens his eyes and shakes his head. "My manager says she wants to come to San Diego with Min-Kyung, and the studio thinks it could be a good idea."

"What? But why would they come here?" I'm not sure why I'm panicking. But I don't want Jacob to have to go through this. And I can't be held responsible for what I'll do to that Min-Kyung person if she comes here and does anything to hurt Jacob. (Despite the fact that she's an excellent actress, and I'm obsessed with her portrayal of Sun-Hee on the show.)

Jacob shrugs. "I don't know. I never know. I don't think the way she does or the way the studio does. I don't do politics. I just want to put in my time for the show, get paid, and move on to the next one. I'm tired of all this micromanaging. Sometimes I wonder if I want to even do this anymore."

His admission shocks me. "Really? But you're so good at it," I say. I can't believe what a shame it would be to waste his talent.

He chuckles. "Thanks. So, I take it you like the show? I mean, was that really the first time you've cried in three years?"

I scrunch my brows, thinking. "Yeah. But can you blame me? That show is emotional. A person can only go through so much. Why does life have to throw every curveball at them at such a young age?" I catch myself getting drawn in again and blush.

Jacob tries to hide his smile. I appreciate the effort. "Welcome to the world of K-dramas. Hey, let's forget about the show for now and go have some fun at this party. What do I need to know?"

I scrunch my face at him, not certain what he's asking.

"Oh, sorry. I'm just used to being set up for an event.

Like, what role do I need to play, who I need to be for it to be a success, what color I should wear to get higher approval ratings."

This is Jacob's existence. He's never just free to be himself. The expectations and pressure are always at the top of his mind. I can't even imagine what that does to a person. I'm seeing glimpses of what it's doing to Jacob, and I'm not okay with it. But what can I do to help him?

"You don't have to be anyone but you. It doesn't matter who else is there. You and I are gonna have a great time."

"Cool. It should be fun," he says, the perfect actor's smile painted on his face.

I decide in this moment that for tonight, all that matters is that Jacob gets the chance to let go and have fun. I don't care about Nate or Soo-Yun or fangirls or Minky. I only care about Jacob being able to be himself, even if I have to remind him who that is. If I can give him that, then maybe, just maybe, he'll be able to see that everything can and will be okay.

We make our way through Liz's house and hear the music and most of the talking coming from the backyard. The moment we step through the sliding doors, all eyes are on us.

"Why didn't you tell us you know Kim Jin-Suk?" Brady Lyons grabs my elbow, pulling me slightly away from Jacob as she whisper-shouts her question in the direction of my ear. I look over my shoulder, and Jacob is being pulled in the other direction by another group of people. "How do you know him? Is it like some Korean connection?" she asks.

What "Korean connection" is she talking about? "Are you asking me if all Koreans are related or something?"

"No, no, not like that. But don't all Koreans trace back to only a few dynasties? So, is that how you know him?"

"Sorry, I don't have my 23andMe results handy," I say. The nerve of this girl.

Something catches Brady's eye, and she lets go of me to head towards the shiny new object. Uh-oh, that shiny new object is Jacob, and he's suddenly surrounded by groupies fawning all over him. I can't believe I thought these people were my friends.

But were they ever really?

I make my way towards him to save him from the growing crowd, only to be suddenly blocked by a huge mountain standing in my way.

"Hey, Hannah, glad you made it to the party," Nate says. He looks down at me with a sparkle in his eye.

"Hey, Nate." I try and look around his mass to make sure Jacob's okay. Something wet drips on my arm. Nate's holding a Bud Light in his hand. Great, not this all over again.

Nate looks over his shoulder and back at me, jaw tight, determined. I'm suddenly very worried about what will happen next. *Please don't go and kick Jacob's ass.* That face is his moneymaker.

"How've you been?"

"Good, thanks. You?" The conversation feels weird. Forced. I suddenly don't remember how to play this game. I used to always make myself into a version that someone else wanted. Kind of like Jacob tonight, when he asked what role he was to play at the party. I realize I'm always playing a role, too.

Except for these last few days hanging out with Jacob.

"I saw you came to the party with Kim Jin-Suk. And you two were just at LEGOLAND yesterday?"

"Yeah," I answer. I try to think of something to add, but my mind draws a blank.

"Anyways, Hannah, about us..." My eyes lift to meet Nate's, and my back straightens at the expression on his face. His eyes are warm, his eyebrows slightly raised in a question, and a small smile forms at the corners of his mouth. "I miss you. I know I said I didn't think we had anything in common. But now that I know you're, like, into K-dramas and stuff, I see that we actually do."

Wow, Jacob was right. Spending time with him really did make Nate take notice, and it really does make him jealous. Boys are such Neanderthals.

I want to tell Nate that he's mistaken, that I'm not into K-dramas. But I think back to just this afternoon when I was immersed in the world of *Heart and Seoul*, and I'm not so sure that's the case anymore.

Nate leans in towards me. "Hannah, I've been thinking about us." Okay, I guess this is happening right now. This is good, right? I'll have to tell Jacob that his plan ended up working better than any plan I made to try and win Nate back. Oh, he'll get a kick out of that. Jacob loves to be right.

Nate is trying to tell me he wants to get back together. And I want...

Jacob's face crosses my mind.

I break eye contact with Nate, distracted. I lean to the

left to look around him, just to make sure Jacob is doing okay on his own. I see him over by the pool with a different group of girls now. I can hear the annoying trill of their giggling over the music and conversations. Jacob's eyes meet mine and then scan their way to Nate. His brow creases, but he quickly looks away and laughs. Whatever Sarah Martin is saying is apparently the funniest thing ever.

Heat rises to my cheeks, and I roll my eyes. I'm way funnier than Sarah Martin.

"Hannah, are you listening to me?" Nate asks.

"Huh, oh, yeah, of course. You were saying..."

"I was saying that now at least I know we have things to talk about. We share some of the same interests. Like, take Kim Jin-Suk. It's cool that you know him."

"What about him?" Honestly, if Nate only wants to get back together because of my connection to Jacob, I may just scream. "You know him, too. We both grew up with him."

Nate cocks his head to the side, eyes narrowed, not understanding. "What are you talking about? I only just met him a couple days ago at the pool." Can he really be this dense?

I shake my head. "No, you've known him for years. Kim Jin-Suk is Jacob Kim, my best friend growing up." I leave out reminding Nate how he used to torment and pick on us. I don't know why. I often do wonder if he remembers any of it, because he's never once mentioned it to me. Selective memory for self-preservation, maybe. I'm guilty of that, too. I blamed Jacob for leaving but chose not to remember how I'm the one who cut all ties.

Nate jerks back as a lightbulb of recognition goes off in

his head. "No fucking way! That's Jacob Kim? That small kid who followed you around everywhere?" He shakes his head back and forth like he's trying to loosen the memory or trying to make all the puzzle pieces fit. "Come to think of it, that kid totally just disappeared right before freshman year, right? I forgot all about him. Wow, he left town and is now back as a big star. That's epic." Nate nods in appreciation. "But he's going back to Korea at the end of the summer, right? So, he'll be gone?"

I feel a zinger in my heart, and I wasn't prepared for the sudden hurt. Jacob will be leaving again. Right when I just got him back. But we have so much more to do, so many more things left on his list.

"What list?" Nate asks.

Shit, I said that out loud. "Um, well, he's got this bucket list of stuff he wants to do while in San Diego for his break. You know, like normal stuff. Things he can't do when he's busy working in Korea. And I've got to, I mean, I *want* to take him to do it all. He's my focus right now. I just don't have time for anything or anyone else."

It's my way of telling Nate to "hold please" while I spend the summer with Jacob. Nate and I can resume when school starts, because Jacob will be gone. Ouch, there's that ache in my heart again. Maybe I need an antacid.

"Oh, okay, well, that's really cool of you. But I still want to get together to talk about us."

It's exactly what I was hoping for, to get his attention, to win him back. We really do have stuff to figure out. Right? I just would rather it not be right now. Not when my so-called friends are pawing all over Jacob.

"For sure, Nate. We definitely should talk," I say. "Text me."

I turn to leave, but Nate reaches out and pulls me towards him, tucking me in under his arm. I'm caught off guard and reach my arm out against his chest, catching my balance and giving myself some space.

Out of the corner of my eye, I see Jacob rush over towards me and Nate. I look down at his ankle as he maneuvers his way through the crowd. It must be feeling better for him to move this quickly. He follows my attention, and his eyes widen. Suddenly, he's limping again. It looks almost worse than it did weeks ago. His face scrunches up into an agonized wince, and a small cry of pain comes from his mouth.

I release myself from Nate's hold and go to Jacob. "Jacob, are you okay? Is your ankle hurting? Shit, I thought it was starting to feel better. You should have worn your boot."

Jacob wraps his arm around my shoulder and leans in. "Yes, um, it really, really hurts. Let's go sit down somewhere, maybe inside where it's quiet, away from him?" Jacob lifts his chin towards Nate as he narrows his eyes and skewers him with a glare.

"Oh, okay, yeah." I wrap my arm around his waist and help him make his way inside.

Some people ask if he's okay. Others try and snap pictures of him. I look up to check if he's still in pain, but he's looking down at me, smiling, the kind that reaches his eyes.

"What?" I ask.

He shakes his head but doesn't answer me. Just keeps on smiling.

"Weirdo," I say, hiding my own smile. For someone who has an injured ankle, he sure is happy.

We walk through the house and back out to the front porch, where it's empty and quiet. I help Jacob take a seat in a rocking chair, and I sit in one next to him.

"Let's have rocking chairs on our porch when we're old," he says.

I don't even question that he's made plans for us when we're old. It's how we've always talked to each other, a given that we'll be friends forever. Minus the three years we weren't. But that seems to be old news.

"I saw you talking to some girls," I say. I don't mean for it to come out with such a bite.

"I saw you talking to Nate," he says calmly. He's better at hiding his emotions than I am, I guess.

"Yeah, I guess you were right. Seeing me with someone else made him take notice."

"Great," Jacob says. His voice is flat.

I change the subject. "Do kids have house parties like this in Korea?" I don't want to talk about Nate right now.

The moon is huge and bright, and it illuminates Jacob's face just enough so I can see his eye roll. "The only house parties I've attended are with my mom and sister and a quart of ice cream, some chocolate sauce if we really wanna get wild."

"I know this will sound weird coming from me, but I've always wanted to go to Korea, see what it's like. I want to eat tteokbokki at one of the night markets, and sit at a café drinking too-sweet coffee, and cool off with patbingsu with fresh fruit and condensed milk and ohmigod those little mochi balls."

Jacob barks out a laugh. "All the best parts of Korea, for sure, especially if you have someone to do it with."

I nod my head slowly, realizing that it probably wouldn't even matter where Jacob was living, as little freedom as he gets to enjoy anything, to live life.

"You and I can try some of those same things together here in San Diego. Or we can drive up to Koreatown in LA. And then, who knows? When I come to Korea, you can show me some of the other fun stuff."

Jacob pushes off the ground with his foot and rocks back and forth in the chair.

"I'd love for you to come to Korea. And our list for the summer keeps getting longer and longer. Can we get it all done before I go?"

It's the second time tonight someone's brought up Jacob leaving. I wasted so much time being mad at him. And now I barely have any time left to enjoy him. I wish he didn't have to go back at all.

My eyes well up. The freest spirit I've ever known, strangled by his allergies as a kid, shackled by his job now.

"Hey," he says, his voice soft as he turns towards me. He stands up and reaches for my hand. I take his, and when I get to my feet, he pulls me closer, looking down into my eyes. His thumb rubs the top of my hand back and forth, soothing and calming me. He searches my face, his attention captivated by the tear that's escaped down my cheek. "Don't cry. You held them in for so many years, the tears are gonna fall at the drop of a hat now."

I try and smile, but his words are so kind they sting. I've forgotten how to breathe. I can't look away. I search for the boy that I've known inside and out growing up, and I find him everywhere on Jacob's face. But I'm drawn in deeper to the care and the fire in the eyes of the young man now.

"I've missed you so much," he whispers. He swallows, and the tip of his tongue peeks out to lick his bottom lip.

My breath hitches.

"Maybe if we stand closer, Nate will notice," he says.

"Yeah, he's probably watching now," I say. I don't bother to check.

Jacob takes a step closer, not that there was much room left between us.

"Can I?" he asks. He doesn't need to ask.

"Yes," I breathe out.

His lips meet mine, and they're warm and feel like home. Maybe he thinks he's doing me a favor, trying to make Nate jealous. But in this moment, I don't care about anyone else but Jacob. My heart races, and my mind searches for everything that could be wrong with this and lands on only what's right. My fear threatens to break through, taunting me that this can never last, but my belief that Jacob will never hurt me wraps me up and silences the doubt.

His hands hold each of my elbows gently, a soft caress. I lift my chin a little higher, closer. I wrap my arms around his neck. His arms drop down around my waist.

The pressure intensifies, and I open my lips to invite his tongue in. It's sweet and delicious. He explores my mouth, a part of me he never knew before. I hang on tight, wordlessly telling him how much I want this.

We pull apart to catch our breath, Jacob leaning his forehead against mine, eyes closed. His lashes flutter slightly.

I raise myself up on my toes and gently kiss each of his eyes.

"Oh. My. God. That was so hot," a voice says.

We jump apart, our bubble broken.

"He never kissed Minky like that," someone else notes.

"I'm gonna watch this video all night and dream about this kiss."

Out of the corner of my eye, I see two of my classmates videotaping us. The violation makes me feel dirty and, frankly, a little pissed off.

Jacob shifts our bodies so his blocks mine from the unwanted visitors. I'm too afraid to look at him, to look in his eyes, terrified of what they'll reveal. If one of these girls posts this video and it gets back to his studio, will Jacob be in trouble?

Jacob's warm hand wraps around mine, and he squeezes. It's a gesture to soothe me. To tell me it's okay. I look down at our joined hands, which gives me just enough confidence to look up at his face. The corner of his mouth raises in a small smile, and he gives me a slight nod.

"Don't worry. We'll be okay," he assures me.

We.

We'll be okay.

We have things to figure out.

I'm feeling emotions I'm terrified of.

He's leaving in a few weeks.

We'll be okay.

The question is, do I believe it?

CHAPTER 12: Jacob

Holy shit. I kissed Hannah Cho. I play the scene over and over again as I fall asleep smiling.

Hannah

I toss and turn in my bed, unable to get comfortable, unable to find sleep. Holy shit. I kissed Jacob Kim.

Jacob

The smells floating from the kitchen hit me as soon as I walk in the front door. Loud voices fill the house, and it's clear everyone is awake earlier than I had planned. I hide the bouquet of flowers behind my back. Maybe I can sneak them upstairs before anyone sees me.

Or just lay them on Hannah's bed for her to find.

Is that cheesy? Why did I think to go get flowers for Hannah…the day after our first kiss? That is the dorkiest thing ever. But it was the only thing on my mind this morning. Hannah and our kiss. I hope she wasn't doing it just to make Nate jealous. I don't think that's something she'd do. And she looked genuinely worried about the pictures and videos being posted and what it might mean for me. But I'm not worried about that. In fact, I'm not even giving it another thought.

A few weeks ago, the most I hoped for was Hannah to say five words to me. Now, my head is spinning. I can still feel Hannah's lips on mine. As kids, we shared everything. But we never shared…that. Last night was the closest I've ever felt to her, both physically and emotionally.

The clanging of pots and pans along with the melodic chatter of two Korean moms breaks me out of my thoughts. To the untrained ear, it might sound like they're arguing, their voices modulating from high to low, hitting key notes like cymbals. But it's more likely animated gossip and teasing. It's comforting.

I realize I haven't heard or seen my mom this happy in a long time. Korea, despite the success we've found there, has been hard. This trip to San Diego is good for us all. But what happens when the summer's over?

My heart tightens when I think about how little time Hannah and I have together. I know we'll stay in touch this time. But I don't know that it'll be enough. I need to talk to her, but for now, I'm just going to enjoy spending time together. And hopefully more kissing, a lot more kissing.

I walk past the kitchen to head up the stairs and notice Hannah standing at the counter with a knife in her hand, chopping something. Jin-Hee is standing next to her, talking up her ear, and Hannah's smile as she looks down at my sister lights the room. I stop in my tracks. I have always loved Hannah's smile, but having been without it for years, every single one now is a gift.

Seeing the people I love the most all in one place makes my heart stretch in an almost painful way. It's a scene I haven't witnessed in so long, and I didn't realize how much I've missed it, how lost I've felt without this connection.

"Oppa, Hannah says that we'll go back to LEGOLAND and I can come, too."

"Is that so?" I ask, doing my best to sound disappointed. "I'll think about it."

"Yeah, well, while you're thinking, Jin-Hee and I will go and have a great time without you," Hannah says, the slightest lift of her mouth showing me she's kidding.

"Yeah," Jin-Hee says. She raises her hand for a high five, and Hannah taps it with her elbow, her hands full with a knife and a bushel of green onions.

"Are those flowers?" Jin-Hee asks. "Who are they for?"

I widen my eyes and press my lips together at her, begging her to shut up.

My sister does not get the message. "Oh my god, are those for Hannah?"

"What?" Hannah asks, turning to look at me.

I stand there stiff and awkward, wishing that the earth would open up and take this lame bouquet of flowers away, and since it's open anyways, me with it. But instead, I pull the flowers out from behind my back and hold them in front of Hannah. "These, um, are for you. Just because, you know."

I quickly scan the room and see four faces, jaws all on the ground.

Clearly guys don't randomly buy girls flowers after a tiny first kiss outside of K-dramas. Not for the first time, I kinda hate that I have zero life experience or points of reference other than scripts I read.

"Daebak," Jin-Hee whispers in awe, dreams of every happy ending she's ever watched playing through her head.

"Yeppuda," Mrs. Cho says. I'm sure she means the flowers are pretty and not me. But she can't take her eyes off of me.

My mom stands with her hands clasped at her heart, looking at me with such pride you'd think I won an Academy Award.

Hannah's eyes are fixed on the bouquet I'm still holding out for her. She's frozen with a knife in her hand held up like she's wielding the weapon. I walk over slowly, place the bouquet on the counter, and remove the knife from Hannah's grip. Her hand remains raised, but her eyes turn to meet mine.

"You bought me flowers?"

If we didn't have an audience, I'd kiss her right there, the surprise on her face the cutest thing I've ever seen.

"Yeah, uh, I went for a run this morning..."

"But what about your ankle? Was it okay?" Hannah asks.

My stomach does a little flip. Having someone worry about me, and not because it'll impact how I look in front of the camera, is new for me. I want to kiss her where her brows are furrowed with worry. That's all I keep thinking about, kissing Hannah. I clear my throat and try to stop the haze of lust my mind is in. "Yeah, I'm fine. It's the first time I put this much pressure on the ankle without it hurting. A little sore, but I'm good." I give her a reassuring smile. "Anyways, I, um, passed that flower shop by the grocery store. You know, the one run by that old man who looks like Gandalf? I can't believe he's still there." I stop my rambling before I confess that the flower shop was nowhere near the path I was jogging this morning. "Wanna put these in water?" I ask her. I guide her hand out of the air and down to the bouquet.

She nods, still in shock.

"I'm gonna take a quick shower before breakfast," I announce.

"Yeah, no sweaty boys at the table," Jin-Hee teases.

I walk over and stand behind my sister, wrapping my arms around her and pushing her into my armpit.

"Ewwwwww! Let go of me! Blech, blech, blech," my sister screams. Her fake vomiting makes all of us laugh, including Hannah. The sparkle in Hannah's eyes as she looks at me makes me feel like I can fly.

"Now I have to go and shower, too. You are so gross," Jin-Hee whines. But her own smile gives her away. I squeeze her one more time and head to the shower to clean up and change.

I can't get back to the kitchen fast enough.

Hannah

I'm not a nostalgic person. Self-preservation, really. There just aren't a lot of people in my life to share memories with. They all seem to…leave.

But sitting around the dining table eating breakfast, mi-yeuk gook that we all prepared together, with my mom, Mrs. Kim, Jin-Hee, and Jacob, makes me surprisingly warm inside. Memories of these same moments from the past explode in my head, mundane back then, but something to be cherished now.

The flowers Jacob brought me are in a vase serving as the centerpiece of our meal, surrounded by little dishes of banchan. I stop myself before sighing out loud.

I've become a sap. Jacob Kim kisses me and gives me flowers, and now I'm an emotional weakling.

Last night's shared moment between me and Jacob flashes in my mind, and I bite my lips to keep from smiling. Honest to god, Jacob Kim stole all my cool. And I'm totally okay with it… I think. I may need him to kiss me again just to be sure.

I try not to let myself wonder if he meant it all, though. Was he really trying to help me make Nate jealous? Or was that just his way in?

I look at the flowers one more time and smile. I have a feeling I know the answer to my own worries.

I sneak a peek at him from under my lashes and meet his gaze aimed directly at me. We haven't talked about last night. What if he regrets it? What if he's freaking out? Do *I* regret it? Am I freaking out? It's all a lot. But looking into Jacob's eyes, I know he's been thinking about it, too, and by the expression on his face, everything's okay.

"Uh..."

I glance over at Jin-Hee as she looks back and forth between Jacob and me and then to the bouquet of flowers. She's had a huge, goofy grin plastered on her face all morning.

At least she has the sense not to make a scene.

Instead she stuffs another heaping spoonful of rice and seaweed and soup into her mouth, trying to chew around her smile.

I look back at Jacob, and he gives me a tiny shrug. This is all new territory for us. But apparently, we have the twelve-year-old's approval. At least there's that.

Mrs. Kim & Mrs. Cho

"The miyeuk gook was very good today. Not too salty," Mrs. Kim says as she washes the dishes.

"Yes, you were right not to salt the gogi before we put it in the soup," Mrs. Cho adds as she puts the lids on the various containers of banchan and piles them in the refrigerator.

"The weather looks like it will be pretty today," Mrs. Kim says.

"Not too hot. That's good," Mrs. Cho comments.

"What time shall we leave for church tomorrow?" Mrs. Kim asks, as if they haven't already found a rhythm in schedule over the last few weeks.

"I think ten thirty will do," Mrs. Cho answers, without missing a beat.

The silence lasts a beat.

"He brought her flowers! You've raised him so well," Mrs. Cho says excitedly.

"What a good boy. And did you see how Hannah and Jacob looked at each other?" Mrs. Kim asks, her voice two octaves higher and five beats faster than before, not able to wait one second longer to comment on this morning's events.

"How could I miss it? I knew they'd forgive each other. I knew they'd admit their feelings," Mrs. Cho says, eyes sparkling, hands held together in delight.

The dishes are washed, and the food is put away.

The two women turn to look at each other and smile.

"It's finally happening, my dear friend," Mrs. Kim says.

"Yes," exclaims Mrs. Cho. "Everything we've prayed for…"

"…and planned for," Mrs. Kim adds, a glint in her eye. "I hate to say it, but my Jacob's ankle injury happened at the perfect time."

"It was the exact excuse we needed to get you all to San Diego," Mrs. Cho says.

The two women nod, and their smiles grow wider.

Mrs. Kim reaches out her hand and grabs her friend's,

giving it a squeeze. "Could it be that our children have finally begun to realize they're in love?"

Mrs. Cho squeezes back. "Yes," she says, barely containing her squeal. "It seems like they have. And it's about time."

CHAPTER 13: Jacob

"Hannah, be careful driving the winding parts of the road. People drive too fast through the mountains," Mrs. Cho says.

"Everyone drives too fast compared to you, Mom," Hannah says with an eye roll and a smile.

In fact, all of us are smiling. The mood is light in the house, and it's as if everyone notices the shift. I don't want to read too much into it or else I'll have a panic attack. There seems to have not only been a cease-fire, but Hannah and I might just be on track for something more.

And everyone, meaning our moms and my sister, knows about it. Awkward.

I don't know that I ever believed this could have happened when we planned this trip to San Diego for the summer. I can barely wrap my head around it, it all happened so fast. But I'm happy, and it's a great feeling.

"Ready?" Hannah asks me.

Hannah is taking me to one of the items on my bucket list I've been most excited about, the Borrego Springs

Sculpture Garden. It takes a drive through the mountains and back out the other side to get to a vast desert with a surprise plopped in the middle of nowhere. Twenty-plus-feet-high rusted-to-red iron sculptures are spread out across the sand: scorpions, serpents, camels, a dragon even. I've only seen pictures on Google. But I've always wanted to see them with my own eyes, and better yet, sketch them with my own hand.

Hannah's never been either, so I'm excited we get to experience this together.

"Hannah, can you stop in Julian on the way back and bring us some apple pies?" her mom asks.

"Oh yes, Jacob loves apple pie, don't you?" my mom asks. I don't think I've actually ever had apple pie, come to think of it. What's she talking about?

"Can you bring me back some apple pie?" Jin-Hee's sulking again. Today I really would have taken her along with us, but it's the last day of VBS at church, and she can't miss it. I'm glad she's made some friends her age, though. Hopefully she'll be better at keeping in touch with them than I ever was.

My heart feels heavy for a brief second, like recall of the pain I've been carrying around for the past few years. But I remind it to chill. We're good now. Better than good.

"Uh, I guess so. But it's like an hour out of the way," Hannah points out.

"Oh, but you have all day. There's no rush," her mom says. She turns to meet eyes with my mother, and the two women smile.

"Let me make sure it's okay for Jacob to eat," Hannah

says. She's still looking out for me. Back into old habits and old roles.

"Our Hannah is going to make such a wonderful doctor one day. Immunology is an important field, and she's been so passionate about it for years," Mrs. Cho brags to my mom.

I whip my head around to face Hannah. "What?"

Hannah's eyes widen in surprise. She never told me. She opens her mouth to respond, but closes it back up again. Her face looks like she's been caught keeping a secret. In a way, it feels like she has. "I..."

"You want to be an immunologist? Since when?" I ask.

"Since we were kids," she says quietly as she drops her eyes. "I, you know, if, well, if there's anything that can be done, that I can do to maybe help kids who have bad allergies, I want to..."

I let out a deep breath. My heart squeezes tight, but is pounding like it's trying to make its way out of my chest. She wants to help kids with bad allergies. Like me.

"Wow, that's daebak," Jin-Hee says.

"Hannah-ya," my mom calls out, her voice reverent.

We all know how much this means.

I reach out my hand and take hers. I pull her towards me and drag her out the front door. We don't say goodbye to anyone. I just need to get her alone. I need to let her know how much this means to me.

I need to breathe or I'm going to pass out.

I buckle into the passenger seat after three tries. This damn seat belt.

"Are you mad?" Hannah asks.

I turn to look at her. Her face is so unguarded in this moment, I know with all certainty how I feel about this girl. I take her hand into mine and rub my thumb over her knuckles. "I'm…floored, Hannah. I can't believe that this is what you want to do with your life. And I can't tell you how much this means to me, to my family." I swallow back the lump in my throat and the swell of emotions with it.

"I think the stuff you're doing with the clinical trial is so fascinating. I want to ask you more about it, if you're open to telling me," she says. She has a small smile on her face, and I can't help it. I lean in and gently touch my lips to hers.

I pull back just a little. "I'll tell you anything and everything you want to know." There's that lump again. I've never had this, someone to be physically intimate with. In fact, for the past three years, I haven't had someone to be emotionally tied to, either. A brief moment of anxiety starts to tighten in my chest as I think about what happens when summer is over, when I have to go back to Korea. Does life go back to the lonely, regimented shell that it was?

Hannah pulls back this time and nods. "Alright, we've got a long day ahead of us. Do you have everything? Your sketchbook, pencils?"

"Yup, let's go," I say. My hands buzz with excitement. I don't want to think about the end of summer. For now, I just want to experience as much as I can and do it all with Hannah.

"This one is incredible. I think it's my favorite," I say as I crane my neck back to look up at the massive metal dinosaur. Despite being an inanimate object made out of iron, movement and emotion are captured so precisely, I'm in awe. I flip to a new page and without taking my eyes off of the sculpture, I start to draw. This is what freedom feels like. Not worrying about making mistakes. Creating off of instinct and trusting yourself to get it right for your own eyes.

Working on K-dramas, each scene is so carefully choreographed, each emotion calculated and precise. I thought I loved it because I knew what was expected of me, and I could just focus on delivering it. But being in the open out here in the desert, I realize it's the exact opposite of what I want in creating something.

"Yeah, I think you've said each one we've seen so far is your favorite," Hannah teases. Her smile is so pretty. I'm momentarily distracted by her rather than the sculptures. "I'm so glad you wanted to come here. I never would've if it weren't for you, I don't think. I'm not gonna lie, I'm slightly terrified of these things. They're massive and not exactly...welcoming," she says. "Can you imagine living in one of the homes nearby and looking out your window one night, seeing the outline of a huge serpent?" Her body shakes with a slight shiver.

"If we have time, I definitely want to come back and bring Jin-Hee here. Although it might be too scary for her," I say.

"Are you kidding me? She's the bravest kid I know. She'll be fine. She'll love it. We'll definitely come back," Hannah says. Each time she shows this side of her, the generous side, the one where she'd drive all the way back out here so that my sister can see it, too, I want to hold her forever and kiss her even longer. Jesus, I'm a sap.

Hannah turns around to take a picture with her phone, but it slips out of her hand. We both bend over to pick it up.

"Ow, fuck," she says.

"Shit, that hurt," I say at the same time as our heads bump on the way down.

We both stand up, holding our foreheads, rubbing our wounds. "That's gonna leave a mark," she says, laughing.

I reach down to grab her phone.

She reaches down and grabs my sketchbook that I dropped when we collided. Hannah's eyes scan the page and grow huge. Her mouth drops open as she examines the drawing. I reach out to try and grab it from her, but she brings it to her chest and raises her eyes up to mine.

I swallow.

"Is…is this me?" she asks, holding out the book opened to a page with a picture of a girl sitting cross-legged in the grass, long hair blowing in the wind.

My cheeks heat. "Um, is it creepy that I drew you? I know it's not that good…"

"It's incredible," she says in an almost whisper, awe in her voice. "It's like you took a picture of me and Facetuned it to fix the bad parts and then put a filter on it."

I have no idea what she's saying, but I think it's a good thing. I take the book back. I don't flip to any of the other pages of pictures I've drawn of her. There are more than a handful, and I don't want to freak her out. "You're the perfect model. I just wish I could do you justice." My face heats, realizing how cheesy I must sound gushing over

Hannah right now. "Um, I'm still practicing and learning. I'm not very good yet," I say.

"Don't do that. It's such a Korean thing, the modesty, not letting yourself celebrate your own talents. I'm amazed at how incredible your sketches are. I never knew this was something you wanted to do, or even could do. Though come to think of it, you were always doodling random action figures and characters on napkins."

"Yeah, it's fun. I haven't had time, or inspiration, to draw in a long time. This summer back home has given me the chance to work on it some more," I say.

Hannah bites down on her bottom lip, trying to hide a smile. Seems she likes me calling San Diego "home" as much as I do. "Hey, let's take a few pictures so you can draw them later, too. Get up close and capture some of the detail that you can't see from other people's shots on Google Images."

"Good idea. And then let's go pick up some of that apple pie."

"Yes, cool. We'll bring some home for everyone. I think we'll go to Moms Pie House instead of Julian Pie Company. I know for sure they're careful about cross-contamination. But, just in case, how does your body react now if you're exposed?" She asks all the right questions, and I swear it's the sexiest thing I've ever heard.

"I still need to avoid nuts, but with the treatment, it helps lessen the effects of exposure and prevents more severe reactions," I explain.

She nods. "Okay, that's good. Let's grab the pies and maybe a couple of caramel apples, too. We'll eat them at home with everyone together. Oh, and we need a picture of the two of us before we go." She grabs my hand and pulls me over to the giant serpent sculpture. It looks like the head of the serpent is emerging from out of the sand, the body buried, the tail exposed. We stand a few feet away in order to get everything in the shot with the two of us. Hannah holds up the phone, arm outstretched, and I wrap my arm around her waist, pulling her close. I like the feel of her small body next to mine. She just…fits.

"Smile," she says, taking a few shots. We both look down at the screen, and I see two happy people looking back at me. She tucks her phone back into her pocket.

"You're not gonna post it?" I ask.

"Nope," she says, shaking her head. "That one's just for us." She turns and starts walking back towards the car.

Just for us. Not to make Nate jealous. Not to make our families happy. It's a picture capturing a happy moment between Hannah and me, during a day filled with good ones.

I let out a sigh and watch her as she walks away.

She looks back over her shoulder and yells, "You coming?"

I nod and smile as I realize I want to have a lot more of these happy moments with Hannah. "Right behind you," I say.

My phone buzzes in my pocket. I look down at the screen, Hae-Jin's name in the caller ID. I wonder what thing I've done wrong this time.

I press Decline. Not now. She doesn't get to ruin this day.

I pocket my phone and head to catch up with Hannah.

When I get close enough, I hear her. She's on the phone with someone. And she's not happy.

"I knew you'd do this," she says. "You know what? I don't even care. It doesn't matter. Don't come."

I slow my pace. I want to go up and make sure she's okay, to comfort her, to hurt whoever is on the line making her angry—no, sad. To someone who doesn't know her, she would sound angry. But I hear the truth in her voice. Her words. They're similar to the ones she said to me years ago. She's pushing someone away.

"I don't want to talk about this, Dad. And I don't want to come to Singapore. Just stay there and take care of your business and whatever. You were the one that always said summers were 'family time.' I actually never cared if you came home or not," she says.

God, she's so good at this, lashing out, saying the words that will hurt. Pushing away.

"Dad, I'm busy. I gotta go." She hangs up the phone and drops her head. I come to a stop behind her.

"Hannah?" I say, reaching out and softly touching her arm.

She jumps a tiny bit, startled, but she doesn't turn around to look at me.

I come closer, wrapping my arms around her from behind, trying to offer her some comfort. She's shaking.

"He's not coming home," she says, swallowing the last word with a small sob.

"I'm sorry, Hannah." I don't know what else to say.

She leans back into me, and I hold her a little tighter, letting her know I'm here.

But she pulls away suddenly and glances over her shoulder at me. "It's not a big deal—I honestly don't care. He hasn't been in my life for a long time now. Let's go. It's getting late, and we have to make that stupid detour to Julian. I don't want to get stuck driving down the mountain in the dark," she says. She starts walking to the car.

When she looks back at the pictures from this day, what will she see? Will she remember the happy moments? Or will she remember the disappointing ones?

I decide then and there that it's now my turn to make this the best summer for Hannah, and that's exactly what I'm going to do.

CHAPTER 14: Hannah

I need coffee. And a donut. Or maybe a bagel. If I can sneak out before Mom starts cooking breakfast, then she won't guilt-trip me about buying something instead of eating whatever she makes. I mean, she *will* guilt me, but it will be too late.

We're all supposed to pack up and head out to Mission Bay right after breakfast for a Fourth of July picnic and fireworks. In San Diego, if you don't find a spot early and lay claim to it all day, you're screwed. But honestly, this is my favorite day of the year. The smell of people barbecuing, the squeals of kids running around, kites in the air, and all my favorite memories from childhood.

I won't let my call with my dad ruin it for me. So he can't come home…again. So he's missing out on family tradition. That's on him. I'll feel sorry for myself about my broken family another time.

I'm determined to have some fun today. We've got the Chos and the Kims reunited, celebrating once again with Korean barbecue, our little grill, various pickled banchan, and a lazy day out in the sun. I don't even mind that it will be Korean food over hot dogs and burgers. That's how excited I am.

I tiptoe past the guest room, where the door is closed. Jacob must still be sleeping. I smile. And then I catch myself and reprimand myself for all these smiles. My face is sore from all this stretched-out emotion. It's very unlike me.

I am not a romantic, so why am I suddenly so swoony? Possibly because yesterday was one of the most romantic days of my life, even with the backdrop of terrifying sculptures in the desert heat. It was just *nice* to be able to spend time with Jacob. And god, thinking about that picture he drew of me. Is that how he sees me? Because the girl in that drawing was beautiful. Wow, I am crushing, hard. I need to check myself pronto before it's too late and I'm doomed to a broken heart when Jacob leaves.

But not today. And definitely not this morning.

Because I need coffee, and nothing will stop me.

I stayed up late and watched four more episodes of *Heart and Seoul* last night. I'm hooked. This show is addictive, and Jacob is so damn talented. Pride swells in my heart with every episode as he puts his acting chops on display. He makes it all so *believable.* I definitely see why everyone's rooting for Won-Jin and Sun-Hee, and even why they're rooting for Jin-Suk and Min-Kyung. But that's not what Jacob wants. And a small part of me is happy about that. Okay, a bigger part of me than I'm willing to admit.

I carefully open the front door, making sure not to wake anyone with its squeaky hinge. I try to hold back my scream as I run right into a sweaty chest.

Jacob.

"Hey," he says, eyes bright, sexy AF. "Where are you sneaking off to? Haven't you learned yet? This is what got you into trouble in the first place." His smile teases me, and my knees barely hold up my body.

I think back to how he caught me sneaking in from lifeguard camp. How he blackmailed me into driving him around for his bucket list. How that bucket list led to us making amends and finding our friendship again. How he kissed me, and it was real and wonderful and...darn it, my smile is too wide for this early in the morning. Too wide for before coffee.

"I was gonna go and get some coffee and a donut," I stumble breathlessly. You see, Jacob is standing before me, and his T-shirt is wet and clinging to his chest. And his hairline is wet and shining in the morning sun. And that should be gross, but I can't quite get my wits about me.

He takes a step closer, and I have to tilt my head back to look up at him. He puts a hand at the small of my back and draws me nearer. I put both my hands on his chest and instinctively rise up on my tippy-toes as he bends down.

The lightest brush of his lips on mine.

I lean in for more, pressing my lips harder against his and then opening up for him. A mewl escapes from my throat, and Jacob responds with what can only be described as a growl. I've never felt this wanted before. And yet so cherished, too. It's because it's Jacob and he knows me, accepts me as I am, and still desires me. There is something so completely intoxicating about that.

My hands curl, and his wet shirt bunches in my fists.

I feel his hardness grow against my hip. I let out the tiniest of gasps.

He pulls away slightly and presses his forehead to mine. "Sorry, um, these shorts don't uh, do a lot for, the, um..."

I let out a contented sigh and smile wide, giving him one more peck on the lips before pulling out of his hold.

"I need caffeine, desperately," I say as I walk towards my car. "And you—" I throw Jacob a look over my shoulder and lift my chin, eyes dropping to the noticeable bulge in his shorts "—need a shower, apparently a cold one."

His face scrunches in frustration. It's adorable.

"Can I at least get a chocolate donut with sprinkles?" he asks.

"Anything for you," I say as I unlock the car. And I mean it.

A voice in the back of my head whispers, "Do you hear yourself? You're in too deep. Abort. Abort." But the sound of my heart screaming that I want this, that I want him, drowns out the caution signal.

As I open the door to get in, another car pulls up next to the curb. The back passenger seat opens, and out steps my sister, Helen. She thanks the Uber driver, and as he takes off, she turns to look at me and then to the boy standing by the front door. She looks back to me, back to the boy, and smiles.

"I'll get to you in a second," she says, pointing at me. "But first..."

She walks up to Jacob. "Jacob Kim. As adorable as always, I see. Are you keeping this one in line?" she asks as she lifts her chin in my direction.

"Helen noona!" Jacob says as he bends to kiss her on the cheek. "I'm super sweaty, so proper hugs saved for after my shower. But it's really good to see you again. I've missed you." His cheeks are redder than I've ever seen, the very awkward timing of my sister's arrival to blame.

"Good call," she says with a laugh. "I can't wait to catch up and hear all about Korea. But prepare yourself for a grilling. I need you to tell me what happens at the end of season one. Have you seen the script yet for next season? I have to know.

"And let me guess." She turns to me. "Donuts?" She walks over to me and wraps me in a hug. I hold her tight and squeeze. My sister is here. My sister is home.

"Wait, what are you doing here?"

"Well, according to Mom, there are shenanigans afoot, and I couldn't wait to get home. Decided to take advantage of the long holiday weekend and come to see for myself." She waggles her eyebrows at me while tilting her head towards Jacob.

My cheeks flush. And I twist up my face, trying to give her a dirty look to stop embarrassing me. I don't think it's working.

"Dad bailed again," I say.

"Yeah, he called to tell me. Also said you were pretty disappointed."

"It's Fourth of July," I whine.

"He'll make it up to us," she says. She's more confident than I am.

The front door opens, and my mom comes shuffling out. "Helen!"

"Hi, Mom," she says as she walks up to give our mom a hug.

"Uhmuhna, Helen." Mrs. Kim is outside now, grabbing my sister for a hug.

"Helen unnie." Jin-Hee's squeal joins the mix.

Arms reaching for my sister, a mix of Korean exclamations and questions, and little girl joy all fill the morning air.

Welp, everyone's awake now. No sneaking away for coffee. A little piece inside of me dies. But I shrug it off, close my car door, and join in the lovefest of welcoming my sister home.

"I'm gonna take a quick shower," Jacob announces. He searches for my eyes and meets them. I'm really starting to love that, how he always looks for me, just to make sure I know. And I do, I know.

He's got me.

"So," Helen says, throwing an arm over my shoulders as we walk into the house, "looks like summer is going well?" That knowing smile she's giving me irks me. I'm just waiting for the accompanying "I told you so."

"It is," I say. "How long are you here?" I ask, changing the subject, as I do.

"I'm here through Tuesday," she says. Something passes in her eyes that I can't quite read, but then it's gone. Is there another reason Helen's come home?

"Everything okay with you?" I ask.

"Yup, yup," she says. But I'm not convinced. I raise an eyebrow in question, but she ignores me.

"Let's get inside. If you're not getting donuts, I'm gonna need some Korean food stat. And I can't wait to hear all the details of what's really going on," she says. "I have a feeling tonight's Fourth of July fireworks aren't the only ones happening around here."

Looks like I'm not the only one who's mastered the change of topic.

We score an awesome spot close to the water, but still in the grassy area. It's a perfectly clear, sunny San Diego day, and the blue of the sky is a twin set with the blue of the water in the bay. The locals have come out en masse, but it still feels cozy and uncrowded.

Jacob is playing Frisbee with Jin-Hee, and with his sunglasses and ball cap on and in this setting, no one even notices him. The carefree joy on his face warms my heart. No studio execs, no managers, no fans to ruin it for him. I wish this for him all the time, despite knowing it's not what he'll face when he goes back to Korea.

I look at Mom and Mrs. Kim pulling out various plastic containers and setting up our table with snacks and fruit. The smell of charcoal and barbecues fills the air, and it reminds me of every summer growing up as a kid, our families, including our fathers, together, enjoying the day while waiting for night to fall and fireworks to begin.

For a second, I wish my dad was here for this. I wish Jacob's dad was here, too.

"Are you whistling?" Helen asks.

Wait, was I? Do I even know how to whistle? "What? No. I don't even know how to whistle."

"Uh-huh." She smiles with that knowing look of hers, one she's speared me with so many times while we were growing up. "I'm just glad you're happy," she says. She gives me a tiny nudge as she grabs a water bottle and goes to join in with Jacob and Jin-Hee.

Helen says something to him I can't hear, but Jacob throws his head back and laughs as Helen continues on with her story. Jin-Hee has joined them and is in stitches, too.

"It's good to have Helen home," my mom says. She's manning the little charcoal grill we brought to cook the galbi.

"My kids look happy," Mrs. Kim says as she pulls the tops off the small containers of banchan and organizes them on the table. I help her get the plates and wooden chopsticks and napkins.

My mom grabs her scissors and cuts a long piece of spare rib into bite-sized pieces. She puts them onto a napkin and passes it to me. "Jacob bought all the groceries for today. Go and give everyone a taste and tell him thank you," she says.

"Yes, go join the kids, Hannah. There's a spot on the blanket right next to Jacob," Mrs. Kim says, playing innocent. I look over, and the three of them have given up on Frisbee and are now sitting on the blanket playing Gawi Bawi Bo, the Korean version of Rock Paper Scissors, except it includes a two-finger slap by the winner of each round on the inside of the loser's wrist. Jacob's skin already has red slashes appearing from the last pass. Koreans are brutal.

As the day goes on, and with our stomachs full from lunch, Jacob and Jin-Hee offer to clean the table while our moms walk down to the water.

Sitting next to me, Helen lets out a deep sigh, eyes closed, head tilted towards the sun high in the sky. "So, are you gonna tell me the truth of what's going on with you two?" Helen's voice is casual, but I can tell she's been waiting all day to get me alone to ask the question.

"I don't really know, to be honest. We talked through all the misunderstandings and hurt from the past. And now, I guess, we're just seeing where it goes?"

"That's unlike you…forgiving and spontaneous."

I shrug. She's right. But I also don't take offense. Maybe I'm thawing. Maybe I'm growing.

"I still can't believe they make Jacob pretend to be into Minky. I knew MinJin was just fanservice. I've seen a few interviews with her, and she's way too slick. I don't trust her," my sister informs me. "But it's good that you and Jacob have made up and moved on." She leans into me with her shoulder, and I lean to push her back.

I nod slowly, pushing my lips out in thought.

"Yeah," I say.

"Yeah?"

"His life is…hard in Korea. And he needs a friend, someone to be on his side. I want that to be me again. And I want to give him a fun and easy summer in San Diego."

"And you want more than that, too?"

I look down, reach for a handful of grass, and let the blades slip through my fingers. "It's been going really well. I… I like him. A lot." My cheeks blush admitting it aloud.

"No shit," Helen says teasingly. Her smile fades away, and she looks down at the ground, tearing pieces of grass up and throwing them into the wind. "He's leaving at the end of the summer, huh? Have you guys talked about what's next?"

I swallow hard. It's the question I've been trying to avoid, even from myself. "I don't know. We haven't really talked about any of it. I'm not even sure what I mean to him. I don't exactly fit into his life. I could just be a summer fling. And you know I don't do well when people leave me." My mouth twists into a wry smile, apologizing to my sister in unspoken words for being such a brat.

"Look, Hannah, I gotta be honest with you. Long-distance is no joke. It takes a lot of work, and it's hard to stay close."

I listen to the emotion in her voice. Is she referring to her and me? Me and Jacob? "Helen? Is everything okay with you?" I ask.

She raises her eyes and has a far-off look as she focuses on something straight out across the bay. "John got into the MBA program at Berkeley. He's moving to California in September."

"What? But you moved out to Boston for him." I can't believe that my sister left for Boston for a boy, and now he's leaving her. As much as I hate the pain of someone leaving me, I'm feeling twice the amount of frustration and worry for my sister at this moment.

She turns and gives me a sad smile. "I moved to Boston for a job, Hannah. The fact that John was there was a bonus," she clarifies.

John Kim from Seattle, not the John Kim we know from Mira Mesa, nor the John Kim we know from Anaheim, nor the one hundred other John Kims just in Southern California alone, is my sister's boyfriend. She moved to Boston for "a job." It had nothing to do with this John Kim fellow being out there. I know I should give him a break. But I can't help but blame him for my sister's choice to move away. To leave me...for him.

"But now that we've been talking about our future, I think it's a lot less clear than we assumed. A long-distance relationship is hard, and he's gotta focus on school and, well, I don't know what's gonna happen." Her voice is thick with emotion, and a lone tear escapes down her cheek. I put my arm around my sister, and she lays her head on my shoulder.

"But why would he do that? He's supposed to love you?"

"John moving to Berkeley doesn't mean he doesn't love me, Hannah. And just because he loves me doesn't mean he has to stay in Boston."

I think about what she's saying. I don't want to see her with a broken heart. But how can a long-distance relationship work, really? It all seems way too hard.

"Look, I don't want you to freak out and push Jacob away. I don't want you to be afraid of what you two might have to face come the end of summer. But I do want you to be realistic. I don't want to see you hurt again when Jacob leaves."

Her words smack me in the face and then take hold of my chest and press hard. What did I think would happen when Jacob goes back to Korea? There's no way we can keep our relationship going. We haven't even defined what it is yet. I don't even know how strong his feelings are for me. What if...what if he's acting and just having some light fun for the summer...at my expense?

I scan through a picture reel of our short time together, the new memories we've made. No, there's no way he's acting. This is real. He's wanted something real, and he's got it with me. But I've wanted something to last. And I can't possibly have that with him, can I?

"When you love someone, you make it work. You make whatever comes your way work," Helen says as if reading my mind. "I love you, and I'm here. I'm here whenever I can be. Dad loves you, and he does his best at work to provide for us. It's just not as black-and-white as you think."

Maybe she's right. Maybe I am looking at things as too black-and-white.

A shadow falls over Helen and me, and we both look up to see Jacob standing there, holding out two bowls of watermelon cubes. "Here, thought you might want a snack. They're really sweet." He smiles down at me as I take my bowl, and then he walks back to cleanup duty.

Helen pops the watermelon into her mouth and smiles. "When someone's worth it, even distance is manageable. At least, that's what I'm hoping for with John. And what I hope for you and Jacob, if that's what you want. My opinion? He's a keeper. Jacob Kim is worth fighting for. And you've never once mentioned trying to change for him. Because you know he's here for you as you are. So no matter what happens, don't give up on him, okay?"

Her words find a crack in my shield of fear, penetrating their way to my heart. I look at Jacob and know. She's right. He is worth it. And right then and there, I make a promise to myself: no matter what happens, I won't give up on Jacob, not this time.

CHAPTER 15: Jacob

I wipe my palms on my jeans and take a couple of deep breaths to try and calm my heart, which is ready to pound through my chest. When the studio emails you directly, including your manager, your mom, and your lawyer in the message, you know it's serious. I'm freaking out. I'm so busted. I can feel it. But I'm determined not to admit to doing anything wrong. I deserve some time off, and what I do with it is no one's business.

So why are my hands shaking, and why is this huge lump in my throat threatening to choke me?

Mom puts a glass of water in front of me and sits down at the kitchen table. We dial the videoconference line the studio sent over. It's the first time either of us has done a video meeting like this, and I'm scared. Can I make it clear enough through this screen that I don't want to do all the things the studio is asking of me, expecting of me?

The last time I had a big video call, I broke Hannah's heart and lost her for three years. It can't be any worse than that, right?

"Don't worry about any of the legal stuff," my mom says. "Samchun will look that over and advise us." Always have a doctor and a lawyer in the family. Well, he's not really my uncle, but rather a close friend of my dad's. Still, he's been a savior with the contract negotiations, marking all the areas where we have a foot to stand on. He keeps insisting he's not a contract lawyer, but without him, we'd be lost entirely. "Just tell them you do not agree to any of the things in Addendum Two." She points at the screen where the list of "Additional Publicity Requirements" is written out. This includes the mandatory off-screen interactions and relationship with my costar. Someone actually had to write that up and put it in my contract. What a job.

Multiple faces appear on my screen in their own little boxes. Studio upper management that I've never seen before sit around a table all on one screen, my uncle the lawyer on another. I pull back in my chair once I see Hae-Jin and Min-Kyung. Every wire in me is on alert. I'd forgotten how tense each of them makes me feel.

"Hi, Jacob. How is your vacation in California going?"

Min-Kyung's voice is casual, not calculating like I'm used to. But I don't let down my guard.

"It's good," I say.

"You look tan and...relaxed," she says with a nod and a small smile. It's disarming. I've never seen this side of her. Is it the real her for once? Or is it a trick, a show for the execs? Or maybe her vacation has done her some good, too?

"We were outside most of the day for the Fourth of July celebration. I got a lot of sun," I say.

"Oh, yes, that fun American holiday. I hope to experience it one day."

"Okay, let's get to work," the studio executive begins.

An hour of conversation to review the contract and expectations of me off camera ends with frustrated powerful people and an enraged mother. If my mom and uncle hadn't been here, I would have just given up and agreed to all their demands. The studio people are scary. But apparently so is my mom when she needs to be, and she fiercely fought for my best interests. I tried to chime in here and there, defend myself, speak to reason. For the most part, I just remained silent, waiting for the verdict. Which, by the way, we did not reach.

"What can you tell me about the situation with Jacob's uncle?" my mom asks.

Glances are exchanged as we wait to see which one of the execs is going to give us an answer. It doesn't look promising. Mom grabs my hand under the table and squeezes. Whatever happens, we'll get through it.

"It's unclear if we're going to be able to come to an agreement. The financial requests on his part are quite extraordinary. Apparently *Dispatch* is willing to a pay a large amount for the story," one of the men from the company says. I've never met him and have no idea who he is. But he speaks with authority, so I guess he's important.

"What's the plan?" I ask. I try to moderate my tone, but I can't hide my feelings. Maybe they'll want me to stay away, to lay low, longer than originally planned. Maybe we can stay in San Diego longer.

"Whatever happens, we'll deal with it. There will likely

be some damage control. You'll possibly have to counter with your own interview to tell your side of the story."

My mom gasps and squeezes my hand tighter. "No, Jacob won't do that. I'd never put him in that position. This is our personal business." I hear the emotion building in her voice. I hate that she needs to even have this conversation. This hurts her as much as it does me. Maybe more. It's her husband's brother. Family. He's supposed to be on our side.

I turn to look at her, but her eyes are glued to the screen.

"Understood. We'll figure out our next steps once we know more. We'll stay in touch about that."

"I would like to bring up the other problem," Hae-Jin says. The extra emphasis and disdain for the word *problem* make it very clear she's talking about something pertaining to me. "This new girl…"

My head snaps up. What new girl? Are they talking about Hannah? But why would they bring her up on this call? I'm not letting them drag her into this side of my life.

The other people on the call all start chiming in with an opinion and it's clear that word is spreading around Korea that I'm spending time with an "American girl" this summer. They can't even get that right. No. I will not let them say anything bad about her, let her be referred to as a problem.

"Hannah isn't a part of this. There's nothing to discuss," I say, finally finding my voice.

"You made her a part of this," says Mr. Kim in Business Relations.

"You changed the narrative," says Mr. Kim in Communications.

"We suggest you post a couple more pictures of the two of you looking cozy and then stage a very public breakup where you come out looking like the victim," says Mr. Kim in Public Relations. "We have some ideas."

"No, no way." I slam my hand down on the table, and my mom jerks back in surprise. No one else on the screen even flinches. "I'm not putting Hannah out on display and then faking some breakup. I'm not exposing her to this life."

"It's a little late for that," Hae-Jin says.

"If you all don't mind, would it be okay for me to talk to Jin-Suk alone? Maybe we can schedule a follow-up meeting next week?" Min-Kyung's voice rises above all others, and her charm is turned to its highest level. The men all hesitate but end up nodding in agreement. She has the magic touch with older Korean men, apparently. Hae-Jin, however, is unconvinced and sits up straighter, leaning in towards her screen. "Please, Hae-Jin," Min-Kyung adds forcefully. Hae-Jin's eyes narrow, but she, too, nods and logs off without a word.

How does Min-Kyung do that?

I'm tied up in knots.

My mom touches my arm and gets up from the table.

It's just me and my costar now.

She looks down at something, possibly her hands, as she thinks. I wait silently. What is this about, even? We barely talk one-on-one when the cameras are off, and when we do, she's usually reprimanding me or insulting me. It's why I can't go on pretending there's an attraction there. I just want to do my job on camera and not have to interact with her when we're not working.

"Jin-Suk-ssi, I can see how time off away from Korea has done you well," she says, finally lifting her head, eyes looking directly into her computer camera. "You look happy and healthy. And maybe a bit in love?"

I swallow hard. Am I in love? I haven't even had a chance to talk to Hannah about this yet, so I am most definitely not going to talk to someone else first. Least of all Min-Kyung.

I don't say a word in response.

Min-Kyung's focus is no longer on me. She uses eye contact as a weapon, but at this moment, she's looked away, gaze focused somewhere off-screen, or somewhere even further away.

A small nod I barely register, and then she snaps her attention back up to me.

"This career, especially in Korea, is not for everyone. To be famous, you have to give your entire self away." She swallows hard, and if I didn't know better, I would think she's battling emotions. Or, as I've learned time and again, she's one of the best actresses out there.

"This is your first time at this level of fame and scrutiny. So I will do you a favor and lay it all out for you. You've been sloppy. You let pictures of you and this girl get posted online. You did what you wanted without thinking about anything or anyone else. You didn't tell Hae-Jin about this development, or the studio. You didn't prepare them for the possible need for damage control. You look like a young, reckless cheater, and our relationship is in peril in the fans' eyes. Which puts our show's ratings at risk. And there is a lot of money invested in this show."

My mind is racing to process everything she's just told

me. Hannah and I have gone viral, and my job is at risk. I open my mouth to justify, to explain, to apologize…

"And if you'd taken two seconds to think this through, you could probably have saved your girl from a load of hurt. But you didn't. You acted selfishly. And now she's the target of the cruelest comments." Min-Kyung picks up her phone and scrolls with her finger. "A slut, a relationship wrecker, an ugly American wannabe. Fat. Too tan. Flat nose. Bitchy."

"Stop." I can't listen to her read off the hate-filled words being posted about Hannah. I won't. They're cruel and untrue.

She puts the phone down and glares at me, eyes narrowed and focused.

"You need to decide what you want, Jin-Suk. You're still new to this, only a few years. But ask any Talent who has been doing this for a while. The price of fame and success is putting your own life on hold. You think I haven't wanted to fall in love…" She stops herself. Her nostrils flare, and I'm uncertain if she's mad at me or at herself for sharing too much. "You have to do what the executives say because they are the star-makers. If you don't want this, then step away. But you will be risking everything for a lot of people, not just yourself or your family. Our show is a hit. For some of us, this is our last chance. Think about what you're doing by being this selfish and stubborn. And think of how this is impacting Hannah."

I look away, unable to hold her stare any longer. She isn't being malicious. She's not accusing. She's speaking the truth as plain as day. This isn't just about me.

"I really mean no offense, Min-Kyung. I am thankful that we've been working together to build something great with our show." Working hard and getting to a place where *Heart and Seoul* is successful worldwide is a huge accomplishment. The fact that I even got nominated for the Best Newcomer award blows my mind. The most I ever had to be proud of before this was a B-plus on my fifth-grade science report. "But you have to agree with me that the fake relationship off camera sends a false message to our fans and can end up backfiring."

Min-Kyung closes her eyes and shakes her head like she just can't believe how dumb I am. Why I thought I could reason with her, I don't know. I squeeze both my hands into fists, preparing for her next verbal attack.

"Look at every couple in the successful K-dramas. There is always speculation and fuel added to the fire that they are dating. Their pictures are snapped as they grocery shop together. They laugh and flirt in interviews. And it makes fans believe in their chemistry even more with each episode. It's even more important for us because we're young and you're relatively unknown. We can't be seen as flighty or easily distracted. We want viewers of all ages to cheer for our happy ending."

I don't actually watch other Korean shows. Mostly because they make me super insecure about my own acting abilities. Some of the actors are just so powerful and talented. But I have overheard Jin-Hee and my mother gossip about other Talent. And I believe what Min-Kyung is saying is true.

I shake my head, trying to figure out a way that this could actually work.

It's the breaking point for Min-Kyung. Her face is hard, and no sign of her charm is left. Like this, I can't see one attractive thing about her.

"You want to be irresponsible and throw that all away? Fine. Because trust me, the studio will not allow you to call the shots. You refuse the demands in the contract, prepare to find yourself without a job. You aren't irreplaceable. Where will you, your sister, and your mother be then? On the streets. And I suggest you start reading the comments on your summer love affair. As I've shared, unhappy fans can be terribly cruel, and that's just a small sample. I wonder if your new 'friend' can survive the public scrutiny."

I look up and mine is the only face left on the screen. The person looking back at me is desperate, scared, and out of options.

Shoulders hunched and head bowed, defeat weighs heavy on my back. I close my eyes and can still see the sparks of fireworks from the night before. The laughs, family, the stolen touches, Hannah. At least I have the rest of the summer. If I can store up enough happy memories in my remaining time, maybe, just maybe, the life that awaits me when I get back won't break me after all.

CHAPTER 16: Hannah

There's this weird thing that happens when you start to fall hard for someone and weird things like the *L*-word start dancing around in your head. Is it that the sun shines brighter, and the birds chirp louder? No, although it is an exceptionally nice day today, and the fact that I want to dance along with the birds outside my window has nothing at all to do with Jacob, I swear. It's that you start to forget that anything else matters and anyone else exists in the world. It's a bubble you want to wrap you and a certain hot Korean guy up in and just hang out together.

So when I get the text on my screen, it takes me a minute to even register who is sending it.

Nate: Hey hey

Who is this "Nate" person, and why would I talk to… oh…

Well, now I'm in a pickle. You see, I'm starting to have very strong feelings for Jacob. And even though I swore to win Nate back this summer, he's kinda become a nonissue. The last thing I want to do is kiss Nate when there's Jacob.

But then I remember how I've basically fallen off the face of the earth the last couple weeks and left Nate hanging at some point at the house party. I guess I just assumed he'd spend the summer with his new Korean boo and I'd spend the summer with mine.

It's what happens when summer's over that has my heart sinking.

And I did promise him we could talk and, if I remember correctly, told him to text me.

I text back suggesting that we meet at Boba and Waffles in an hour. I'll talk myself out of doing the decent thing if I don't get it out of the way soon. Plus, Jacob's on the conference call with his studio today. I hope everything's going well. It isn't helping anyone for me to just hang around and fill the air with worrying.

I gather my hair up into a messy bun and wipe off my lipstick. I put on a too-baggy T-shirt and a random pair of high-waisted pleated chino cargo shorts I found in the back of my dresser. Totally must be Helen's. I pull some white sport socks on and look at my flip-flops. Do I dare? Or is that further than I'm willing to go? I shrug. Might as well go all the way with this look.

Perfect. I'm about as unappealing as it gets. Off I go to meet Nate.

Thankfully, Boba and Waffles isn't busy when I arrive, and Nate is sitting at a table by the window, waiting. His face lights up when he sees me, but then quickly his brows knit together in confusion. Yes, Nate, I look like a hot mess on purpose. Let that sink in.

"Hey, thanks for meeting me. You look great," he says.

I want to laugh. He's either full of bull, or he's just too kind. I feel a little guilty for dressing this way. I do care about Nate, and if it were the other way around (which, come to think of it, it was), I'd want more than a brief conversation at a party. He may never have given me closure, but I feel like I owe it to him. It's what Jacob and I didn't really get to have three years ago. But then again, maybe it's because we didn't want to be closed.

I determine that a more mature approach to this conversation with Nate is a better tactic.

"Your tits look bigger in that shirt for some reason," he says.

Yeah, okay, so maybe not.

I know he's joking, namely because of the twinkle in his eye, and because I know his sense of humor. But also because this shirt is one hundred times too big to see anything and, well, I have nothing to see anyways.

"Gee, thanks," I say. I sit down ready to talk, but I'm immediately drawn to the menu and the smells coming from behind the register. But why delay the inevitable? My stomach growls…loudly. Traitor.

Nate laughs. "I already ordered for us. Got us each a waffle with powdered sugar, and got you a strawberry boba with whipped cream. It looked so good in the picture."

God, he's always so good about taking care of me in the ways that he thinks I need. But I'm lactose intolerant. Jacob would have known never to put whipped cream on anything he orders for me. It's not even fair to compare the two of them.

I always thought Nate and I worked because we had history. But it's like we were in the same history book, not in the same chapters. We were both there. But we didn't experience it together, not really. Not like Jacob and I have. And even years apart couldn't break that bond, a foundation that has just gotten stronger as we've reconciled and grown this summer. Just like years in the same space couldn't really build it for me and Nate. Not in the same way.

I look up at Nate.

"Ouch," he says under his breath.

"Huh?"

He shakes his head and drops his eyes down to his hands, where he's twisting up a paper straw wrapper.

"I thought it would be a good idea for us to talk, you know, to reconnect. But seeing that look on your face, I'm not so sure anymore."

"Nate..."

"Wait, hear me out. I get it. I'm the asshole that broke up with you. But I've been thinking a lot, Hannah. And it was a mistake. Not just because you're into K-dramas now. Or whatever. But when you told me you're taking Jacob all around San Diego, it kinda bummed me out. I thought San Diego was our thing. We're the ones who love it here, who don't leave here. Everyone else does, but we don't."

Nate's words hit me, hard. It's true. My dad left, my sister left, Jacob left. I'm semi-terrified that my mom might one day want to leave, too. And it is just me who's left behind.

I look up at Nate, his eyes open and earnest. He's here. He's stable. He won't go.

But that isn't enough, is it? I don't love him like I love…

"I mean, it's cool you're showing him around and everything. But he's leaving soon, and then maybe you'll be free to bring your attention back to me, to us. When we talked at the party, I thought maybe there was an opening, there was still a chance for us. I don't know. Maybe I was hoping that, well, if you're not sure if we can talk about getting back together yet, maybe we can just go out on a date and see how it goes? At the end of the summer, of course. I know you have some other distractions right now."

Nate is trying so hard. I don't know how to even respond. I think the direct approach would be the clearest message. "I…we…um…" Smooth, Hannah. Clear as day.

"There's that Puerto Nuevo camping trip coming up that everyone's going to. And there's also the end-of-summer bonfire. I just thought it would be cool if we could do some of this stuff together…like we planned. I know you've been busy with Jacob, but that doesn't take up all your time, does it?"

I think about the day I first saw Nate with Soo-Yun at the pool. I try to remember if I was hurt by the shock of it, the suddenness of it. I was. It was like I was so easily replaced, and it made me feel small. So I think I understand where Nate is coming from.

"Well, you know Jacob and I have been friends since we were kids. And I guess now that we're older and he's back, that's starting to grow into something more."

Nate wraps his straw wrapper around his big thumb

three times and unravels it only to wrap it up again. He nods in thought.

Will he fight for me, or will he let me go?

"Oh shit, really? I mean, I guess I understand. He's like a famous star and everything. I still can't believe that *the* Kim Jin-Suk is Jacob Kim. That scrawny kid grew up."

I smile thinking of how tall Jacob is now. He really sprouted out of that too-small little boy stage.

"Yeah, and it's been good becoming friends with him again."

"You two always were kinda the weird kids who hung out by yourselves, talking your own language," Nate says.

For a second, I mistakenly think he's talking about the Korean language, and my first reaction is a spike of rage. I'm offended. I open my mouth to tell him so. But when I look at Nate, it's clear he meant no offense at all. I'm tired of getting defensive about anything and everything related to my Koreanness. It's not a competition to prove I'm Korean enough with my non-Korean friends. I get it now. It's actually kinda cool that the rest of the world is finally taking notice that Koreans have got it going on.

I realize, instead, that Nate's talking about the closeness Jacob and I had, that we have, that makes us just get each other the way other people don't. It's the language of familiarity that we share.

"I guess I always figured since we're both the ones who've been here the longest, we were kinda meant to be together," Nate explains. "Destiny, you know?" I want to tell Nate I don't believe in destiny. But I think that would be a lie. "But damn, Jacob's back, and you have way more history with him."

Yes, we've got more history, and despite all my fears of how our lives don't fit on paper now, Jacob and I just make sense. We always have, and we always will.

"I'm sorry we never really sat down and talked it out between us. I guess, well, it was a good thing that we broke up when we did. Like fate was making room for Jacob to come back. And I've seen you talking to Soo-Yun at lifeguard camp. Maybe there's something there between the two of you?"

Nate shakes his head. "It was fun that we share the same interests, and I could talk to her about K-pop and K-dramas. But she was way more into all that stuff than I am, and she's kinda borderline obsessed. That's all she talks about. Plus, she thinks Lee Min-Ho is a good actor. And, well, she's just not as cool as you are."

I try not to, but my chest expands, and I smile. That was really kinda sweet of him to say. "If it makes you feel any better, I *did* have a plan to try and get you back. It's just that, well, Jacob kinda showed up and I realized…you know…"

"Oh, so is that why you still ended up at lifeguard camp? I was wondering…" Nate looks surprisingly shy at the realization. He really is a decent guy.

"Hey, well, I just started getting into *Heart and Seoul*, ya know, for reasons." I can't help my smile. "So, if you ever wanna talk about that show, I'm hooked."

Nate's face lights up. "Awesome. And if you need any recommendations for a new show once you're done, hit me up."

"Deal."

"Oh, and you and I signed up to give the end-of-camp toast at the bonfire. If you're down for it, do you think Jacob would be okay if we still do that together?"

It's cute he thinks I need Jacob's permission. But I will run it by him first so he's not surprised by it. You never know how some things can be misinterpreted without context. I don't want Jacob to feel out of the loop. "Yeah, I'm still down. Thanks for reminding me."

"And hey, who knows, maybe we can talk again before school starts. It would be weird, both of us single during our senior year," Nate says.

"Single?"

"Well, Jacob won't be here to take you to prom or hang out with on Senior Day or bring you flowers for graduation. All the fun stuff, ya know?" He waggles his eyebrows. "I could be his stand-in when he's gone."

I've faced Jacob having to leave at the end of the summer. I've thought through the fears of how we'll continue on long-distance. But I haven't considered what life will be like without him on a day-to-day basis. Jacob and I have only ever done every-waking-moment or nothing at all. What does the in-between look like for us?

My face falls, and my heart is heavy.

Nate reaches out and puts his hand on top of mine. He's still trying. Either he cares about me more than I thought, or he's not used to not getting what he wants. Maybe a combo of the two. "Hey, I might not be a famous actor or anything, but I'm a pretty decent pick for a regular ol' boyfriend, don't you think?" His smile is kind, and I smile back. Too bad my heart already made its choice and isn't budging. I realize that even if Jacob can't be here, I'm not interested in anything with anyone else.

"You are a good guy, Nate. And I'll probably be a little jealous when some lucky girl steals your heart next year." I turn my hand over and squeeze his. "Thank you for being so cool about all of this. I'm really glad we're friends."

"Ouch, I've been friendzoned." He grabs his heart like he's in pain, and I laugh. "But I don't give up that easily," he says with a wink.

I want to tell him not to waste his time, but I think he kinda likes the challenge. Better not encourage him.

We give each other a hug and part ways.

I watch all my plans for senior year walk away with him. And I'm left with a lot of questions about the future. Luckily, I have Jacob to figure it out with.

And in my rush home to see my guy, I totally overlook the man with a camera pointed straight at me.

CHAPTER 17: Jacob

"Breathe, Jacob," Hannah's patient voice says.

Most guys my age have done this already and have way more experience. I was almost too embarrassed to even ask Hannah if she wanted to. But she surprised me by being more than eager to be the one to help me with my first time. It takes so much trust.

I'm a little uncomfortable knowing she's already had her first time without me. It couldn't have been that long ago, but I don't want to think about it. I hope she was being safe, at least.

We're parked in the empty school parking lot. I imagine a lot of people have their first times here, too. It's private, no moms or sisters around to interrupt us. My heart is racing, and I know I need to calm down if I'm gonna be able to go through with this. I close my eyes slowly, take a deep breath, and let it out.

"Okay, I'm ready," I say. "Are you?"

"I am," Hannah says.

I look into Hannah's eyes and see an ocean of patience

and a sparkle of excitement. She is so beautiful. She leans in and gives me a quick peck on my lips.

"You can do this, Jacob. I promise. Once you get started, it'll come naturally," she assures me.

I nod.

I press the brake, turn the key, and the car comes to life.

It's my first driving lesson. I hesitated adding this to my list, but when else will I get a chance to learn? No way I'm gonna risk life and limb trying to drive on the crazy streets of Seoul. And no way I'm risking my sanity by asking my mom to teach me. It needs to be here, this summer in San Diego, and it needs to be with Hannah. With the conference call going as badly as it did the other day, I'm suddenly worried I won't get many more chances like this, to be a regular guy doing normal things.

"Jacob, you don't need to grip the steering wheel so tightly," Hannah says, teasing in her voice.

I immediately press down the brake, and the car stops abruptly, jerking us both forward a little. "Sorry, yeah, okay, I won't hold on so tightly," I say. A bead of sweat trickles down my forehead.

"It's best if you ease into the brakes when you want to slow down or when you're rolling into a stop," Hannah says. "Same with the gas. No lead foot. Just gently push and add pressure to pick up speed. Which, you will do at some point, right? Because the whole purpose of driving is to, ya know, move forward."

"Har har."

I gently let off the brake, switch my foot over to the gas pedal, and put some pressure on it. We jerk a little forward, but eventually I'm able to gauge it better, and we're moving. We curve to the right and turn back to the left. We gain speed and slow down again. We do a very slow, very wide three-sixty turn. And eventually, we park.

"Great job, Jacob," Hannah assures me. "I mean, no chance you're gonna get a speeding ticket anytime soon, but you've mastered the basics. Congratulations, you're driving."

I smile and crack my knuckles, massaging some feeling back into my hands.

Hannah and I both jump at the knock on her passenger side window. Standing outside the car is Nate Anderson. What the heck is *he* doing here?

Hannah lets her window down, but before he can lean into the car, I use the driver's control to raise it back up again, leaving only a small opening so we can hear what he wants. Hannah throws me an annoyed look over her shoulder, and I ignore the glare coming from Nate.

He puts his hands on the top of the window, like that's gonna stop me from closing it all the way and crushing his fingers. As if.

"Hey, Hannah," he says. His voice sounds slick and assholey as usual. "I thought you were in here with your grandpa or something, the car was moving so slowly." He cocks his head to look deeper into the car as if he didn't see me already. "Ha! Just kidding. What's up, man?"

"Hey...man." I'm tempted to speak to him in Korean and pretend I don't understand him. It's an easy trick to use to get someone to not talk to you. Unfortunately, I don't get the sense he's here to talk to me.

"Dude, I can't believe that it's you. Jacob Kim, hometown hero, returns after all these years as a big shot actor. It's so cool," he says.

I jerk back at his words. He *knows*. He remembers me and made the connection. I don't know how I feel about that. But clearly, he feels pretty good about being in the know if his arrogant smile is any indicator.

"When Hannah told me, I couldn't see it. Man, you look so different. But good different, ya know?"

The words sting like a slap in the face. So it was Hannah who told him. Which means Hannah's been talking to Nate. But when, and how often? My cheeks heat, and I adjust myself in the seat, uncomfortable sitting in this confined space.

Hannah glances at me quickly and notices me squirming. She turns back to him. "What are you doing here, Nate?"

"Hey, open the window a little more, I feel like a creeper," he says with a chuckle.

I hold back the temptation to reply *"exactly"*, just as Hannah presses the control to bring the window all the way down. Nate's mouth slowly stretches across his entire face, a victory smile, and all the muscles in my body tense up in response.

"That's better," he says. He puts both arms on the door and leans in. "I was getting a couple miles in at the track. I like getting here early before anyone else. Then I saw your car in the parking lot, moving at a snail's pace, and thought maybe it was giving you trouble. What, is this a driving lesson or something? Oh wait, is this one of those things on your summer list that Hannah is helping you with?" Nate asks me.

I freeze. I catch Hannah's back straighten out of the corner of my eye as well. But my attention is solely on Nate. My eyes widen in surprise. Helping me? Like I'm some charity case? And all this time I thought that maybe she was having fun doing it together. Was I wrong?

"Oh, sorry, was it a secret? Don't worry, dude, I won't tell anyone where you are and what you're doing. I can only imagine how privacy is important in your line of work. Hannah just explained to me that she was assigned tour guide duties all over San Diego for you while you're in town," Nate goes on. "But I'm surprised you haven't done most of this stuff already, since you grew up here. It's a great place, right? Is Hannah showing you a good time?"

Is this asshole making fun of me? I try and moderate my breathing. In through the nose, out through the mouth.

Hannah turns to look at me, mouth open and eyes frantic. But I can't, I can't look at her. I just drop my gaze to the emergency brake that seems to grow in size, widening the divide between us.

"I told him a while ago at the party. I was just trying to explain to him..." Hannah starts to speak, but every word feels like a dagger.

I close my eyes and imagine all the right words written for me on the page. Cues of how to react, emotions to evoke, all described for me.

"Oh shit, sorry. I didn't mean to cause any misunderstandings here. I'm just running my mouth like no one has anything better to do," he says. His laugh grates on me, and my heart is racing, not out of fear, but out of rage. But it's not me here. It's a character I'm playing. I just have to get through this scene.

"Naw, man, it's all good. No misunderstandings here. Good to see you again." I stretch my arm past Hannah and hold out my fist.

I want to punch him. But instead I wait for his fist to meet mine.

"Well, I'll let you guys get back to it. Good seeing you again, man. Sorry for butting in on your driving lesson. Hope I see you around again this summer?"

I look at him out of the corner of my eye and force a nod and a cocky smile.

He drops his voice lower. "Hannah, thanks for the talk. I hope all of this works out for you," he says.

I stare at the steering wheel, not wanting to look at them. I try and drown out whatever they're saying to each other. The boulder-sized betrayal lodges itself in my chest, and I'm finding it difficult to breathe. She's been talking to him about us. What else has she told him? What else does Nate Anderson know about me?

When we were kids, I knew with all certainty that Hannah had my back. We were ride-or-die for each other. No one would come between us. But a lot has changed over the years, and no matter how hard we try and want for that to be restored, it was never destined to happen overnight. I've been an idiot.

"Sorry, Nate." I barely register Hannah's voice, Nate's presence, anything else around me. I'm encircled by a bubble of confusion, hurt. She's apologizing to Nate. Unbelievable.

A hand is on my forearm, but I carefully pull my arm away. I don't respond as I think I hear Nate saying something about a bonfire and catching us later.

It's quiet now in the car. The air is heavy and my head is spinning.

"Do you think you can drive us home? I have a really bad headache," I say. My voice is flat, but I don't have it in me to act this scene out any other way. And I'm not about to let Hannah know how much this bothers me.

I undo my seat belt, get out of the car, and switch sides. Hannah slowly does the same. She stops in front of me. "Jacob..." She reaches out to touch my arm again. I pretend the contact doesn't sear through my skin.

I could be overreacting. I could be totally off about all of this. Hannah wouldn't betray me, would she? But I can't process it or even think about it right now. I open my eyes and look down at her. I force a small smile on my face. "It's okay, Hannah. I just need some rest."

I pull away from her touch, get in the car, close my eyes, and wait for her to take us home.

I hole up in my room for the rest of the day, door closed. My mom was not thrilled when I said I didn't want to come down to dinner. But she didn't push it. I told her I wasn't feeling well, but really, I just don't want to face anyone right now. I imagine Hannah and Nate Anderson laughing at me and the sad, sheltered life I've come to live, no experience with things other people my age should have.

I think about the studio execs meeting to figure out how to fire me. I think about all the cruel things written about Hannah in the comments and how I can't shield her from them. I think about days going hungry and cold when the electricity wouldn't come on.

I should just go back to Korea.

The thought fills me with dread, and I pull the too-short covers over my head, in turn exposing my feet. Stupid blanket.

There's a knock at the door, and my traitorous heart jumps, hoping that it's Hannah.

The door opens slightly, and Hannah peeks her head in, but she doesn't meet my eyes. "Can I come in, just for a second?" she asks tentatively.

I want to scream no and stay hidden underneath the blanket.

I want to scream yes and ask her to hide with me from the world underneath the blanket.

Instead, I don't say anything.

"I heard you still weren't feeling well. I brought you a bae," she says, stepping inside and holding out the round Asian pear in both her hands, like some kind of peace offering.

Damn it, she knows me too well. She knows I can't turn down a bae. I grumble to myself as I sit up in the bed and take the deliciously sweet and juicy-looking fruit from her hand. I push out my bottom lip and pout before lifting it to my mouth and taking a bite. I am so weak.

The corner of her mouth lifts. "How's the headache?"

"I'm okay," I say.

She looks at the spot next to me on the bed, and after some internal struggle, she goes and pulls out the desk chair and faces me. She pulls both of her feet under her, sitting cross-legged on the small chair. She's so tiny and so adorable, and I want to forget everything that happened today and just pull her into my lap and kiss her.

I take another bite of the pear instead.

"Can we talk?" she asks.

I nod.

"But I want to talk to Jacob, not Jin-Suk the actor or some character you think you're fooling me by playing."

Ouch. I duck my head and try to hide behind my bangs.

"I wanted to explain about today, about the stuff Nate said."

"Have you been, um, spending time with Nate this summer?" I can hear the hurt in my own voice. Asking the question cuts up the inside of my throat, words slashing, fighting not to be spoken. But I have to know.

"What? No. Jacob, of course not. In fact, the only reason I told him about you, helping him make the connection and explaining what we've been doing together, is so that he'd understand. No one who knows us, especially not Nate, would question why I'd choose to spend my time with you over him."

"But he wants to spend time with you."

"I mean, I guess, yeah. We didn't really have closure after we broke up. I think he just wanted to talk."

"Does he want you back?"

"I don't know. It doesn't matter right now, does it?"

It doesn't matter right now. But will it matter when I'm gone?

"Why *him*? Why Nate Anderson out of anyone you could have dated?"

She hesitates, turning her head to the side as if she'll find the right words there to explain to me why she chose the one person she knew would hurt me, had hurt me. "You asked me that before. I told you that he was nice to me. But he also told me that I was pretty. Me, with my small eyes and round face, my flat nose…for some reason, among all the other girls who were perfect, he liked me. I know that sounds pathetic."

"You're the one who's perfect, Hannah. You don't even realize how beautiful and amazing you are. And it breaks my heart that you'd settle for a guy like Nate Anderson just because he has some kind of Asian fetish."

"That's not fair, to me or to Nate. Nate's not a bad guy. He really isn't. Sometimes I think he just didn't know how to handle being such a big kid when we were growing up. Kinda like how we both fell into these expected roles as the Korean kids in the neighborhood. He just took on the role as the bully because of his size. People were already afraid of him. But, Jacob, give me some credit. I wouldn't let myself be disrespected and treated like shit. He's grown up, changed. He's one of those people who will do anything to help someone. And he's always trying to take care of me. He doesn't always get it right, but he doesn't stop trying."

"You don't let anyone take care of you, Hannah. You're always trying to take care of everyone else." It's the truth.

And the fact that Hannah would even consider letting Nate do anything for her hurts me more than I expected.

This entire summer has been a battle between past and present, hurt and forgiveness, memories and reality, complicated by the fact that we're older. We're old enough to feel things and understand what they mean. Not old enough, maybe yet, to understand the repercussions of our words and actions.

I'm so tired. Longing for the simplicity of what life used to be here in this room when the hardest thing we had to decide was who would play Mario and who would be Luigi in our video games.

"I was gonna, you know, um, give myself to him," Hannah says. Her voice is barely audible, and I close my eyes, trying to convince myself I didn't hear her. I never expected to hear those words, and even if I had, I never could have guessed how much they'd hurt.

"What do you mean, 'give yourself to him'?" I surprise myself that I don't scream.

"I was going to have sex with him, if he wanted." Her voice sounds small, barely a trace of the strong, spunky, confident girl I know. The air in the room is stifling, and I shake as I let out a breath to release the tension building up inside of me.

I want to kill Nate Anderson.

"Hannah, please don't say that," I say.

"Why?" she asks.

Because it hurts me to hear it.

"Is it just because you think he'll 'take care of you'?"

Hannah scrunches her mouth tightly, trying to hold back

her reaction. "This is embarrassing to talk about, okay? I don't know why I just told you that. It was just a thought."

"But do you love him?" No.

"Do I have to? I like him. And sometimes I hate how people make such a big deal about sex and the first time. There's nothing stopping me. Next you're gonna tell me I shouldn't be planning this because I'm a Christian and not married yet."

Everything in me wants to run away from this room and not hear what Hannah has to say about this. I can't handle the words *sex* and *Nate* in the same conversation. But I also miss these times when Hannah wants to debate something she's feeling passionate about. It's when she's at her best and one of the things I like so much about her. That conviction.

I egg her on. "Well, I hate to state the obvious, but you are a Christian, and you aren't married yet." This is territory I can maneuver in, getting her to work through her arguments and point of view. "Are those things you personally feel you should take into consideration before making this decision? Or are they things you've been *told* to take into consideration?"

"The idea of waiting till marriage is outdated and problematic," she says.

"How so?"

"We all know Korean Christian girls are the worst. They force themselves into the good girl narrative and end up being so repressed they lose it and become the crazy insecure girlfriend: breaking into phones, reading their boyfriend's texts, keying their cars, having meltdowns, faking pregnancies..."

"What kind of Korean Christian girls are you hanging out with?" I'm shocked at what she's sharing with me.

"Jacob, these are the same girls we were singing songs with at church on Sundays when we were kids. You'd be shocked at what's happened to some of them. And the same stuff is happening in LA, too. The Korean church has some real issues."

My eyes widen. "I had no idea. But I see what you're saying and how it could happen, I guess."

"I just think that the longer we guilt ourselves into lives of repression, the longer we stew inside until we eventually blow. I don't want to be one of these girls. I don't want to be a statistic."

"So, you're just gonna have sex to avoid being a statistic? And worse, you were gonna do it with Nate Anderson?" I almost vomit on the words. I don't want to ask her *what about me*, but I wonder it nonetheless.

"Like I said, I just don't think sex is that big of a deal." She throws up her hands in frustration. "It doesn't have to mean something, does it? I mean, it can, I'm sure. But does it have to be life-altering?" She shrugs. "I don't know. I just don't get why it all matters so much."

This is a side of her I never knew. But I'm curious and feel like I could talk to her for hours about it. "This is all really fascinating. But can we maybe keep talking through this without ever mentioning Nate Anderson's name again?"

"Ugh. Everything is all so confusing. This entire summer has been emotional whiplash. First Nate breaks up with me for no reason I can fathom. Then, you." She points at me with a murderous look in her eye. I lean back a little in a move of self-preservation. "You suddenly appear after three years when I fully locked you away as gone and dead to me." She stands up and begins to pace. "So of course, Nate shows signs of being jealous, which obviously he would because look at you, all tall and manly and perfect-smiley and—" she looks my way and gives a little grunt of frustration "—hot without trying. And then there are all these memories that make me smile. God, *why* am I always smiling? And it makes me want nothing more than our friendship back because, to be honest, I have no friends. None like you were to me, at least. But I hated you for years, right? And then I just didn't anymore. See? This is where I'm so confused. How does one so easily change their mind with just a burrito and a peek at a sculpted, albeit entirely too pale, chest?" This time she takes both her hands and rakes them through her hair.

I'm totally entranced by the entire thing. It's the best monologue I've ever seen. She's on a roll. I can't say a word in response, and I wouldn't dare stop her now. *Continue*, I think to myself, making sure I don't say it out loud but offering it up to her through my eyes.

"And then I, clearly being a pushover, just forgive you and let you back into my life like that." She snaps her thumb and forefinger, and the sound reverberates through the air. "And let's get real, everyone could have seen a mile away that this would turn into something more interesting because, I repeat, look at you, and duh, I'm an emotional mess. Very dangerous combination."

Hannah flops herself back down on the bed and covers her eyes with her arm. "So now, I'm pretty much screwed.

And confused. And exhausted. And in this stupidity, I got all blabby and told Nate shit you clearly didn't want me to, and now I'm worried you think I might have betrayed your trust. And I'm just so angry at myself. Gah, this life!"

Wow, that was something. I look over at Hannah still lost in her thoughts. I can't help smiling down at her. What a ride it is, following her train of thought. I try to think of what to say to her to tell her it's all gonna be okay. But I don't have the words. And I can't stay mad at her. It's impossible.

"Please don't have sex with Nate Anderson," I say. *And don't ever talk to him or look at him again*, I plead in my head. It's just a part of what I'm feeling, but it's the only thing that comes out.

Hannah laughs, but it's more sad than happy. "Not gonna happen, I promise. But, Jacob, what are we doing here?"

"I don't know," I say softly. "I just know I'm crazy about you. You mean so much to me. And I know we're working through our messed-up past and making up for all the lost time. And we definitely need to figure out the seemingly impossible and complicated future. But right now, I don't want to waste any minute that I can have just enjoying spending time with you."

Hannah sits up and puts her head on my shoulder. My arm instinctually wraps itself around her, drawing her closer.

"I don't want the summer to end. I'm scared," she whispers into my neck.

God, so am I. I don't know how this can end up working for us. But I can't think about that. And I don't want Hannah to think about it, either.

Hannah lifts her head to meet my eyes, and the tenderness laced with fear is more than I can bear. I lower my lips to meet hers. I hold her tighter, not wanting to ever let go. She opens her mouth to me, and I deepen our kiss, not caring to ever take in oxygen again.

"Jacob," she whispers between our kisses.

"Hannah," I whisper back.

We don't say them. We don't tell each other with words. But in the shared breath of our kisses, everything unspoken spills out, and all that's left is love. And what happens next for us doesn't seem to matter.

CHAPTER 18: *Hannah*

This panda hat I'm wearing is ridiculous.

But a bet's a bet.

Last night, after a very competitive round of Go-Stop, a Korean card game, I was neck and neck in points with Jin-Hee, who I completely underestimated, because she is way too young to be a card shark.

Before our last hands were dealt, she stopped everyone and insisted we agree upon a penalty for the loser. Brutal.

"Whoever loses this round does the dishes for a week," my mom suggested.

"The loser buys us all lunch tomorrow," Mrs. Kim threw out.

"The loser does laundry for a month," Jacob said, staring at his sister. His faith in me warmed my heart.

"Or maybe everyone pays the winner five dollars each?" Everyone turned to stare at me, shaking their heads in disappointment. Apparently, Koreans take punishment way more seriously and with much greater pleasure than they do reward. Noted.

Jin-Hee scanned the room and noticed something in the corner. A smile crept over her face. She looked at her brother with a wicked grin. "The loser has to wear that panda hat all day and take one hundred pictures to post online."

"Aw, twelve-year-old punishment is cute," I thought to myself.

That was until an epic upset happened with the last cards and I found myself at the bottom.

And thus, here I am, left wearing this fuzzy hat. It's eighty degrees out, and I have to wear a furry panda on my head during our day trip to the zoo today. Sadly, all the real pandas have been returned to their home zoo in China, so I'll be the lone sad panda in San Diego.

I grab the extra sunscreen and stick it in my backpack. Jacob's tan is coming along nicely, and most of the atrocious farmer's tan he was sporting has evened out over the past weeks. But I still don't want him to burn. I grab my Burt's Bees lip balm as well, just in case. Jacob has become addicted to it.

Slinging the straps over my shoulders, I leave my room to head downstairs.

The sound of Jacob's voice whispering catches my attention and stops me in my tracks. He's in Helen's room, the one his mom and his sister have been sharing, and the conversation, at first, sounds intense. But back-and-forth in the Korean language often can be mistaken for arguing, so I listen closer to what Jacob and his mother are discussing, seeing if I can understand enough of the words to make out what they're talking about.

Will ditching Korean school as a kid come back to haunt me for the rest of my life? I mentally shake my fist in the air at my greatest life's regret and tiptoe closer down the hallway.

"Did they say why?" Mrs. Kim asks.

"You know why. The same reasons as always. They want to control my life." Jacob's voice is frustrated. I imagine him pulling on his hair like he does when he's upset. "They weren't happy after the call. I think we pushed too hard. Our demands were too much. I should have just agreed."

"No, Jacob. You stood up for yourself, and we made it clear we won't let them treat you badly. And we'll just tell them we can't possibly come back early. We have airplane tickets we can't exchange."

"Like they care, Mom? No way. They'll say that you and Jin-Hee can stay but still force me to come back," Jacob says.

Go back to Korea early? But why? And when? He's on a break. They can't really force him to return if he doesn't want to. My heart starts to beat faster, and every goodbye scene plays out in my head. No, not yet, please, not yet.

"Sucks, huh?" a small voice whispers from my left. Sitting at the top of the stairs is Jin-Hee, looking like someone stole her puppy.

"Hey there, what's going on?" I whisper back, hopeful that the shakiness in my voice goes unnoticed.

"Hae-Jin, Jacob's manager, called this morning. She told Jacob that he has to go back to Korea tomorrow. They're mad about..." She stops herself.

"Mad about what?" I ask.

But a hand lands on my shoulder, and I jump back in surprise. I cover my mouth to stifle the scream.

"Sorry, I didn't mean to scare you," Jacob says. His face looks miserable, and I want to wrap him in a hug and not let him go. I want to tell him he can't leave, that I won't let him, that I'll talk to the studio and explain that he needs to stay, that his ankle isn't better yet. He can pretend it's still hurting like he did at the party. Or I'll sic my mom on them. She can guilt-trip them into backing down. She's a pro.

But instead I just stand there, my hands fisted at my sides, unable to look into his eyes.

Jacob reaches out and lifts my chin, and my eyes meet his.

"Hey," he says, "nice hat." He smiles, but the muscles around his mouth are strained. It's not his on-camera smile, but it's not one that actually looks happy, either.

"What's going on?" I say, swallowing the lump in my throat. "Are you…leaving?" The last word feels like a boulder blocking my airway.

"Hasn't anyone taught the two of you not to eavesdrop?"

I look at Jin-Hee, and she looks back at me, both of us wearing matching expressions of worry.

Jacob grabs my hand, pulls me into his room, and shuts the door. He leads me over to the bed and sits down, inviting me to sit next to him. Just last night, we were kissing and cuddling on this bed. Memories of the skin just above the waistline of his jeans flood my mind.

But now, I'm afraid of what will happen here next. I look at him, his profile with the strong jaw and chiseled cheekbone, something I can stare at for hours. But right now, that profile is a wall put up to keep me from looking into his eyes.

"You know that call I had with my management team and the studio the other day?" He hesitates. "It didn't go well. We refused to sign the new contract with all the added details around marketing the show." He swallows, and it pains me to watch.

"And apparently the pictures of our summer have gone viral, gotten way more traction than any of us anticipated," he starts to explain.

He's speaking about "us" again, but this time it isn't me and him. It's like corporate jargon or something, and he feels far away as he says it.

"And they're not happy." I state the obvious.

He lowers his head, eyes closed, pained.

"The studio wants me to come back to Korea to start working on press for the next season of the show," he explains. "There's some, um, damage control to the image of me and Minky's relationship that they think we need to work on." His voice is barely audible at this point. I don't know if it's because he's whispering or if it's the pounding in my ears.

"Your relationship? With Minky," I say. It's clear to me now that he's just repeating someone else's words. Jacob never calls her Minky. It's too familiar. He only ever calls her Min-Kyung.

"I mean, you know, not for real. Just the press and the fans and..."

He's not making any sense, and I'm not sure what to think.

"What aren't you telling me, Jacob?"

"Before we left for America, my uncle tried to sell a tell-all interview about my family to the press. The company was supposed to take care of it. But it'll cost them to keep his mouth shut. And, well, if they're gonna go to that much trouble for my family, for me, they're clear that I need to play the good company soldier now. No more avoiding calls and responsibilities. No more complaining and making mistakes."

What mistakes is he talking about? "Am *I* a mistake?" I ask. I hold my breath, too afraid to hear the answer.

He slumps his shoulders and drops his head to his chest. He won't look at me. "You know that people have already posted pictures of us online, and the studio found out. Well, they think that it could have a negative impact on my reputation. It makes me look like a cheater, and it makes my and Minky's relationship look in jeopardy."

"Um, but there is no relationship. It's all fake, right? Sounds like it's already in jeopardy."

"You just don't get it, Hannah. This is how things run. Fanservice, speculation, manipulation of the truth are all part of the game."

"You're right, I don't get it. And you hate all that stuff. So just tell them you won't do it anymore."

"It's not that easy. I can't fuck this up, Hannah. My family depends on me. This job is all that we have."

"That's not true. You have so much more." I stop myself before I say it, before I offer up that he has *me*, that I'm here for him.

"And other people, all the staff who I work with, they

need it to be a success, too. It's not just a stupid little TV show that doesn't matter. What I do to jeopardize it matters. You don't understand what I'm going through."

"But what about us?" God, I hate even asking this question. I hate how pathetic I sound. Jacob never promised me anything. We never even talked about what was really happening between us. I don't know what's going through his head, and it's making me question everything going through mine.

"Hannah, you know how I feel about you, but I can't just say no to the studio. It was stupid for us to have been so visible this summer like I didn't have anything to lose. I didn't think through all the consequences, and now I'm fucked. The studio's pissed. Min-Kyung is threatening to leave the show if I continue to make her look like a fool. There's a lot of money on the line. And my fans..."

"Jacob, you're miserable. This show, this life, eats you alive. You don't get to do any of the things you like. You don't have time to try new things and see new places. You don't even have the time to work on your art. Anytime you talk about Korea and your work and the lifestyle, your entire face drops, and I see it. I see how unhappy it makes you. Why do you do it? You're a gifted actor, for sure. But you don't want everything that comes along with it. Isn't it too steep a price to pay? Forget them. Forget Min-Kyung's threats. She needs this as much as you do. Tell them you're not playing their game, and they can take it or leave it," I plead with him. I can't stand to see him unhappy like this. And I selfishly can't stand the thought of him walking out of my life...tomorrow.

"I tried." His outburst startles me for a second, and I lean back. He takes a deep breath, clearly waging an internal battle to get himself under control. "You don't know what you're talking about," he says. He opens his eyes and turns to look at me, but they're resigned, empty, a deadness inside. They're his actor's eyes. "Hannah, this is my job, but it's also the life I've chosen for myself. It's not perfect, but it's better than what most kids our age have. I'm famous and make money, and everyone wants to know me."

"Are you listening to what you're saying? Those aren't the things you want. It's the lie the studio is feeding you, you're feeding yourself, to put up with everything that makes you miserable. It's not you. This life is a well-crafted lie, Jacob." I grab his arm and give it a squeeze trying to wake him up out of this false narrative.

He shakes his head and pulls his arm away. The tension is so tight, like a stretched rubber band waiting to snap. His nostrils flare, and something sparks in his eyes.

"Not like your life, huh, Hannah? Not like how you dye your hair and do anything you can to not be the 'Korean' girl in school. And now, suddenly, when everyone loves all things Korean, you're so bitter because you changed everything about yourself to avoid who you really are. And it's gonna bite you in the ass. Maybe if you'd just be yourself for once and not what you think other people want you to be, then you wouldn't be alone."

My mouth opens, but nothing comes out. His words slash at the most tender parts inside of me. I'm not ready for this attack, not from Jacob. I try and process everything Jacob's just said. Is this how he sees me? Fake and trying too hard? How dare he...he doesn't even know me. My body shakes in anger.

Slash back. Hurt him back.

"That's rich, coming from you. That's exactly what you're doing. When was the last time you were ever truly yourself to anyone? Do you even remember who that person is? Or are you so bought in to how the world sees Kim Jin-Suk that you've lost Jacob in all of that? How about you take your own damn advice and maybe *you* wouldn't be alone. Because you sure as hell do not have me to come crying to," I say.

"There you go again. Pushing people away and then running as fast and as far as you can. Your MO is cutting people out so they can't hurt you. You pushed me out of your life and didn't look back. You're even trying to do it to your dad. I know we've hurt you, Hannah. But your dad is alive and well. My dad is the one who's dead, who will never come back."

Jacob's words hurt too much. They're not tiny cuts. They're daggers piercing me. I can't listen to this anymore. I turn to storm out of the room.

But Jacob rushes to the door and blocks my way.

"Get out of my way," I scream at him. I don't care who's listening. I don't care if Jin-Hee, or our moms, or the whole damn street can hear me. "Move," I yell.

"I'm sorry. Fuck, Hannah, I'm sorry."

"Get out of my fucking way or I swear to god, I will scratch your face off, and you try explaining *that* to the studio." The rage boils inside of me, exploding out of every pore. I'm too angry to let myself feel any pain. I just need to get away.

"Hannah, stop, please," Jacob begs. His hands grab my arms, and the pleading in his eyes shuts me up.

I stop yelling, but I look away, turning my gaze to the floor, breathing heavily through my nose.

"I'm sorry. I swear, I didn't mean it. You're not fake. I'm the one who's fake. I'm the one who has no idea who I am. And it scares the shit out of me, and I'm taking it out on you. God, I'm a dick. I'm so, so sorry," he says, dropping his chin to his chest.

Tears flood my eyes.

Seconds pass, maybe minutes, and neither of us says a word. We don't look at each other, too ashamed to face the hurt we've caused.

And then Jacob finally lowers his hand and touches mine. I pull away at first. His touch stings my heart. But then he reaches again, farther, and he wraps his long fingers around my hand, pulling me in. I don't jerk away, but I can't look up, either. His words still repeat themselves in my mind. Even with his arms wrapped around me, I'm alone.

"Let's not repeat history, feeling hurt and then hurting each other. It cost us so many years, and I can't go any-more without you."

I want to deny it. It's too raw, this much honesty after that much pain. But I know he's right. Tears fill my eyes again, but I close them, forcing the salty drops back before they fall.

"It just hit me that we really don't know each other like

we used to. I mean, you know me better than anyone, but…"

"We've changed," I say.

"Yeah, we've changed," he agrees. "But for the record, Hannah, I seriously love your hair. I don't know why I threw that in your face like it was something wrong."

"Well, for the record, Jacob, I seriously love my hair, too, and don't need your approval," I tell him.

He tightens his hold on me, and I feel his head nod against mine. "Badass," he whispers. I'm not sure if he's saying it to himself or for me to hear. But I'll take it. He releases me and pulls his head back, a smile on his face, all signs of his previous facade gone.

"I have to remind myself that we're not fourteen and fifteen anymore. Each of us has baggage we've been carrying over the last years," he says. "And we have some unresolved anger that we default to when we don't know how to handle our feelings now."

"You're good. If this acting thing doesn't work out, you should be a therapist." I pull myself out of his arms and go to sit on the bed. He follows me and sits next to me, pulling me in to his side.

I grab his hand and hold it on my lap. "Jacob, I'm so sorry if my disappointment with my dad has triggered any kind of feelings about you losing yours. I… I never even considered that. I don't know why I've been so selfish in that regard. I wasn't there for you then, when your dad passed. And I haven't been there for you now." I swallow the shame.

He kisses me on my head. "Thank you for saying that. But I'm okay. And if I did or do need to talk to someone about it, I know I can talk to you. This was something that I got through with my mom and Jin-Hee, though. We relied on each other a lot the past few years."

I'm so grateful that he had someone, his family, to see him through this. But how much of the burden was he carrying around on his own shoulders? And how much of that is forcing him to make this decision to go back to Korea now?

"We may have both changed in ways. But you're still the smartest, most loyal, and…most stubborn person I know," he says.

"You're still the sweetest, funniest, and kindest person I know," I say back.

He leans in and gives me a peck on the lips.

"Jacob, I can't always read your mind like I thought I could when we were kids. But I still feel like I know who you truly are," I say.

He nods.

"I'm not trying to tell you what to do. I just want you to be happy. I don't think acting or the life you're living is doing that for you. And you're right. You know me, too. Maybe I've been doing my own acting, just not in front of cameras like you. I haven't been happy, either. I can admit that. But this summer, spending time with you and reconnecting, it was like finding a part of myself that had been missing. I feel as complete as I have in a long time, and I honestly can say with all my heart that being with you makes me happy."

I don't know why I'm admitting all of this so freely to him, but the words won't stop themselves. I have to let him know before he leaves…which could be as early as tomorrow.

I wait, my heart on my sleeve, hoping that he'll tell me I make him happy, too.

Jacob closes his eyes and squeezes them in a pained expression.

"I'll lose financial security, I'll lose everything, if I'm not Kim Jin-Suk. It's who I am. It's everything I have. Without these fans—" he hesitates, opening his eyes "—no one will love me." His voice cracks.

I don't quite believe what I'm hearing. Has the road been so lonely for him that he believes only the fans will love this made-up version of who he is?

"I love you," I whisper. My heart is completely still. I say it without volume, but with all the conviction in my heart. I said it. I mean it.

Jacob's eyes snap to mine, wide with shock and then narrow in disbelief.

But before he can say anything to refute me, before he can tell me I don't know what I'm talking about, I say it again. "I love you, Jacob. I always have. I always will. And the scary thing is, the way I love you feels like it's changing, but I know more than anything that in many ways, it's exactly the same. I love the person you are. I want more than anything for you to be happy. I want to be the one to make you happy. I want to be that for you."

As I say the words, I come to realize that every person I've ever said "I love you" to has left me, my father, my sister, and in a way, my mother always gone at church. He could be the next to go. But I don't want to be afraid of that. I'm more afraid that he'll never know how I feel about him before he leaves.

He shakes his head, and goose bumps appear all over my arms. I can't give him the chance to reject me. I can't give him the chance to convince himself that I'm lying.

"I may not be fandom, but I have always been your biggest fan," I say.

I don't have time to process his movements until his hands are gently holding my face and his lips are on mine. Warm, wet. Emotions buzz within our connection so powerfully, I want to believe it'll never be broken. I turn my head slightly for a better angle, and he increases the pressure. I wrap my arms around his shoulders, drawing him closer to me.

It's every kiss I've ever dreamed of, but never knowing that the face was Jacob's. Or maybe always knowing but never fully allowing myself to see it clearly.

Without disconnecting our kiss, he leans into me, pushing me back onto the bed, cradling my head as he comes down on top of me. I lift my chin, asking him for more. His mouth covers mine, and our tongues wrestle to get deeper, closer.

His hand reaches under my shirt and caresses me up my side and across my belly. His thumb makes its way under my bra and gently over my nipple. I gasp into his mouth and he swallows the sound.

I ignore the concern that our moms are just downstairs, and shit, his sister might be sitting right outside the door, eavesdropping. But I can't stop.

I wrap my legs around his, trying to draw him closer, needing more friction.

Jacob presses up onto his hands, straightening his arms and raising himself, looking down into my eyes. His pupils are blown, his lips swollen and red from our kisses. He's breathing heavily, and I can't tell if he's willing himself to stop or trying to plan what he'll do next.

He answers my question, moving downward and kissing my stomach, making his way up with soft caresses of his lips. He kisses my breast on the outside of my bra. He kisses my neck and behind my ear. I reach for one of his hands, and he props himself up on his elbow as he continues to kiss me wherever he can find skin. I pull his free hand down and lead it under my skirt where I'm wet and throbbing.

His hand takes over, and he pulls my underwear aside, dragging his finger along the wetness until he finds the most sensitive part of my body. A ragged breath leaves my lungs. I've forgotten how to breathe normally.

"Jacob," I moan, louder than I intend to. I freeze, waiting to see if anyone has heard me, if anyone is going to interrupt us. My mom loves Jacob, but she'd shit her pants if she saw us now. She'd pull us both by the ears and drag us to church to get a prayer from the pastor. Now, that would be awkward.

Jacob's gaze meets mine. We stare at each other in silence, eyes wide, waiting for motion outside our room, for any sound warning us of our impending doom. But after a few beats, we both relax and smile.

"Alexa, play Spotify," Jacob says.

"Here's Spotify," Alexa says back as the sound of Ed Sheeran begins to play in the background.

"Wait, Alexa? I don't want her listening to us, you know…" I say to Jacob, eyes huge, realizing that Amazon might be recording our shenanigans.

"Sorry, I don't know that one," Alexa says back.

I groan. Oh god, Alexa is listening to us…

Jacob drops his head, and his back starts to move up and down. He lays his head on my chest and continues convulsing. He looks up at me, tears in his eyes…laughing.

"Jacob, stop laughing. This isn't funny. It's an invasion of privacy. You invited Alexa—" I whisper the name "—into this…"

"It's not a threesome," Jacob says as he continues to crack himself up.

My lips pull into a smile, and I, too, realize the absurdity. I start cracking up with him, Jacob's head bobbing on my stomach as he tries to control his giggling fit.

I wrap my arms around him and let my fingers play with his hair. The laughter dies down, and it's just the two of us, holding each other, breathing in unison. We may not have gone all the way, but it was still the most intimate, beautiful, and ridiculous moment of my life. That is so us. Jacob pulls the Pokémon comforter up and repositions himself as the big spoon around me on the tiny bed. I smile and dream of Jacob as I doze off.

When I wake up and open my eyes, Jacob is gone, the space next to me on the bed empty and cold.

CHAPTER 19: Jacob

I tiptoe out of the room and lean against the door, already missing the beautiful girl napping on the other side.

I've loved Hannah Cho since we were three years old, and I built her the biggest house I could with my Magna-Tiles and promised her we'd live in it together forever.

But when faced with her beautifully open and honest face telling me she loves me, Jacob Kim, not Kim Jin-Suk the actor, I froze. I didn't say it back. I tried to show her in every way possible, though Alexa foiled that plan. Freaking technology.

But I didn't say the words.

I keep playing it over and over in my head. *I love you, Jacob. I always have. I always will.* Hannah's voice is on repeat in my mind. My heart is so full, it feels like it might explode.

And I know exactly what I have to do.

I stare down at my phone, finger hovering over the send arrow.

The bedroom door opens, and Hannah stands there looking confused and adorably rumpled, sleep still in her eyes.

"I fell asleep," she says. "You were gone when I woke up." The small whine in her voice makes me want to pick her up and take her right back into the room.

I smile. "I had to send a quick message," I say. "I think our moms and Jin-Hee have escaped somewhere. Because no one's home." I waggle my eyebrows and hers rise up quickly to her hairline.

"Pervert." Her smile widens, and then she drops her eyes. Is fierce Hannah Cho suddenly feeling shy? I love seeing all the new expressions from her that I never knew before.

"Do you still want to go to the zoo?" she asks. "We can probably get a couple hours in before dinnertime. It's one of the last things left on your list."

I'd rather mess around some more in the bedroom. But I look at her and know that I'd do anything for her and with her. "Yeah, definitely," I say, determined more than ever now to fight back against the studio. To fight for us.

She nods and passes by me, brushing her hand against mine as she does. "I'll meet you downstairs in ten," she says, heading to her room.

I try and think of the perfect way to tell Hannah that I love her, too. Maybe at the zoo by the flamingos. Or by the turtle exhibit. She loves turtles. Or maybe I'll wait until tonight or tomorrow night and take her up to Mount Soledad, overlooking all of San Diego, and tell her. It's a perfect city in which to fall in love. And it's got so many amazing places to tell someone you love them.

I'll come up with something good. I have time now.

I look back at the message I've drafted on my phone.

Sorry, can't come back early.

I press Send and head downstairs to get ready to go.

"Don't forget the panda hat," I yell up to Hannah. It's gonna be a great day.

We rushed home to get back in time for dinner. But traffic was awful, and Hannah's mom told us to take our time. Catching the sunset as we drove along the freeway heading home was worth it, even though I'm starving now.

As soon as we step inside, laughing, arguing about which of the orangutans is most like each of our personalities, we hear voices coming from the living room before we turn the corner. I give a questioning look to Hannah, and she shrugs.

"Church people maybe?" she guesses.

But when I look up, I stop in my tracks.

Sitting on the sofa are Hae-Jin, her assistant, Young-Mi, and Min-Kyung. They're drinking coffee and nibbling on fruit cut into the shapes of flowers along with Korean gwaja on a plate. I have trouble reconciling in my mind that the people from my Korea life are sitting here in the midst of my San Diego life. It takes my brain a few seconds to catch up.

There are strained smiles on my mom's and sister's faces. Mrs. Cho, however, is playing the ultimate host, lifting plates to her guests, asking them to eat more biscuits and fruit. Hae-Jin is completely out of place here in her black pantsuit and perfectly pressed white silk blouse, her uniform. Min-Kyung is in a floral sundress, and her face lights up in her rehearsed way when she sees me.

"What are you doing here?" I ask, still in shock at what I'm seeing. Hannah comes up and stands beside me, hand on my elbow as a sign of support and solidarity, I assume. I can feel her hands shaking, and the anger begins to boil inside me. How dare they come here and make her afraid? Thank goodness for the anger, or else I, too, would likely be terrified.

I only sent Hae-Jin the text that I wasn't coming back to Korea this morning. There is no way she could've gotten here so quickly in response. That means...she knew all along that I wouldn't agree. So they came to me.

"I got your message," Hae-Jin says. Not acknowledging the fact that she was already likely midflight by the time I'd sent it.

Min-Kyung stands up and skips over to me. "Jin-Suk-ssi, it's so good to see you. I've missed you very much," she says. She reaches to hug me politely. But I stand awkwardly, my body completely stiff, and don't return the embrace. "Hi, I'm Min-Kyung. You must be Hannah. I've seen you online. What a fun summer you are having," she says in perfectly rehearsed English. She holds out her manicured hand and Hannah looks down at it for a beat. Min-Kyung is a damn good actress, and I worry for a second that everyone here will fall for it.

Hannah steps closer to me, possessive this time. She's not fooled.

“Hi,” is all she says back before reaching her hand out to shake Min-Kyung’s. She doesn’t smile.

Min-Kyung narrows her eyes slightly at Hannah as her lips tighten. To the naked eye, she’s as friendly as always. But I see exactly what’s going on. She is pissed. And when she’s pissed, she’s nasty.

I brace myself.

Min-Kyung’s eyes scan Hannah, from her head to her toes, examining her. She purses her lips in thought. “I wouldn’t worry about all the comments online. Fans can be so brutal and cruel. They are just really invested in seeing Jin-Suk and me end up together. On-screen, of course.”

Hannah’s body stiffens next to mine. “I make it a habit not to read the comments,” she says. Her voice is strong, bold, but I hear the tiny shake in it, too.

“No? Oh, you’re so smart, and much stronger than I am. I can’t avoid seeing what the reaction from the fans will be. Or maybe because they’re mostly written in Korean, and you can’t read it? That’s a shame. I always wonder how Koreans who don’t know their native language survive, especially these days when everyone loves all things from Korea. Our fans especially are so very loyal. But I honestly didn’t think they’d believe there was something between you and Jin-Suk.” Min-Kyung’s expression sours, but she quickly puts her fake smile back in place.

Hannah’s entire body is strung tight, and I wrap my arm around her to protect her from the words shot in her direction.

“Don’t worry. Your skin really isn’t that bad in person. And there are worse things to be called than a…what was it? Oh yeah, I think the correct translation is 'relationship-wrecking slut.'" She cocks her head to the side with a satisfied grin.

"Stop," I say. I look down at Hannah next to me, but she won't meet my eyes. "There are always bad comments mixed in with the good. It's the worst part about being famous, having to expose yourself to what anyone and everyone thinks. Please don't worry about any of it. They don't know you; they don't know us."

She gives me a small nod and squeezes my hand.

"Jin-Suk, it's one thing to have a summer fling play out publicly. But how are you handling the shame of the betrayal? You seem to be taking Hannah's indiscretion quite well. Especially considering you must still be raw from your uncle's betrayal. Maybe you're more Americanized than I was led to believe. The fans sure aren't happy about that secret meeting...at a boba café, was it? How romantic."

"What are you talking about?" I ask. I'm so sick of Min-Kyung's game. She is just spewing nonsense at this point.

She shoves her phone in my face. Before I can see what's on the screen, Hannah tries to grab it, but Min-Kyung pulls it away and offers it, again, to me.

"Jacob, I can explain." I take a second to register Hannah's voice and the fact that she clearly knows what Min-Kyung is getting at. Wait, how does she know what Min-Kyung is getting at? I slowly lower my eyes to meet Hannah's and then move to the photo on the phone. I take it from Min-Kyung, despite Hannah trying to reach out to stop me.

On the screen is a picture of Hannah...and Nate. They're

drinking boba, and smiling, Nate's hand placed on top of Hannah's on the table. I look at the posting date. It was two days ago. I quickly scan the comments, trying to find someone to explain to me what the fuck I'm looking at. Comment after comment of people calling Hannah awful names and crying out for me to come home to Korea and be reunited with Minky.

My entire body grows cold, and I'm frozen to the spot. She told me she hadn't spent time with Nate this summer.

Hannah grabs the phone and looks at the picture. A tiny cry escapes her throat. She grabs my hand, but I don't grab back. "It's not what it looks like," I think I hear her say. "Jacob, let me explain," I may have heard her plead.

"Oh, I think it looks like you're having multiple summer romances, Hannah," Min-Kyung says. "And it's not only our fans in Korea. Our fans here are also not okay with seeing their Jin-Suk with a broken heart. You might want to lay low for a while. A few months should do it. Not like how Jacob was supposed to lay low with his ankle injury but pranced around San Diego all summer anyways. It's evident our popularity has crossed over to America as well, and I'm not sure how long it takes fans here to forgive a cheater."

"Hannah," Mrs. Cho calls out.

"Jin-Suk," my mom calls out at the same time.

"Oppa?" Jin-Hee sounds worried.

I don't move. I don't speak. Hannah was with Nate when she was telling me she loved me.

"Jacob," she says, her desperation in a whisper.

I slowly turn my head a fraction, daring to look at her from the side of my eye. Her face is panicked.

"Enough." The word gets all our attention. It is decisive. It is final. Hae-Jin's anger is clear. "Since you refuse to come back to Korea as requested, we've come to get you," Hae-Jin says. "Your behavior this summer has made a mess of things, and we have some rebuilding to do of your image."

It's just like Hae-Jin to try and gaslight me, making it seem like I'm going to be the downfall of the show, of the entire studio for that matter, for not doing what they want. But I don't say a word. I can't get the picture of Hannah and Nate out of my head.

"It's a lovely backdrop, San Diego. We'll get some press photos for the new season around here. Maybe even write a vacation into the script if we can. But I think first, we'll have a photographer and cameraman follow you and Minky around town as the two of you complete some more things on your summer list. We can take it from here. No need for amateurs anymore." Hae-Jin doesn't even look at Hannah, but the shot was fired, and the deflation of Hannah's shoulders shows it hit its target.

"I've always wanted to see California," Min-Kyung squeals.

My sister looks to my mom, who looks to Mrs. Cho, who looks to Hannah, who looks up to me. But I don't meet her eyes. I can't. I'm too stunned. Too confused. I'm being pulled in all directions, and I'm going to rip apart. A single tear escapes from my eye, but I don't feel it. I let it drop and don't give it another thought. Discussion of the rest of my summer happens around me, arguments from my mother, my sister calling my name, and I don't register any of it.

Hannah grabs my hand again. "It's not like she's making

it seem. I told Nate about you earlier in the summer, but I actually did go and meet him a couple days ago to explain to him my feelings for you. I thought it was the right thing to do. I should've told you, but it honestly slipped my mind. That was the only time, I swear. I'm so sorry."

I want to believe her. I don't want to jump to conclusions. But I'm not sure. I don't know. The camera can lie and twist a story. But can Hannah? The confusion courses through me like a poison eating away at me from the inside out.

I shake my head.

Hannah takes a half step back, making room between our two bodies. She releases my hand, or maybe I let go first. I don't know.

"Jacob," she pleads again.

"I can't do this right now," I say. I mean this whole thing, this whole scene. But Hannah's face drops. She thinks I mean her, us.

"I… I…understand. Of course. I'll let you guys get to planning," she says, voice breaking. Hannah turns around and escapes upstairs. I try to get my body to turn and go after her, but it doesn't move.

Someone grabs my arm.

"Jin-Suk, I can't wait to see all the things around San Diego that you grew up with," Min-Kyung says, pulling me towards the sofa to sit down. I'm dragged along like a rag doll.

Hae-Jin takes out a leather-bound notebook and pen from her briefcase. She pulls out a very official-looking document and turns it facedown on the coffee table. Clearing her throat, the message is obvious…she wants to talk to me alone.

My mom comes over to the sofa to stand next to me.

"It's okay," I say to my mom. "I'm okay." I nod to reassure her.

Mom, Jin-Hee, and Mrs. Cho leave, and I'm here on my own to fight the Korean wolves.

I try to stop Hae-Jin before she gets started.

I try to pull out of Min-Kyung's grasp.

I try to go and check on Hannah.

But I'm rooted here on the spot. I can't get my feet to move. I'm stuck in every way possible.

Hae-Jin's disapproving expression and the fact that they sent a very expensive camera crew and a team from the studio, and Min-Kyung, all the way out here makes it clear that I'm in some big trouble. I've messed things up royally. And I better suck it up and do what they want, or this could all go very wrong for me.

At this point, I don't even care. If I'm not fighting to stay here with Hannah, I might as well go back with them. Have I gotten the whole thing wrong? She told Nate everything. She's spent time with him behind my back. Was she playing me all along? Or maybe she's keeping him around for when I'm gone?

So I sit there, watching Hae-Jin write up plans without hearing what she's saying. I'm a statue made of stone, and I'm stuck.

For the next two days, I'm swept away into work mode.

Min-Kyung and I are thrown together at Belmont Park,

where we're shot in front of the old wooden roller coaster, eating cotton candy. I put on a smile when the cameras are filming and am a removed, disinterested robot the moment they're off.

"Put some effort into this, Jin-Suk," Hae-Jin hisses at me under her breath. "The studio is very interested and invested in how this turns out. No one is happy that you put us and the show at risk by carelessly letting yourself be all over the internet this summer with that girl."

"Don't talk about her," I say. "I'll let you treat me like your dog, but you do not get to say anything about Hannah." Hae-Jin raises an eyebrow, clearly surprised that I've spoken back to her, that I'm defending the girl she believes betrayed me. I can't tell if she's pissed or impressed. Likely just annoyed to have to be dealing with me.

The publicity team must have gotten the word out, because fans show up at every location we go to. I don't feel like I'm in San Diego anymore. It might as well be Seoul.

Next we go to SeaWorld, where we're shot feeding the dolphins and rubbing the heads of the killer whales. No one cares about the controversy of keeping the killer whales captive at SeaWorld. All they care about is that they get the shot of MinJin looking like we're having the best time. I slap on my actor smile and do as I'm told, going through the motions.

I haven't seen or talked to Hannah in two days. She's been ignoring my texts. I'm desperate to talk to her. I didn't trust her, so why should she trust me? And when Hannah is hurt, she pushes people away. That's what I'm scared of most of all.

"I think we got the shot here," the cameraman says.

"Good, let's pack it up and call it a day. We'll shoot at Old Town and at the Korean dessert shop on Convoy tomorrow," the director says.

"It's a lot of work for just a few promo shots," Min-Kyung says to me. Her voice is strained, and it's the first time I've seen her facade break. She pulls the umbrella shading her from the sun closer to her face. She's frustrated. I don't know that I've ever considered what she got pulled out of in order to get dragged to San Diego to save face for our on-camera relationship.

"How's the hotel?" I ask.

Her head jerks up, and she gives me a distrustful look. "It's nice, I guess," she answers.

"Min-Kyung noona, I'm sorry for being such a jerk about all of this. It's just… I had plans for the summer, and this all kinda took me by surprise." I can do this. I can at least try to make peace and be friendly. We're in this together.

"I warned you on the video call. Your carelessness and selfishness put everyone in a bad situation, including your girlfriend. And then she's caught with another guy? Jesus, Jin, get with the program. We can't have 'normal' lives in this business, no matter how much we may want them. We have jobs to do, and that includes an image that our fandom wants to eat up. The moment that veneer is gone, and the hope of our relationship is unbelievable, we're ruined. So I'll say it one more time, because you were clearly too slow to understand it the first time I told you. Unless you want to go back to being jobless and poor, I suggest you figure out how to be an actor…for once." She storms off, straight into the waiting car.

Welp, so much for an olive branch.

I look down at my phone. No messages from Hannah.

Are you around tonight? Can we talk? I type out.

Still nothing. I'll keep sending them until she answers. She can't avoid me forever. She has to come home eventually. And when she does, I'll be waiting for her.

I missed family dinner again. So I sit down to a warmed-up plate of leftovers while the moms watch a Korean variety show with current music stars competing for audience votes by singing old-school hits. It's a fun concept, and the moms are really getting into it.

I have one eye on the screen and the other on my food while my mind wanders, thinking of what I want to say to Hannah. She's upstairs in her room and has her music blaring, which means *stay away*. But I've stayed away for two days now, and I can't let it go on any longer without talking to her.

I finish dinner and wash my plate. I run upstairs and brush my teeth and change out of my clothes from the day. Taking a cue from earlier in the summer, I crawl under my bed to the electrical outlet and listen to hear what Hannah's doing.

"Having fun down there?"

My head hits the bed as I react to being caught spying.

"Ow," I yelp, rubbing the spot where my head knocked the bed frame. "You scared me."

She's standing at my door, leaning on the frame, legs

crossed at the ankles. She's in her flannel pajama pants and a tank top. I love that Hannah can wear just about anything and be the cutest one in the room every single time.

"Sorry," she says. "So, how was your day with Minky? Get all those fun things crossed off your list?" Her voice is mocking, irritated, and my heart aches that I've made her feel this way.

My mouth opens to say, "How was your date with Nate?" But I shut it and stop myself. We're not in the hurt-each-other-on-purpose phase anymore. We've grown past that. We need to talk this out.

"I'm so sorry it all turned out this way. I'm sorry about them showing up here, on your turf, no less. I'm sorry about all the internet trolls and the comments. And I'm sorry the most for not trusting you. I was wrong. I am wrong about all of it." I swallow hard, pushing back all the emotions and trying to stay focused on Hannah, being here for her.

Her face crumples, and I stand up and go to her, wrapping her in my arms. But I struggle to find a solution for her pain. In two weeks, I'll be heading back to Korea. So if these two days hurt her, I can't even imagine how hurt she'll be when I leave.

Well, I can imagine, because I'll be hurting, too.

"Can we talk?" I ask.

"Isn't that what we're doing?" She wipes away her tears and keeps her eyes lowered, hidden. She's not gonna make it easy on me.

"Hannah, I'm so sorry it's all happening like this. I didn't know they were coming, and I'm pretty much up shit creek with the studio. So, I have to play nice and do what they want from me or else..."

"Or else what, Jacob? They fire you? You're the star of one of their most popular shows. How could they just fire you?"

What she's saying makes sense, really. But she doesn't know the industry and how competitive it is. There's a new K drama popping up every day, and as long as it follows the formula of maximizing screams, tears, and tugging at heartstrings, then it'll be a hit. And that means even more young actors are auditioning for all these parts. Who knows what will happen once *Heart and Seoul* is done? The fact that they're planning a second season is almost unheard of. Most shows only run for one. I'm lucky to have a job. And with Hae-Jin bringing a revised contract for me, holding it hostage until I do everything they want of me this summer, I'm out of options.

"They could. Or they could just make life really hard for me and my family," I say.

"Don't they already? The way I see it, you're pretty miserable doing their bidding as it is. How long can you last like this?" She's frustrated. And she hurts for me. I hurt for her. I wish things could be different.

"Jacob, shit like the misunderstanding over the picture with Nate will always happen. Us needing to trust each other more and talk things out will be part of our growth. That's all real life. But this perception and fear that the studio owns you and can make you do whatever they want is not. It's not real."

"Hannah, I know this sounds outrageous to you. But

it is how it works with these Korean studios. They won't hesitate to cut me if I don't cooperate."

"They can't be the only company for actors in Korea. And every company can't be just like this one. Maybe you can work with someone else."

I've thought of that, too. But I know the truth. "The expectations are all versions of the same thing no matter where I go."

I look up at her and my eyes plead for her to understand. But the confusion in her own face tells me everything. I'm in a no-win situation.

She tightens her lips and nods.

"Jacob, I wasted three years because I was hurt and stubborn and blocked you from my life. But now that we've reconnected, I know how I feel. I told you I love you. The thing is, that's only gonna make it even harder when you leave. It hurt the first time. But I'm in deep now, and it's gonna be impossible this time. So I think you should just rip off the Band-Aid and go back to Korea with everyone, and let's just remember this summer as a nice memory and move on with our lives."

"Wait, what? You want me to go? And you don't want to try and make this work?" I know I sound desperate, but this wasn't what I expected from her. Sure, I've been thinking that it will be hard, but I wasn't ready to just give up.

Tears form in my eyes, and they match the ones in Hannah's.

"I can't do it, Jacob. I'm just not strong enough to see you with someone else, even if it's just acting. I can't watch how they treat you and how miserable you seem. And hardest of all is knowing that I can't help you because you'll be six thousand miles away. I don't know how to do this."

"Hannah, please. You say that everyone leaves you. But really, you're the one who ends up cutting all ties when they do. Don't push me away this time. Why won't you even try to make relationships work? What are you so afraid of?"

The tears flow more freely down her face now. "I'm afraid of being alone. I'm afraid of being left behind. I'm afraid of not being enough to make someone choose to stay."

I wish I had a clearer response for her. "Hannah, you're enough. You're more than enough. It's just that the situation is messed up. I don't know what to do. Please..."

She shakes her head. My words aren't enough. "I'm sorry," she says. "Goodbye, Jacob."

"Hannah," I say to her back. Don't leave. Don't give up on us. Don't go back to Nate Anderson. Don't.

I may be an actor, but this is the most drama I've ever experienced in my life. And the heartache is the most real emotion I've ever felt. Maybe Hannah is right. Maybe it's not worth feeling anything for anyone in the first place, and maybe it really is easier to just walk away.

CHAPTER 20: Hannah

It's a San Diego cliché, driving out to The Cliffs, overlooking the ocean, to think and clear your mind. But it's the first place I thought of to get away to be by myself, along with the twenty or so other people here by themselves attempting to ignore one another, and trying, but failing, to not look at the naked old men down below enjoying Black's Beach, San Diego's only "clothing-optional" strip of coastline.

I close my eyes and let the slight breeze blow over me. The waves roll in and out, and the sound is attached to so many of my memories growing up.

I think back to when we were kids, Jacob and me. I can't remember a single day where we weren't laughing. I was always happy to be with him. He was the small, sweet, loyal friend. He felt things deeply and expressed them openly, and he brought me out of a shell built up by my insecurity and need to be liked. The fear I was not enough for people started when my dad left for Singapore and would only get worse when everyone else in my life left me.

Including Jacob.

The person who I felt safest with to be myself, argumentative and stubborn and bossy and scared and damaged, left me, too. I didn't feel safe to be me anymore. I always played to be who someone else wanted me to be.

We never talked about it. But even apart for three years, we both seemed to find the same fate. He, too, was always pretending to be who someone else wanted him to be.

Until he came back. And I can say with confidence that we both are a lot more ourselves than we've been in a long time.

I'm not sure if I'm happy to have had the summer with Jacob or if I wish he'd stayed out of my life. His smile lights up my world. His kisses make me feel adored. His laughter ensures me that I'm not lame. The way he looks at me tells me I'm worthy of being loved.

His choice to stay in the life that makes him miserable and leave me to go back to Korea shatters my heart.

I don't want him to leave. But really, there's no room in that life for me, is there?

I sit down towards the edge of the cliff, bring my knees up to my chest, wrapping my arms around them and balling myself up as tight as can be, keeping everyone else on the outside.

"I knew you'd be here."

I look over my shoulder and see my mom standing behind me. She has on a huge visor that protects her whole face from the sun. Her hair, pulled loosely into a bun, shows signs of graying. She wears her plain khaki pants, with a plain white T-shirt, a plain long gray cardigan, and a fanny pack. She's about as unassuming as one can get. She is every Korean ajumma, nothing setting herself apart.

She became this way, slowly losing herself, once my dad moved away. She gives and gives of herself to others without asking for anything in return. Since when did that become something to be admired? Who watches out for you then?

She walks over and takes a seat next to me, ignoring that everyone else is here alone, in solitude, not talking. My mom doesn't have an inside voice, so I prepare myself for all these strangers to be exposed to my personal business.

Great.

"Daddy loved this place," she goes on to say to me, and to everyone in a two-mile radius, including the naked grandpas below.

I cringe a little. Not just at her volume, but at memories of my dad here in San Diego. She talks about him in past tense, like he's dead. Maybe that's why I do, too. But Jacob's right. I have a dad who is alive and well. Yet somehow, it makes it feel worse.

"He loved living in San Diego and near the ocean. He felt like a rich man," she says. "And then he moved. Living in Singapore makes him feel like a more rich man."

I hear the sadness laced with a bite of bitterness in her voice. It still amazes me how much pressure my parents put on themselves to be seen as successful. Is it because they're immigrants? Is it cultural? Jacob is successful by every indication, and yet he's miserable. Who cares about success if you can't be happy?

"Daddy is rich. But it makes me feel poor," she continues.

Maybe success isn't as important to my mom, either. Not at the cost we pay for it.

I swallow the lump in my throat. We don't talk like this often, me and my mom. So any little nugget she shares with me feels almost too much, too important, too precious, too painful.

I tuck my lower lip under my teeth, forcing back the emotion, ignoring the pain the scrape creates. I no longer care that anyone else can hear. For the first time, my mom tells me that she's lost something, too, and I hate myself a little for not seeing that in her. For only thinking about my own pain. My dad and sister and the Kims left her behind, too.

"I'm sorry, Mom," I say.

She grabs my hand and squeezes it, still looking forward out over the horizon. The crashing of the waves doesn't sound so peaceful anymore. The waves sound angry and hurt, lashing out against the rocks.

"I was so mad. I thought about divorcing Daddy."

The words strike me across the face. I didn't see the blow coming. I'd never heard my mom say any of this before. Divorce is not acceptable in the Korean culture, nor in the church. Is my mom stuck because she believes she has no other options?

I think about Jacob and how it must be exactly how he's feeling, too. Stuck in an impossible situation.

I squeeze my mom's hand.

"But how can I divorce him? I love him. He loves me. Maybe sometimes he loves himself more. Or maybe working in Singapore is his way of showing he loves me, loves us. I don't know. But I don't want to be with anyone else. Being so far apart from my husband is hard, but I wouldn't choose any other way if it meant I'd lose him. Even if the church said it was okay to divorce, I wouldn't do it. I love your dad. I love him."

Her voice breaks, and it tears my heart open, causing all the tears to flow. It's not what I expected to hear. I wipe my face with my free hand while grabbing my mom's hand even tighter, holding on. A deep, agonizing cry builds in my throat, but I refuse to let it out. I sit and keep listening to my mom's words.

"You being so far apart from your daddy is also hard."

I close my eyes and conjure up my dad's face. He is always smiling when he looks at me. I try to imagine his face without that joy, but I'm unable. I can't because I love him. And his face always shows love back to me.

"Daddy doesn't love you any less because he left for Singapore," she says.

It pains me to hear.

"Helen doesn't love you any less because she moved to Boston."

I shake my head, trying to ignore her words.

"Hannah, I don't love you any less because I work so hard with the church and helping others," she says through her own tears. "But I'm so very sorry if I made you feel like I do. You're my strong, independent, confident girl, and I'm sorry if I took that for granted and left you on your own."

My entire body shakes, but I press my lips together, holding back any sobs that might escape. I don't feel strong or independent or confident. I feel all the hurt I've carried around my entire life envelop me. The pain is too much to bear. The loneliness, the uncertainty, never feeling good enough for anyone crashes over me like the waves below.

Mom wraps her arm around me and pulls me in, comforting me with her shushes and kisses to my head. I soak in her comfort and her love. I try to let go of all the anger, my defense mechanism. I'm so tired of being angry at everyone, at myself.

"Jacob has very difficult choices ahead of him. His whole family relies on his job financially. But he puts the pressure on himself most of all. Losing his dad so young, fighting his own medical issues, trying to be the man of the family, he carries so much burden. Don't you see? He was always the one taking care of everyone, even you. I have to thank him for being there for you when I wasn't always paying attention. He is such a good, good boy."

I let my mom's words course through my mind. I always thought I was the one taking care of Jacob while we were growing up. I protected him from bullies. I made sure no one picked on him and no one gave him anything to trigger his allergies and no one took advantage of him.

But Mom's right. Jacob was also always taking care of me. He was there for me when no one else was. He was my safety net. He loved me when I believed no one else did, even myself. He always has. And now, when everyone continues to need and want and take from Jacob, who's there for him?

I walked out on him last night.

When I had the chance to be there for him, to support him, to take care of him, I turned my back. When he wanted to talk, to find a way to make it work, for him to take care of me, of us, I shut down and left.

"I've been really selfish," I say.

My dad leaving for Singapore wasn't about leaving me.

My sister leaving for Boston wasn't about leaving me.

Jacob leaving for Korea isn't about leaving me.

I wasn't the reason people left. It was the unfortunate outcome to difficult decisions they had to make for their lives. And me, only a child, trying to carry around this shame, this belief that people's choices were made because of me being unlovable.

The truth, the realization, starts to release years of hurt and loneliness coiled up so tightly inside of me, unraveling here in this moment with my mom.

I look out and strain my eyes to find where the sky meets the ocean, but I can't see it. I'm always looking for the end, but why does there have to be one? Does love have to come to an end?

I love Jacob. And if he has to go, what then? Can we make it work long-distance? Maybe. Maybe not. But even if we can't be together romantically, shouldn't I be there for him as a friend? No matter what his choices, don't I need to support him and not abandon him? Haven't I learned my lesson from last time?

I'm not willing to lose him. Not again.

I let out a deep, cleansing, healing sigh. I can feel the physical ache leaving my body. I don't have all the answers to what happens next in life. But I know for sure what I have to do now.

"I love you, Mom. Thank you for coming here to get

me," I say. I lean into her and absorb her strength, her love, her compassion, her power. She stands up and offers me her hand. I take it and stand, too. She gives me one more kiss on the head and walks away towards her car. I watch her go. I want to be there for her, too. And I want to receive her love in whatever way she knows how to give it.

I turn and take one last look out over the ocean. I may not be able to see Singapore from here, but my dad is in my heart. I can't see Boston from here, but Helen is always with me. I strain my eyes to see what stretches past the horizon. But I don't see anything. I don't see Korea from here. But I know with all confidence that Jacob is and always will be with me.

I nod to myself and turn to go catch up with my mom. I am my mother's daughter, and she is stronger than I ever imagined.

And so am I.

CHAPTER 21: Jacob

I force the zipper a little harder, praying it doesn't break. Sitting on my suitcase trying to get it closed exacerbates my frustration over leaving San Diego two weeks early.

I'm not ready to leave.

I don't have a reason to stay. Hannah made it clear she wants me gone.

How did it come to this? I should never have put Hannah into this position, exposing her to the studio, to my management, to the fans. God, the things they said about her in the comments and to her face. The things they're accusing her of. And me, unable to stand up for her, not strong enough to make choices that won't break her heart.

Dread consumes me every time I think about going back to Seoul. For three years I lived with all the ups and downs of being in Korea. I handled the life of being an actor on TV and the restrictions created by having a fandom. I survived a life with almost no freedoms. I had to. It's what we needed.

I didn't always hate it. But I lost myself, my identity, in

it. I look down at my sketchbook and think of all the drawings I've filled it with. I've now tasted things I want in life, I've experienced it rather than acted my way through it.

A summer in San Diego, a summer with Hannah, a summer watching my mom and sister look happier and more relaxed than I have in a long time, has changed me. Or, rather, it's reminded me of who I really am. And I don't know how I'm going to go back to my old life. The things I've tried to focus on—getting lost in the work and the craft and challenging myself with the acting, being able to financially support my family—don't feel like they'll be enough anymore.

But it's the choice I make.

Just put your head down and work, Jacob. Be the corporate robot and do what the studio tells you to do. Play the part. I think about Min-Kyung. That's what I'll become. Fake, uncertain of what the truth of who I am is, acting my way through life, even off camera. Why do I need anything more? Accept the schedule and do what I'm told. I can do it. I'm going to work harder than ever before. And when I'm done, I'll land another show and another one and keep doing what's expected of me.

It doesn't matter what I want. It only matters what I do.

"Are you all packed?"

My mom stands in the doorway, a mug in her hand. She offers it to me, and I take it, looking inside. It's shikae, the sweet rice drink I associate with summers of my childhood in San Diego. Funny how I never drink shikae anymore despite it being readily available in Korea. So much compartmentalizing of my life before Korea and my current life. Separating Jacob Kim and Kim Jin-Suk.

"I think I have everything. If I forget something, you or Jin-Hee can bring it back with you later?" The words catch in my throat. Not only am I leaving Hannah, my family won't join me in Korea for another two weeks. I really will be truly alone. Who will I even talk to?

Mom searches my face for something. "Jacob, are you sure you want to do this, to go back to Korea early?" she asks. "We can figure out a way to make it work."

I'm not sure what "it" is that my mom is talking about. Can we figure out how to make it work if the company is furious with me? Or even bigger, can we figure out how to make it work if I don't do this anymore? I want to believe her, take comfort and confidence in her words. But I don't see a way out of this.

My mom comes over and squats next to me, hugging her knees as she balances. She puts her cheek against her knees. She looks small and young and beautiful. She's been through so much with the loss of my dad, the lack of support from his family, and now, the blackmail by my uncle. I can't add to her concern, her stress, by losing my job.

I give my mom a small smile. There's no humor behind it, but I try. "Umma, I don't think I have a choice," I say. I'm talking both about the studio's demands…and Hannah's wishes. I don't tell my mother that, though. "I need to go back. I need to get back to work."

"Jacob, you always have a choice. I know sometimes it doesn't feel like it. This life, it must not have felt like you had a choice to do it or not. It all happened so fast, and at a time when we were in need. And it took off and grew so quickly, but…" She hesitates, eyes on the ground. The familiar worry lines around her face that seemed to have disappeared throughout the summer have found their way back.

"It's okay, Mom. I'm okay," I try to assure her.

My mom stands up and walks over to take a seat on the bed. She pats the spot beside her, inviting me to sit. I walk over and sit down. I feel like I'm a little kid again as she takes my hand in hers and holds it in her lap.

"You must have been so frightened, the day you had to leave and go into training," she says.

It's an odd thing to bring up. It was so long ago, and we've never really spoken of it, how it made me feel. I think we all just needed it to work. "It wasn't bad," I say.

"I'm so proud of you, Jacob. My strong, brave, kind, supportive son."

And here come the waterworks. My mom doesn't often share her feelings freely with words, and I don't know if I can take much more without crumbling. The first tears break the barrier and drop down my cheeks. I wipe them away, but they're replaced with fresh ones.

"You had to become a man before you even finished being a child. Working to support our family. Taking on the responsibility not only for your own well-being and health, but for ours. Daddy left us much too soon. And I wasn't strong enough to figure out how to take care of us all. But you—" she squeezes my hand "—you were. Strong. I want to thank you for all you've done for the family.

But—" her voice drops off "—I also want to say I'm so sorry for putting all of that burden on you to carry."

"Mom, I'm the first son. It's my responsibility..."

"No, let me finish," she says. "Watching you this summer, I knew our life in Korea was stressful. But I never knew how much it really took away from you. Here, you're so happy, so carefree, so alive. You're laughing. You're drawing. You're like the Jacob I remember from your childhood. You get to be a teenager here. You get to explore how you want to grow up and live...and love...here. I didn't realize how much I'd taken away from you by staying in Korea until I watched you this summer."

I think about the things I got to do this summer, mostly things I missed out on while in Korea because of my job. Things I could have and would have experienced if I had a normal childhood. But what is "normal," really? What I do now affords us vacations like this one, and apartments in safe neighborhoods, and Jin-Hee's education, and more. Everything comes at a cost.

"It was a great vacation, a much-needed break, for sure. I've had a wonderful time. But that doesn't mean I suddenly can't go back to Korea and get back to work, Mom." I give her hand a squeeze, wiping away the continued tears with my other hand "You don't have to worry. Everything is going to be fine." But even I don't believe the words entirely.

The two of us sit quietly, the only sound our sniffles and sobs.

Mom turns to me, and her eyes are wet but bright, sad but certain. "Jacob, you're old enough now to make choices that suit you. And it's time I take some of the choices for this family back into my own hands. So, I want to ask you, what do you want to do? Not what you think you have to do. But if there was no burden to carry, what would you choose for yourself? Is this life the one you want to live? Is acting what you want to do? Is Kim Jin-Suk the person you want to be?"

I look over at my mom, confused. She's never asked me these questions before, and frankly, I've never taken the time to even consider the answers. I don't know what to say. My life is certainly restricting. I'm not always happy. But do I want to give up acting, the fame, the financial security, the creativity? Do I even have the guts to walk away? And even if I did, would I be able to, contractually?

I've never explored the what-ifs. I'm too afraid of wanting something different, something I can never have. I think of Hannah, I picture her laughing with the sparkle in her eyes, and my heart pinches. This is what I mean. What's the use of thinking about someone else's life when all I have is being stuck in mine?

"I don't know," I finally answer.

A small smile forms on Mom's face. "This is the answer you need to find before any other. The rest we can figure out after," she says.

It can't be that easy. Wanting something and then...doing whatever it takes to get it?

"It's okay, Mom. We don't have to think about these things. I'm really lucky to be able to do what I do."

She shakes her head and puts her hands on my cheeks, looking me straight in the eye. "Jacob, you *do* need to think about these things. You deserve to have the life you want as much as anyone else. I want you to be happy. Stop, for just one minute, thinking of how to take care of everyone else. What do you want and need to take care of yourself? Forget Min-Kyung, Hae-Jin, the studio execs, the fans, even me and Jin-Hee. Think of yourself for once."

She stands up and looks down at me, a look full of love. "Mrs. Cho has invited us to stay longer, for however long we'd like, really. And we've been talking seriously about opening a business together. Something Hannah's father has said he is excited to support. Lots of choices for our family, lots of opportunity, lots to think about and discuss. It won't be easy. But when did our family ever run away from a challenge? We're fighters. But for you, Jacob, there's really only one thing to consider: What will make you happy?"

My mouth opens in surprise. When did all of this happen? And what does it mean? But I don't say anything. Mom just nods and smiles and leaves the room.

If I no longer *have* to work, do I still *want* to? Is that what she's asking me? Is that what I have to ask myself? Could I go to a regular school? Could I maybe pursue art and drawing? Or acting, but without the pressure of fame?

I think of what life would be like as a regular student attending school with other kids. I picture life without security and cameras and fans screaming at me. I imagine a life where I don't have makeup on my face and I'm not told what to wear every day.

I see Hannah's face.

I grab my phone off the desk and immediately type out the message.

We have to talk...please.

I press Send, feeling equal parts unsure and totally certain. I don't know what this all means. But if the choice ahead is mine, if I get to make it for myself, then the road in front of me feels lined with possibilities.

Be brave enough and take that first step. Walk that road, Jacob.

CHAPTER 22: Hannah

Why I let my mom take the lead is beyond me. Driving up the 15 freeway at exactly sixty-three miles per hour is skyrocketing my blood pressure. Mom never drives the speed limit. She worries she'll accidentally press the pedal too hard and it will take her over sixty-five, so she drives sixty-three just in case.

Some might find this endearing. I find it infuriating. I need to get home. I need to talk to Jacob. And Mama Cho is in the way.

The super slo-mo video montage set to a sappy love song plays in my mind. Jacob biting a California burrito, guacamole on his cheek. Jacob ripping off his T-shirt only to reveal a horrid farmer's tan, but with a huge smile on his face as he runs into the water. Jacob screaming like a little boy while riding the roller coaster at LEGOLAND, his too-long legs bent so his knees are up to his chin. All the best memories of the summer flood my mind clear as day. I'm running towards him, hair flying behind me in the wind. And he's running towards me across a field, ankle boot on one foot and seullippo on another, grabbing me and spinning us around while he kisses me breathless.

I've clearly been watching too many K-dramas as of late.

But I'll be thirty by the time any of this happens, the way my mom is driving. I make the decision that will likely invite a major lecture later, but I put on my signal and move into the left lane, pressing the gas and passing my mom's car. I don't look at her. I just go faster, seventy, seventy-three, seventy-seven, and then cross over two lanes to get closer to my freeway exit. My goal is waiting at home, and I need to tell him how I feel. I need to tell him to go and be a superstar but that I'll be here for him when he needs me. I'll always be here for him.

I exit the freeway and speed through a yellow light. If I get pulled over by the police now, I'll know for certain that the world truly is against me. But no lights, no sirens. Oh god, if my mom sees me, she'll have a heart attack. I take a quick peek out my rearview mirror, and there is no sign of my mom's car. I've left her in the dust. No honking, no crashes.

I am in the clear.

I turn onto my street, pull into the driveway, and shut off my car. Our front door, which is always unlocked, is slightly ajar, and I don't hesitate as I run inside and take the stairs two at a time. I'm out of breath by the time I turn the corner to Jacob's room.

"Jacob," I call out, panting. I stop in my tracks.

The room is empty. The bed, made. Perfectly tidy. Always leave a place cleaner than you left it. No phone charger on the desk. No suitcase in the corner.

No.

I turn around, not knowing where to look.

"Jacob?" I call out loud enough for the whole house to hear.

Jin-Hee walks out of her room, and the look on her face tells me all I need to know. The corners of her mouth are turned down, and her red-rimmed eyes drop to the ground. "He's gone. He left a little while ago with Hae-Jin and Min-Kyung."

"What? No. He can't be. Gone where?" I hear the desperation in my voice. I'll go find him. I'll go wherever he is. I'll go to the airport and park in the drop-off zone even if the traffic cop yells at me and blows his whistle. I'll run past TSA and hurdle over the rows of connected seats in the waiting areas to get to him. It will take ten men to bring me down. I've seen the movies. I know how this plays out.

"I think they're at the hotel. Their flight leaves later tonight," Jin-Hee says. Oh, thank god. It occurs to me that my legs are too short to hurdle chairs, and running past security would land me in jail. That would suck and really foil my plans to get to Jacob.

"Jin-Hee, do you know what hotel they're staying at?" I ask frantically.

Why didn't I pay closer attention when everyone was talking about the details? Oh yeah, because I was too busy woe-is-me'ing and storming out of the room, letting them beat me down.

"They're at the InterContinental Hotel. They always stay at InterContinentals when they travel." Good girl. "Min-Kyung refuses to stay anywhere else."

Huh, must make her travel options pretty limited. I don't remember an InterContinental at the base of the Grand Canyon or at Joshua Tree. Her loss.

My face stretches into the biggest smile, and Jin-Hee's eyes brighten as she smiles back. She knows exactly what's about to happen, and I hope that I can pull it off for all of us. The fate of all young love yet to bloom one day is in my hands. "Thank you so much," I say, rushing up to her, taking her face in both my hands, and kissing her on the forehead. "I'm off to storm the castle," I say as I turn towards the stairs.

"You guys are so weird," I hear her say behind me.

I stop to tell Jin-Hee one more thing. It's a teaching moment after all. "Just remember, it's okay for the girl to chase the boy. It's okay for the princess to save the prince. It's okay for..."

"Hannah unnie, I've seen *Wonder Woman*," she says. "I know what a woman kicking ass looks like."

I reach back for a fist bump, trying not to harp on the fact that Diana's love dies at the end of the first movie. "Don't use bad words," I call out as I run down the stairs.

"Hannah Cho, you drive too fast..." my mom calls out to me as she walks into the house.

"Sorry, Umma, I have to go. I have to tell Jacob I love him," I say, running past my mother and out the door.

"Oh, well, okay, good. But remember, don't speed on the way," she says.

Great talk, Mom.

I hustle into my car and take off for the InterContinental. I think about texting Jacob, but I don't have time. I have to catch him before it's too late. And it's not safe to text and drive.

Why don't hotels ever have parking that's easy to find?

I contemplate parking in the drop-off roundabout by the hotel lobby entrance and letting them figure out how to move my hand-me-down Camry. But the last thing I want is to get towed. When I get Jacob, we're gonna need this bad boy to help us ride off into the sunset to our Happily-Ever-After.

So I grab a ticket from the machine and park in the visitor parking area—I'll worry about the cost for the garage later—and make my way down the three flights of stairs, finally running through the front doors of the hotel.

The lobby of the InterContinental is massive and sprawling, and I scan the entire area, looking for my man. There are various people dressed in business suits peppered around, having conversations, waiting with their luggage, generally minding their own business. This, thankfully, makes finding Jacob much easier.

Over in one corner, near the hotel bar, is a group of Asian people making more commotion than any of the others. Eyes of curious bystanders look their way as a couple of cameramen take shots of the two young people standing next to each other. They're in a semi-embrace, bodies facing one another, arms held out mirroring the other's with hands holding elbows. It's as awkward-looking as a forced prom pose, and a sense of relief consumes me as I remind myself that they're just acting.

Right?

Jacob and Min-Kyung are not a couple. I say it to myself once more. With all the pressure put on him lately by the studio, and the looming contract renewal, Jacob isn't thinking straight. And there's the disappointment of me walking out on him. And there's the fact that Min-Kyung is freaking gorgeous. So it doesn't hurt for me to put it out into the universe a few more times. They are not a couple. They are not a couple.

I look at the two of them in their embrace again, and this time it seems a little less forced. Am I seeing things? Stop. It's not natural to be in this pose in front of cameras and fans. This is not real.

The irritation stabs me once again that Jacob has to do this when the cameras are on and all eyes are focused on them. But as I determined before I took off on this wild ride to win my man, I'll support him through it. And I'll be there when it gets too frustrating to bear. I have to trust him and not fly off the handle like I have in the past.

Flashes go off, and the clicks of the cameras are loud even among the general conversation of the groups around the lobby. Hae-Jin stands off to the side like an angry watchdog, and I take in the entire situation to plan my next move.

I can't just walk up there and make a scene, telling Jacob I love him, I support all his choices, and we'll figure out what happens next when we're long-distance, all while he grabs me in his arms, dips me low, and bends to lay the most romantic, sloppy kiss of all time on me. Note to self: maybe figure out a way to work a dramatic slap to Minky into the mix of my imaginary scenario while we're at it. It would be so satisfying.

But I also can't just stand here, frozen, staring. Because that's just creepy. Plus, I'm paying for parking by the quarter hour.

I make my way closer to them, walking along the perimeter of the lobby, and hide behind a large potted ficus draped with twinkle lights. No one will see me here.

Hae-Jin leans in and whispers something in Min-Kyung's ear. Her eyes scan the lobby, and I swear they land on me, hidden behind this tree. But it's only for a brief second, and they pass over me, so I rebuke myself for being so paranoid and watch for my opportunity to make a move.

What are they gonna do, kick me out? I'll go and reserve a hotel room on the emergency-only credit card my mom gave me. I have every right to be here.

Min-Kyung gives a small nod back to Hae-Jin. But that's neither here nor there to me because all that matters is that Jacob has taken this moment to type something into his phone. He's smiling, the sweet smile that seems to hide a secret. That smile belongs to me.

I look down at my phone and open up our iMessage conversation. My heart does a loop the loop as I see three flashing dots next to Jacob's name on the screen. He's typing, probably professing his love to me in text. Aw, that's romantic.

I want to jump up and down and get his attention. I want to scream *yoo-hoo!* and have him notice me, recognition on his face, as he takes off across the lobby to run to me, lifting me into a *Dirty Dancing* pose.

I look back down at my phone, and the dots have disappeared. No new message. When I look back up, I freeze.

Min-Kyung has stepped in closer to Jacob. Too close. Alert. Danger. Step away from my man.

She raises both her small, perfectly manicured hands to his face, holding his cheeks in a tender caress. And before I can blink, before I can scream, she grabs him and pulls him into a kiss. It's passionate. I can tell it's wet. And much to my horror, he doesn't pull away.

This is more than the studio is asking of him, right? I mean, he's not stopping the kiss, but he's not technically kissing her back. If he was, his arms would be around her.

But he's not pushing her away, either.

Shit.

Doubt crashes over me like the largest wave in the sea, pulling me under its current. Maybe Jacob's feelings have changed after all?

I think through all our moments together. Our shared kisses. Our laughs. Our conversations. The realization knocks me in the face as I continue to search my playback reel to prove myself wrong.

And it hits me. Jacob never told me he loved me back.

I said the words.

He never returned them.

And why would he? I was dating his childhood bully. I went to get boba with the guy whose mere presence torments Jacob, and I neglected to warn him about it. I told him I loved him, but I didn't show him how much I cared about him. And then I told him to leave and walked away.

I pushed him away in every way possible, just like I did three years ago.

And Min-Kyung stepped in to help him pick up the pieces.

He doesn't need me. He has…her. Jacob isn't acting. Or maybe he's acting like he's acting. I shake my head quickly, trying to loosen all the doubts. But they've taken hold of my neurons and won't let go.

One thing's for sure. I'm not the only one kissing Jacob Kim. And that makes me the biggest fool in the world. I step back away from the plant and feel the room spinning.

A tap on my shoulder knocks me out of my freak-out.

"Miss, we're going to have to escort you off the property." The deep voice of the security guard in the dark suit pounds in my brain.

"Wait, what? Why?" I've never been escorted out of anywhere. Will they grab each of my arms and throw me out the front door to fall on my hands and knees, screaming at Jacob to take me back, to pick me? Will they handcuff me?

"We've been given notice that you're not authorized to be here, that you're a threat to one of our guests."

A threat? I'm five feet tall, one hundred pounds soaking wet.

My mind scrambles between irritation and fear, all mixed with confusion. Do they think I'm one of those sasaeng fans and that I might be dangerous?

I quickly look back at Jacob and his entourage. His back is to me, but he's leaned in, and his arms are wrapped around Min-Kyung in a hug. Her eyes meet mine just as she whispers something into his ear. I can't read lips, but in dramatic form, it looks like she's saying... *I love you.* She's not looking at him. She's not looking at the camera. She's looking straight at me.

No. No, it can't be. It's a scene. They're acting. This is not real. He doesn't even like her. He likes me. He may not love me. It's hard to know, you see, because he never said it back. Why didn't he say it back?

"Miss, I'll ask you one more time to leave before we..."

I can't stay here and watch this play out. Jacob kissing her, the two of them sharing words of love and affection for each other. Possibly the same words he's said to me, minus the word *love* since, well, I remind myself again, he never professed that to me.

Nausea swirls in my gut and makes its way quickly up my throat. I have to go; I have to get out of here. I'm not welcome.

I run away without looking back. The quickest route to the door is a straight shot across the lobby, right past Jacob. It doesn't matter, though. He's probably still lip-locked, eyes closed. I think about his long, thick lashes and how they lie across his face when his eyes close. I want to take a pair of scissors and cut them off.

"Hannah?"

His voice breaks through the chaos in my head, and I stumble, the marble flooring consuming my vision. I'm about to crash and it's gonna be epic and it's gonna hurt like a bitch. There may even be blood. I'll lose teeth. The dentist bill will be enormous.

Suddenly, hands are on me, saving me from my fall and near demise.

Jacob.

I turn around, prepared to give him a piece of my mind, followed up with the most passionate kiss, branding him as mine for all the world to see. I can fight for him. I will fight for him!

But when I focus on the hands around me, an unfamiliar face looks down at me with slight concern.

"Hey, are you alright? You almost ate it." A random act of kindness by a complete stranger, saving me from landing face-first on the ground.

"Um, I'm fine, thank you," I stumble to say.

"You should be more careful. You could get hurt," he says.

I should be more careful…with my heart. With my expectations. With my trust.

"Hannah," Jacob's voice calls out, closing in.

I shake myself free from the hold of the stranger and take off. I can't talk to Jacob now. I can't confront him. I'm too ashamed, I'm too hurt, I'm too scared of the truth.

I run.

I run through the doors.

I run to the parking garage.

I hear feet behind me, but I'm scrappy and mortified. It's a combination that can't be caught.

I climb the stairs to the third floor of the garage and jab my ticket into the payment machine, followed by a five-dollar bill. I don't wait for the change. I can skip Starbucks tomorrow and maybe still survive.

I start the car, ready to drive far away from the past that stings, the present that confuses, the future that can never be. Forget the long-distance romance. Forget the reunion of childhood best friends who've fallen in love. Forget the face that makes my heart stretch beyond capacity.

It's all too hard. Love shouldn't be this hard.

Maybe I should just lick my wounds and do what it takes to make my life easy and make sense again. Say goodbye to this summer.

I maneuver my car towards home, the exact opposite direction from Jacob Jin Suk Kim.

CHAPTER 23: Jacob

I can't get the look on Hannah's face out of my mind.

I was surprised to see her here at the hotel. Then freaked out watching her about to fall as she ran across the lobby. And pissed as all get-out when that guy put his hands on her to save her from injury.

But it was the look on her face when she turned back for just a second, the confusion mixed with hurt when her eyes met mine. I shiver and swallow away the worry. I need to find her so we can talk.

What is taking this Uber so long?

"Jin-Suk, just wait for Hae-Jin to get the car. It won't be but a couple minutes," Min-Kyung says from behind me. I don't turn around. I don't want to look at her. What the fuck was she thinking when she kissed me? She whispered "I love you" into my ear, and I immediately pulled away. She can barely stand to be near me, so what was with the "I love you"? I don't believe her excuse for one minute that she thought the cameras were rolling. I know her manipulative side too well, and the one thing Min-Kyung is not is absentminded. She calculates every move. But what was that one about?

And is that why Hannah was running? Did she see us?

Even so, Hannah knows me. She knows it's not real. I've told her about what the studio wants me to do and how much I hate it. My head is spinning trying to figure it out. Where is the damn Uber?

The black Suburban pulls up in front of us, and a man in a black suit jumps out to open the door.

"Get in," Hae-Jin says.

The look on her face says I don't exactly have a choice, so I scramble in, and Min-Kyung gets in after me.

"We'll take you to the Cho residence. But you have thirty minutes, and then we leave for the airport. I mean it, Jin-Suk. I will not tolerate your childish tantrums and your teenage drama." Hae-Jin's voice is a carefully controlled even tone, but the tension in her jawline and around her eyes gives her away. She is pissed off and is pretty much done with me.

The relief I feel surprises me. Maybe I want her to be done with me. It could simplify my life.

"What was Hannah doing here anyways? And why did she make such a scene running off like that? People were probably all wondering who the crazy, emotional fangirl was. If I was her, I'd be so embarrassed," Min-Kyung says. "Really, how many times can one girl make a total fool of herself?"

Rage builds inside me and tests the bounds of my patience. My nostrils flare, and my breath is harsh even to my ears, as I try and keep my mouth shut. She does not get to talk about Hannah like that. Not at all.

"Please, please. Shut up," I say.

If she says anything back, I won't be able to control myself. But I don't want a fight right now. With my luck, Hae-Jin will force the car to turn around and go straight to the airport. I can't risk it. I have to get to Hannah.

The sky has darkened by now, but there is still some traffic on the freeway. The red brake lights that come on and off at random intervals give me something to focus on until we get home.

Home.

Not Seoul, where my job is. Here, in San Diego, where Hannah is.

I think about my mom's question. What do I want? I know the answer. I want to be home.

The car pulls up into the driveway and I'm already out, fumbling to get inside. The house is warm and smells so familiar, scents of garlic, spiciness, well-enjoyed meals. And the laughter from the family room as Korean variety show hosts talk in the background washes over me in waves of comfort.

Home.

All eyes turn to me as I hustle into the room. Eyebrows raised in question, mouths open in surprise at what I must look like right now, frantic to find Hannah. But she's not sitting here with the moms and Jin-Hee.

"Where's Hannah?" I ask, out of breath.

"She's not here," her mom says.

"She left not too long ago," my mom answers.

"She went to the lifeguard camp bonfire, um, with that guy Nate," Jin-Hee says, eyes wide with concern. "But she swore he was just her ride and nothing else."

"Where is it?" I ask. My voice is too loud for this space, even with the TV volume at remarkably high levels. I don't care about Nate. I need to get to Hannah.

Mrs. Cho stands up and shuffles past me to the kitchen. She hands over a flyer with surfboards and waves drawn on it, "Say Goodbye to Summer" written across the top. The bonfire is at Torrey Pines Beach with an after-party at Mount Soledad. I briefly think of how a visit to Mount Soledad at night is on my bucket list. It's supposed to have some of the most remarkable views of the city. It's where I wanted to tell Hannah how I felt about her.

"Okay, Jin-Suk. You've come, and Hannah is not here. Time for us to go to the airport," Hae-Jin says.

"The airport?" The surprise in my mom's voice catches me off guard. "Tonight? I thought you're scheduled to leave tomorrow." She looks at me with concern, brows furrowed.

"Sorry, Umma. It was all last-minute. I was going to call you." I look back at Hae-Jin's stern face and Min-Kyung's furious expression, and right then and there make the decision that might screw me over, but feels one hundred percent right. "But since I changed my mind and decided to stay, I didn't bother. I didn't want to worry you."

"Jin-Suk." The warning in Hae-Jin's voice cannot be missed.

"You're a fool," Min-Kyung adds in. "It's your funeral. You're basically digging a grave for your career. Don't you get it? With all the competition out there, one wrong step with the studio and you can be replaced like that." Min-Kyung's snap rings through the now-silent room. The TV is off now. All eyes are on us. My mom stands up but doesn't make another move. It's my call. She's giving me the choice to make it.

"I do get it. I get that you're impossible to work with, and you'll be lucky to find someone to take my place. But I'm sure there will be another new kid coming out of the Training Program, and then another, and another. You should probably worry about your own career instead of harping on mine. You don't have to keep repeating yourself. I got it the first time. It just took me a minute to decide. But now I know." I stop myself and close my eyes, taking a second to really think through what I'm about to do. I open them again and feel like I'm seeing clearly for the first time in a long while. "I have limits. I know what I'm willing and unwilling to do for the studio, for this career, for myself. And the last few days have been beyond the call of acting and publicity for a show. I'm willing to play the part. I am unwilling to hurt those I care about."

"Don't be ridiculous. Think very carefully about what you're doing here, Jin-Suk. You might find yourself in a position you don't want to be in, and you can't take back," Hae-Jin warns. "Plus, you're under contract."

"About that," my mom chimes in. "I've had some time to review the contract and get a second opinion from a lawyer friend of ours at our church here in San Diego, one who specializes in Talent contracts. Lucky for us, it seems Jacob's only obligation in his existing contract is to record the show and do marketing and publicity within reasonable expectations. I can't imagine anyone believing that some of these things being asked of my son lately fall under reasonable expectations. I'd hate for the public to hear about how the studio has been trying to manipulate them with a false love affair. And since we haven't signed on for the next season, how will they explain him missing in the storyline? You really do want us to cooperate, which, I believe, would require you to meet us halfway here."

Hae-Jin narrows her eyes, and the look she gives my mom could cut steel. My mom smiles back in return, unfazed by the anger shot her way. "You'd be ruining any chance for Jin-Suk to be hired again. Say goodbye to his career, with this studio and with any other."

My mom's eyes meet mine, and I let out a sigh of relief as I nod my head. That's exactly what I want.

"Well, thanks for the information. Now, it sounds like you all have a flight to catch back to Korea, and we wouldn't want you to be late. My son, however, will remain in my care for the rest of his scheduled holiday. We'll return to finish the season as originally planned."

Two more weeks. Mom bought us two more weeks.

The silence in the room is deafening. No one moves except for my little sister, whose head is going from my mom, to me, to Hae-Jin like watching a three-way tennis match.

"Very well," Hae-Jin says. Her voice is cold, matter-of-fact, and gives nothing away. "We will see you back in Korea. Please make sure to come straight to the studio the first day back. I anticipate the executives will have something to say to you about this...mess...you've created this summer. We already had the headache of dealing with Jacob's uncle and now…this? I would definitely have your lawyer ready. But until then, enjoy your holiday."

She bows slightly and turns to leave. Min-Kyung glares at me, eyes like daggers. But to my relief, she is silent. She just puckers her lips in disgust, shaking her head in disappointment. "You better bring it from the moment you get back," she says.

If I wasn't so relieved she was leaving, I'd laugh. But watching them both put their shoes on and walk away releases all the tension. I collapse into the sofa and let out a deep breath.

"Well, now that that's finished, shall we all grab our coats and be on our way?" Mrs. Cho asks.

I sit up and shake my head. "I have to go and find Hannah," I say.

"Yes, exactly. And who do you think is going to take you there?" She waggles her eyebrows at me.

I consider my options. I can call an Uber, but I don't exactly know where I'm going. It could take me too long to look for Hannah, and since she's with Nate, I don't have time to spare. The thought of Hannah and Nate together is like a vise on my chest. I clench my jaw, absorbing all my rage.

But if the moms and my little sister drive me, it could be a terrible hit to my cool factor, possibly hurting my chances to win back Hannah. How will she feel if her mom shows up to an event with her friends?

"Jacob, c'mon. Don't just stand there like a deer in headlights. We have to get Hannah back. Get your Prince Charming shoes on and let's go," Jin-Hee says.

Decision made.

I hustle towards the front of the house, put my feet into my seullippos, and turn to open the door.

"Ay! No! You can't wear seullippos when you're going to win the girl. Didn't I teach you anything?" My mom hits me lightly on the arm and leans down to grab my very shiny, very uncomfortable dress shoes.

"Umma, no! He can't wear those. He'll look like an ajusshi. Hannah and all of her friends will make fun of the old man shoes," Jin-Hee says, slapping her forehead with her hand.

"Here, Jacob, take these," Mrs. Cho says, handing me my Chucks. "Hannah likes these. She has a pair in the pink color. Now, let's go, everyone." She pushes me a little and shuffles us all out the door.

Okay, Hannah, I have no idea what happens next, but I hope whatever it is, you'll give me a chance to tell you how I feel...and that it all ends with a kiss (preferably *not* while our moms are watching).

I fidget in the back seat as I look at the clock. My heart beats a mile a minute, which makes at least one thing that's moving at a decent pace. Mrs. Cho, however, is the slowest driver in all creation, and I begin to wonder if Hannah will be home and in bed...two days later...by the time we reach our destination. Hannah, of course, would likely argue that I'm one to talk since I'd give her mom a (slow) run for her money with my own driving.

A smile spreads that I can't contain just thinking about Hannah teasing me. How could I have even considered leaving early? And how did I survive the last three years without her in my life? What I know for sure is that it's not gonna happen again.

"This whole 'win the girl' thing is cute, and I'm super excited that it's Hannah, but, um, could you wipe the creepy smile off your face? It's making me uncomfortable." Little sisters. Sheesh.

We make our way up the winding road until we get to the parking area atop Mount Soledad. Growing up, I'd always seen the cross lit up at the top and heard about what people "do" up there at night. But this is actually my first time here. It's gorgeous, and I take a second to just look at it and get my bearings, when I notice the large group of people off to the side of the parking lot, making quite a bit of noise with laughter and too-loud conversations. Way to ruin the ambience.

I unbuckle my seat belt, but before I open the door, my mom reaches back and puts her hand on my knee. I'm prepared for a stern speech about being careful and how drinking alcohol is a sin and The Sex before marriage is bad in God's eyes. What I'm not ready for is the kind smile she gives me.

"Jacob, you know what you want. You know what you deserve. Now, go tell her everything you're feeling. It's going to be okay," she says. She squeezes my knee, and I nod, swallowing back the lump in my throat.

I meet Mrs. Cho's eyes, and she gives me what I think is an approving smile.

I look at Jin-Hee, and she gives me a thumbs-up.

"Here goes nothing," I say.

I walk over towards the group of kids and see familiar faces from random meetings throughout the summer. It's dark enough that no one notices me, or at least notices that Kim Jin-Suk is in their midst, right away. I scan the crowd and find Nate Anderson's huge head.

Standing in front of him is Hannah. My breath catches as I see her in the light of the moon and the Mount Soledad cross. She's beautiful. And judging by her expression, she's not happy.

My heart at first begins to crackle with a fiery jealous rage. Then it squeezes with a sadness that I pushed Hannah in this direction. But then it starts to lift like a hot-air balloon realizing that it's crystal clear what's happening here—Hannah does not want to be with Nate.

I take a deep breath and start walking to where they are.

As I get closer, Nate's hand circles around Hannah's arm, and he pulls her in towards him. Oh no. He's leaning, bending his gigantic noggin, going in for the kiss. But at the last second, Hannah lowers her head. She doesn't raise hers to meet his lips.

He puts his hand on her cheek, trying to maneuver her face up to look at him. Get a clue, buddy. She is not feeling it, not feeling you.

I pick up my pace, weaving in and out of the crowd.

"Oppa, you're here. You came," a high-pitched, slurred voice says. A girl grabs my arm.

I shake off the weak grip only to run right into another embrace.

"I love you, Won-Jin. You have no idea how obsessed I am with you," the girl says. Her face is too close, and her lips touch my ear. She can't even see me past my character on the show. I gently push her off me, looking above her head for Hannah.

She has both her hands on Nate's chest, and I freeze. No, don't do it, Hannah. Don't touch him. But her brow is furrowed, and her lips move a mile a minute. Nate raises his hands like he doesn't understand what she's trying to say.

Then he grips both her arms, and the move jolts her body in surprise.

I break into a run, and when I reach them, Hannah turns, eyes wide in shock. I'm blind with rage at this point. "Get your hands off of her," I say. Before Nate can process what's happening, but just as he turns his head to see me, I draw back my fist, step in, and punch him in the face.

"Ow, fuck," he says, grabbing his cheek.

"Ow, fuck," I say, grabbing my hand.

There's a commotion behind us, and suddenly, my mom and Mrs. Cho are hitting Nate with their handbags.

"Yah! You don't touch Hannah," Mrs. Cho says.

"Go away, you nappeun saekki-ya," Mom says. Listening to the older women call Nate a bad person and curse at him makes me happier than it should.

"Stop! You crazy ladies," Nate says, arms up, shielding his head. They're not hitting him hard, more like annoying gnats buzzing all around him. But his ego is taking the hardest hit of all, I suspect.

"Jacob, what are you doing?" Hannah screams, positioning herself between me and Nate.

"This jerk couldn't take no for an answer," I say, holding my possibly broken hand. I keep my attention on Nate, waiting for him to come at me, but praying he won't. I knew he'd have a concrete head. There's no way I can hit him again. And the way my hand is throbbing, I don't think I'll hit anyone again in my life, ever.

Luckily the moms have got Nate under control.

"I was handling it," Hannah says. "Umma, Mrs. Kim, stop hitting him. Mom, that's your good Coach purse." She turns back to look at me. Her face is scrunched, and her nostrils flare like a raging bull's. And all that anger is directed at…me?

"He had his hands on you, grabbing you, forcing you to kiss him."

"That's a little extreme. And I can handle myself with Nate, sheesh," she says. "You can't just come up here and punch him like some Neanderthal. He's twice as big as you are," she says.

"Not twice. Maybe only one and a half times bigger," I say. My head drops, and I can't bear to look at Hannah, watching her defend him. I'm too late.

"Listen, Jacob. Nate was trying to kiss me, yes…"

I turn my head away. I don't want Hannah to see the pain in my face when she tells me that she's decided to pick him over me. When she lets me know that I'm too late.

"…but I told him I couldn't. He knows how I feel about you. And even if you, I don't know, changed your mind about me, I wouldn't, I can't, just run into some other guy's arms."

I whip my head back around to make sure, to read on her face, that I heard her correctly.

"Good girl," her mom says. "She's so smart."

"Hannah." My voice is a near whisper. Relief takes away the sound as it rushes out of me.

"I don't want Nate," she says. She looks over her shoulder at the big lug. "Sorry, no offense, Nate. You're a really great guy, but it was never going to work out for us."

"Yeah, I feel like maybe I was too late even before it started," Nate says, looking back and forth between me and Hannah, hand massaging his jaw. He gives Hannah a small smile and winces.

"Uh, sorry, dude. I didn't mean to go all Creed on you," I say.

"Nah, I get it. She's worth fighting over," he says. "And consider it payback for when I was a shit to you growing up. I deserve it."

So he does remember.

He reaches out his hand to shake mine. I awkwardly give him my left hand, the one not currently throbbing in intense pain, and shake his.

"Your hand." Hannah gently reaches out and cradles it in her own hands. "Are you okay?"

"Forget my hand, Hannah," I say. "I'm so sorry for everything. I'm sorry for not being brave enough to stand up to the studio. I'm sorry for not defending you publicly when the comments turned nasty. I'm sorry for letting Min-Kyung take over and ruin our summer. I'm sorry you saw her kiss me. I swear, it wasn't real. I'm sorry I left you three years ago.

"But I'm here now. And I'm going to make it up to you. We're gonna figure it out. Please tell me you're with me on this. That you believe we can make it work." I swallow back all the years of fear of rejection, disappointing people, worrying about failing, missing Hannah. "I may have come to San Diego to heal my ankle, but because of you, I ended up healing my heart."

The crowd around us lets out a chorus of ahhh's.

I touch my forehead to hers and whisper, "That sounds like a line from a script, but I swear it's the truth." I pull back and look into her eyes, so she can be sure I'm being me and not acting.

"Hannah, I love you." They're words shared just between us.

Her eyes glisten with her tears. She searches my face for any reason to be afraid. And when her eyes land on mine, I see all the love she has for me. She wraps her arms around me. I meet her halfway, and our lips touch, releasing the tears in Hannah's eyes that mix with mine.

I barely hear the crowd of kids around us explode into cheers and clapping.

"Good, good, this is very good," my mom says.

"I'm so happy, so very happy," Hannah's mom says.

"Yeah, I do not need to see my brother slip Hannah the tongue. Gross," Jin-Hee says.

Hannah pulls back and looks at me. I miss her lips immediately. Her face is suddenly serious, and for a second, I'm worried she's about to change her mind. But her arms stay wrapped around me.

"You brought our mothers and your twelve-year-old sister to a high school after-party? To win me back?" She struggles to look annoyed, but the scrunch of her mouth fighting off the smile is a dead giveaway.

I shrug. "It was the most important thing I was going to do. Brought out the big guns to have my back."

She nods her head. "I can appreciate that." And she leans in to kiss me once more.

"I love you, Hannah Cho. Always have, always will," I say.

She swallows and looks up at me, her eyes so earnest. "I love you, too, Jacob Kim. And I'm not ever letting you go."

EPILOGUE: Jacob

"I don't know how to tell you this, but I can't keep it from you any longer. I know this is going to be hard to hear, and I'm so sorry to hurt you. But, I'm… I'm dying."

It's a little surreal, playing out a death confession to the character you're supposed to love and have been fighting so long to be with. And just when you're about to finally get together, boom, the worst news is dropped. Man, the writers of *Heart and Seoul* really know how to punch you in the gut and stab you in the heart. I'm even feeling emotional as I play out the scene. But I can't feel too bad about it. It's my ticket to freedom.

I've been back in Korea for three months now, and it isn't as awful as it was before the summer. First, it feels a little bit like a vacation in and of itself since I know, now, that I won't be here much longer. Second, it's tolerable since I've been video-chatting with Hannah pretty much daily since I left San Diego. The difference in time zones has been painful, but we make it work. Seeing her face on-screen isn't the same as in person, but it's better than what I was missing for the past three years.

When I got back from San Diego, the shit had indeed hit the fan. Hae-Jin didn't exaggerate when she told me how much trouble I was in. The studio execs were not happy. But we were able to come to a mutual decision for me to leave the show.

The company worked hard to keep the details under wraps. But they did leak the possibility of my departure to *Reveal*, the big celebrity gossip site. If I'm not an actor in the hottest show anymore, then my uncle's tell-all isn't as interesting. We'll see what happens. But I've heard it's likely they won't be paying him anything. I've got my fingers crossed, since the company is unwilling to pay him off anymore. Looks like he gambled and lost.

And that also put the pressure on the writers to come up with the plot twist to explain my departure, so here we are, at my last big scene with Min-Kyung. My character has an aggressive, incurable, unnamed disease and is dying. After this, the character of Won-Jin will be dead and gone.

"Noooooo!" The tortured scream coming from Min-Kyung's mouth makes all the hairs on my arms stand at alert. The sheer dread and heartache she's able to convey in that one word is impressive. No doubt about it, Min-Kyung is made for this kind of work. I, however, am definitely not, and the relief I feel the moment the director shouts "cut" allows me to breathe again.

"Good job, everyone. We'll take a break and start again in twenty minutes."

Min-Kyung doesn't even say a word to me. She turns

and storms off the stage. She hasn't forgiven me for messing up everything. But I can't be bothered to care. One more day and I'm done with her, done with this show, done with this career, and done with Korea…for now.

What happens next, I'm not entirely sure. But the few things we do have figured out, I'm feeling really good about. I'll be going to a regular high school for my senior year. I'm not excited about having to take core classes like math and science, which I haven't studied in years. But I am excited that I got into the art class I was hoping for.

And I'm excited I'll get to be in San Diego with Hannah.

But luckily, I don't have to wait until then to see her.

I look over into the corner, and it's the face that sets my heart on fire. Hannah's here visiting me in Korea, something I don't think either of us ever thought would happen. Hannah's smile is sweet, and she lifts her chin at me, impressed with everything she's seeing here on set. I can't help but puff my chest out a little bit. I walk over to meet her in the shadows of the soundstage.

"Hey, what did you think?" I ask.

"You're seriously so good. I can't believe that Won-Jin is dying." Her voice is thick with emotion. "And I gotta give Min-Kyung some credit. She really knows how to shut it down. She is good. I *felt* that last scream."

I wrap my arms around her and lean down to kiss her forehead, her nose, her lips. Despite all the video chats, nothing beats getting to hold Hannah and feeling her against me. I sigh into the kiss.

"We don't have much more to film today, and then we can go and check out more of the town tonight," I say.

"And I recall promising you some tteokbokki and patbingsu."

She nods, pulls back, and smiles. "Sounds good. I'd say we're about halfway through my 'Things to Do in Korea' list, so we'd better get to work."

Hannah

The lights are bright and make the soundstage warm despite the air-conditioning running. I recall Jacob telling me that Min-Kyung likes it to be a certain temperature at all times and throws a fit if it's ever too cold. A part of me feels sorry for her. Life must be hard when you're that miserable, despite privilege and entitlement.

Someone comes and brushes some powder over Jacob's face as he rolls his neck from side to side to release the tension. He is all game face at work, and I have to admit, it's super hot seeing him like this.

It's my first time on a television set. It's my first time in Korea at all.

It's gorgeous here, especially during the fall. Honestly, there's no place I'd rather be spending my Thanksgiving week than here with my mom and the Kims.

And my dad.

He decided to make the trip to Korea as well and meet up with us, and it's been great seeing him and catching up. Helen couldn't make it. She's in Berkeley with her boyfriend, John. But we called her to wish her a happy Thanksgiving.

Mom and Dad and Mrs. Kim have been busy discussing the business plan for the ladies to open a small café near the beach in Del Mar where they can cook their favorite Korean comfort foods. It's nothing unique or groundbreaking, but something they both can focus on to support their families and keep busy. And there isn't much competition when it comes to Korean cuisine in that neighborhood. I think it will do well.

Jacob and I have been busy seeing the sights around the city after he's done filming each day. There aren't many press junkets or other demands on Jacob's time now that things have changed. No one is pressuring him to date Min-Kyung. She's moving on to a new "boyfriend" now for season two.

I stand off to the side in the shadows, trying to stay out of everyone's way. Today's scene is pivotal and newly written since the summer break. Won-Jin, Jacob's character, is breaking the news to his forbidden love interest that he's dying. Even thinking of the shift in the storyline does damage to my fragile heart. One, I don't want to watch Jacob tell anyone he's dying, even if it is just acting. And two, I've actually grown fairly attached to and invested in the progress of Won-Jin and Sun-Hee, hoping that the two will finally get together. I am certain Min-Kyung will do a most excellent job of producing tears and screams and playing up the heartbreak. According to Jacob, a new character,

Won-Jin's brother, will step in to comfort her, and a new love connection will blossom for the fans to stan.

And Jacob will have played out his contract and be released to move on.

I look down at my phone, and the lock screen has a picture of Jacob and me during our last day together in San Diego. I actually have a smile on my face. No tears. I admit I was a little worried when it was time for Jacob to leave. Old habits and emotions die hard. But he kept assuring me that it would be okay. And it's been even better than that since.

Because what Jacob helped me realize is that just because someone leaves, it doesn't mean they've stopped loving you. It doesn't mean that you have to cut them entirely out of your life and start fresh with new people to fill the hole. It just means that distance has settled between you, and you have to find new ways to communicate and to stay close.

I FaceTimed with Jacob almost every day until my trip here, and with my dad once a week. Back in San Diego, I make sure to call Helen a couple times a week, and I invite my mom to go out to dinner each Sunday after church. Life feels whole again, and all it took was some patience and care and effort and love.

A lesson learned three years later, but one that's made all the difference. I understand it now. People may move away, but they can remain in your heart. And if you're really lucky, your soul mate will find their way back again one day.

Mrs. Kim and Mrs. Cho

“Korea really is so lovely this time of year,” marvels Mrs. Cho.

“Yes, my friend, it is. We’ll have to come back next year to visit again,” says Mrs. Kim.

“I’m excited for the next step. We’re reunited, we have a business to build, and, well, best of all, Jacob and my Hannah are in love,” says Mrs. Cho.

“Indeed, indeed. We’ve known this would happen since the days long ago when we were two best friends pregnant at the same time.” Mrs. Kim giggles as she thinks back to her younger days.

“Yes, we did. Life is on its own timeline, but it always makes a place for the heart, and the soul, to find love.”

★★★★★

ACKNOWLEDGMENTS

I love reading the author's acknowledgments at the end of a book. It's fascinating and touching to see how many people it's taken to support both the writer and the words through the journey. But now that I'm faced with doing this myself, I'm terrified I will forget someone. So, I want to start with a blanket *THANK YOU.* Thanks to those who have supported me and believed in me. Thanks, even, to those who may have thought this was all ridiculous and I'd never succeed. You all have made this happen in your own way.

Thanks to those who know so much more than me and who patiently and kindly held my hand and directed me through the process.

To Taylor Haggerty, my agent, whom I fangirl all the time. I often pinch myself because I get to work with you. Your generosity with your knowledge and your patience with me and all my questions and concerns are so, so appreciated. Thank you for talking me off every ledge. How lucky am I to have you and the entire Root Literary team, the best in the biz, by my side?

To Stephanie Cohen, editor extraordinaire, with your sharp eye and BTS GIFs at the ready, this book is what it is because of you. And to Bess Braswell, thank you for believing in *Seoulmates* from the beginning. I'm so grateful. And to the incredible editorial, marketing and publicity, and design teams at Inkyard and HarperCollins—it really does take a village. And I'm so glad we're in this together.

This book has the cover of my dreams. And I'm so amazed at and thankful for the talent of Michelle Kwon, illustrator, and Gigi Lau, designer. You brought my vision to life and I want to hug this cover forever.

And now to the friends and the writing community who have truly been the greatest gift.

All my love to my Kimchingoos, Jessica Kim, Graci Kim, Grace Shim, Sarah Suk, and the honorary Mack Gully. You are not only my writing crew, you're my family, my ride or die. I've laughed and cried hardest with you all. I would not have survived this without you. We're gonna change the world with our stories. Hwaiting!

It feels almost too greedy to wish for a group of friends who are incredible critique partners *and* who write books that you love to read *and* who are also funny and thoughtful and insightful and make group chat *the best*. So I, without a doubt, know how blessed I am to have The Coven. Thank you, Annette Christie, Andrea Contos, Auriane Desombre, Sonia Hartl, Kelsey Rodkey, and Rachel Lynn Solomon. I love you.

To The Slackers… I laugh every time I think about how

we ended up finding each other. And continue to laugh on the regular pretty much every single day. You are extraordinary humans and incredibly talented writers and, truly, the best support system out there. Love you, Alexis Ames, Elvin Bala, Ruby Barrett, Rosie Danan, Leslie Gail, Jen Klug, Jessica Lewis, Meg Long, Chad Lucas, LL Montez, Rachel Morris, Mary Roach, Nancy Schwartz, Lyssa Smith, Marisa Urgo, and Meryl Wilsner.

Big thanks to those who were there from the early days. Who tolerated me and all my doubts before the book deal even existed. :) So many steps in this journey might not have been taken if it weren't for each of you: Alexis Daria, Elise Bryant, Gloria Chao, Julie Abe, Tara Tsai, Sarah Harrington, Felice Stevens, BBE, AMMr3, and PW18.

And to those who were there at some of the most impactful grind-it-out moments of writing this book: Tahoe Writing Retreat (Jess, Grace, Sarah, Julie), Ireland Writers Tour (Thao Le, Julie C. Dao, Rachel Griffin, Sarah, Rachel Greenlaw), and Madcap Retreat (Elise, Graci, Tracy Deonn, Yamile Mendez, Yasmine Angoe). I am so grateful for, and inspired by, you all!

To my fairy god agent, Sarah Younger, and fairy god editor, Rebecca Kuss. Each of you has shown guidance and support beyond any call of duty. I love you!

Obviously, this book wouldn't exist without my deep love for K-pop and K-dramas, and getting to share that passion and fandom with Kristin Dwyer, Lauren Billings, Christina Hobbs, Sasha Peyton Smith, Axie Oh, Julie Tieu, and so many others has been *such* a joy.

And while we're here—I've said it before, and I know

many can't quite understand it, but for those who do (IYKYK)...thank you to Bangtan Sonyeondan. :) You've had a huge impact on my life, from finding bits and pieces of my identity I'd thought I'd lost to helping me with my mental health in some of the roughest times. You are each and all a treasure. The world is a better place because you exist. Borahae!

To Jason and Adrian, thank you for loving and accepting me as I am. I'm a better person having you as friends.

Forever grateful to my family: my sister, Sunny, who introduced me to my love of books and is probably the true reason I'm writing them; Wayne; Caleb; my mom, who has the kindest heart I've ever known and has shown incredible support of this career; and to Chrissy, Bear, and Buttercup, my pups who make my heart full. *I LOVE YOU WITH ALL MY HEART.* And to my dad, who is so ingrained not only in my life, but very specifically throughout the journey of this book. I quit my previous career in order to pursue this. And I don't know if he would have approved of that, but he was absolutely the one whose life modeled the courage it took to make these kinds of bold decisions for myself. I owe *EVERYTHING* to him. I love you, Appa. I miss you every day.

And lastly...*huge* gratitude to those who will read this book and take a chance on my story. Thank you so very much. I'm honored and humbled. Let's take this journey forward together! I promise to do my best to make each new book better than the last.